Limestone Cowboy

Limestone Cowboy

STUART PAWSON

This edition published in Great Britain in 2004 by
Allison & Busby Limited
Bon Marche Centre
241-251 Ferndale Road
Brixton, London SW9 8BJ
http://www.allisonandbusby.com

Copyright © 2004 by STUART PAWSON

A catalogue record for this book is available from the British
Library

10 9 8 7 6 5 4 3 2

ISBN 0 7490 8360 3

Printed and bound in Great Britain by
Bookmarque Ltd, Croydon, Surrey

STUART PAWSON had a career as a mining engineer, followed by a spell working for the probation service, before he became a full-time writer. He lives in Fairburn, Yorkshire, and when not hunched over the word processor likes nothing more than tramping across the moors which often feature in his stories. *Limestone Cowboy* is the ninth novel to feature Detective Inspector Charlie Priest.

Also by Stuart Pawson

Acknowledgements

Thanks to the following for their unfailing help, advice and encouragement: John Crawford, Donna Moore, Dennis Marshall, Dave Mason, Clive Kingswood, Margaret Lawrenson, Dave Leach, Kath Gibson, Geoffrey Gibson, Alison at Huddersfield Geological Society (with apologies for introducing a few fault lines where none exist), Mark Crossley and last but by no means least, Teresa and David.

To Doreen

Chapter One

So which was it to be: Balmoral Castle or Sandringham House? This was the sort of decision she hated. Should she choose Balmoral, with its pine trees and purple mountains, or Sandringham, with that impossibly blue sky?

"Oh, for God's sake! Make up your mind," she snapped silently to herself, but still no decision came. Never mind, perhaps she'd do better with the light-bulbs. She turned to go, turned back again, reaching out her hand, then withdrew it and almost fled into the aisle marked Electrical. Her heart sank when she saw the stacked shelves. A lightbulb was a lightbulb, she'd always thought, so why were there so many different types? She read the labels in mounting panic: sixty watt, forty watt, a hundred watt, and so on. Then some were plain and some were pearl, whatever that meant, and others had screw caps and bayonet caps. She felt like screaming. "I only want a lightbulb. A common or garden lightbulb. Any friggin' one will do." Another woman muscled alongside her, picked up a pack of four sixty watts and moved away. For a moment she thought of asking for help, then realised the stupidity of that and gave an involuntary giggle. How could she possibly have explained what she wanted it for?

A female store detective casually walked round the end of the display and watched her. Only two weeks into the job, but she recognised the type: early twenties; hair pulled back and fixed with a rubber band;

spotty complexion from chips with everything but usually by themselves. And wearing a cheap quilted jacket with Michigan emblazoned across the back, even though it was a fine summer's day. Single parent, no doubt, living in one of the project flats after her boyfriend walked out. She'd fill her basket, and perhaps those pockets, with toiletries and hardware here in Wilko's, then walk round to Lidl to buy groceries. Then she'd have to splash what she'd saved by taking a taxi home because she'd never manage everything on the bus. The bus station was half a mile away and the service erratic, whilst there was a queue of taxis right outside the store waiting for fares such as her.

A gaggle of schoolgirls came into the shop and headed for the toiletries, noisy as geese. Wilko's are good at toiletries, often charging half what the more fashionable stores charge for the same branded items. The detective sighed and looked at her watch. There were still three more shops to be visited before she could go home and make the kids' teas. She gave the woman in the Michigan jacket a last look and headed in the direction of the noise.

It was easy, the woman in the Michigan jacket realised. Why hadn't she thought of it before? Choose the cheapest; it was as simple as that. She picked up a bulb – 25p, size and type irrelevant – and placed it in the wire basket she was carrying. What about the tea towels, though? They were the same price, so how would she overcome that hurdle?

She'd choose the nearest. She'd walk round the corner, reach out and pick up the first one. She couldn't remember which it would be, the Balmoral or the

Sandringham, but it didn't matter. Tomorrow it would be a long way away, in the landfill site, so it didn't matter at all.

It was Balmoral. She almost changed her mind because she'd seen a programme about Sandringham on TV when it was the Queen's Jubilee, but she summoned what little resolve she possessed and grabbed the Balmoral. At the end of the aisle she checked in the big convex mirror that nobody was following her and stuffed the towel into one of her pockets. At the end of the next aisle she did the same with the lightbulb.

The schoolgirls were taking the tops off bottles and sniffing the contents, alternately pulling faces or expressing approval. She pushed between them, saying: "Excuse me" and felt a pang of regret mixed with jealousy as their perfume assaulted her nostrils. She wanted to warn them, tell them that there was more to life than boyfriends and pop music and the latest fashion, but she knew that she wouldn't have listened and they wouldn't, either. She picked up a bottle of Revlon shampoo – 95p here, £2.35 in Boots – and dropped it into her basket. Fifteen minutes later she was on the bus home, with a receipt safely in her pocket saying that at 11:59 she had purchased one item costing £0.95.

The flat was on the third floor and she had to rest twice on the way up the stairs. Whoever lived below her was still piling stuffed bin-liners out on the landing, and somebody had peed in the corner. The incessant dum-dum-dum of a drum machine came from the ground floor flat where Heckley's aspiring answer to Bob Marley lived, and the smell of somebody's curry competed unappetisingly with that of stale urine. She leaned out over the wall, took a deep breath of slightly fresher air, and tackled the last flight.

As soon as she opened the door she heard the baby's whimpering. His tears had dried long ago and his crying was reduced to a low keening noise that grated on her nerves like a fingernail across a blackboard. He hesitated for a moment as she loomed over him, but started again almost immediately with renewed energy. She swatted away the flies that were flying and crawling around the carrycot and picked him up.

"It's OK," she said, matter-of-fact, as if talking to an adult. "Mummy's brought something home for you."

The baby wasn't placated. He had a flat face with small eyes, and sweat had pasted his hair to his head. She rested him awkwardly in the crook of her arm until the wetness seeped through and she had to dump him roughly back in his carrycot, her face contorted with disgust. The whimpering escalated to full-blown bawling and she fled from the room, slamming the door behind her.

With the television turned up loud she could hardly hear him. The binmen were due in less than an hour so there was no time to waste. The woman laid the tea towel on the work surface alongside the kitchen sink, the picture of Balmoral surrounded by symmetrical pine trees face down, and laid the lightbulb on it. She folded the cloth once, covering the bulb, and stooped to bring a pan from a cupboard.

The first blow was half-hearted and the bulb didn't break. The second shattered it and the next one reduced the pieces to smithereens. She carefully unfolded the cloth to inspect her handiwork, the shards of glass that clung to the material sparkling in the dilute sunlight that struggled through the uncurtained window. Some too small, most still too large, she decided. Another two blows and she was satisfied with her handiwork.

The binmen came dead on time, the roar of the lorry's engine announcing its arrival as it emptied the dumpsters and compacted their contents deep within its interior. She stood on the landing, watching, as the evidence of her thieving was engulfed by the collective waste of this end of the housing project. Balmoral Castle and lightbulb were swamped and smothered by waste food, empty cartons, disposable nappies and all the other jetsam of modern society. Cabbage stalks and cereal boxes were mashed and compressed with take-away trays, rotten fruit, chicken bones and used cat litter. Jam jars and cigarette packets were mixed with ice cream cartons, ketchup bottles and potato peelings in a stinking stew fit for nothing beyond dumping under the earth, out of sight, out of mind. Powerful hydraulics compressed the tea towel between a semen-stained copy of the Littlewood's catalogue and an unwanted hamster cage, but no one would ever know that. No one at all.

The baby was still whimpering, his throat too dry to cry, his narrow eyes too tired for tears. She picked up a plastic spoon and the tin of peach and banana baby food she'd opened earlier and went into the bedroom. He looked at her, wary and confused, lifting his arms as if reaching for her, then dropping them again. She picked him up, sat him on her knee and let him nestle against her breast. When he was comfortable she dipped the spoon into the gooey mix of fruit and brought it out piled high.

"'Ere," she said, touching the mixture against the child's mouth. "Eat this. This'll give you something to cry about."

The baby felt the moist, sweet fruit against his thin lips and liked the taste. He stopped whimpering, opened his mouth wide and gratefully took in the spoon's contents.

When the Earth was still an infant planet its surface was covered by a vast ocean which teemed and boiled with life. A continent arose out of the ocean and the creatures of the sea came out of the water and colonised it. The ocean was called Tethys, and the land was called Gondwanaland.

No, these are not the ramblings of some would-be J.R.R. Tolkien but a rough approximation of modern geological theory, as I remembered it. The sea was alive with a brew of creatures beyond anything that haunted the worst drug-induced nightmare. Primitive plank-tons and algae competed with and supplied food for life-forms which existed in their billions and have van-ished without a trace. Some of them floated on the cur-rents, others developed the means of locomotion. They wriggled and squirmed or flapped protuberances until they moved into more favourable locations, while oth-ers squirted about on jets of water. They mated to reproduce, or simply divided, then ate each other and their own young. Many were merely a mouth with a digestive tract hanging behind it, while others were ornate filigrees that hung and hovered in the water, catching the sun that gave life to everything. Some pulsed with luminescence while others had eyes that dwarfed the rest of their bodies. Evolution was practising. Most were in blind alleys, doomed to extinction in a handful of generations, because they were not fast or clever enough, or because they tasted too good. Others held tenure for aeons, making Man's visitation on the planet appear no more than a footnote.

Some learned how to convert dissolved gasses and minerals into stone, and developed shells for protection, and for a while they held dominion of the sea. But even these, after a moment or two of life, hardly a blink in geological time, sank to the bottom to join the countless billions of their ancestors. The land rose and sank, rose and sank, in cycles measuring millions of years. Gondwanaland was pulled apart by forces exerted by the Moon and Sun, and by the rotation of the Earth, into a group of smaller continents much like the ones that exist today. Sheets of ice scoured these lands, stripping the soil in some places, depositing it on others, and mountain chains bulged upwards as the new continents crushed against each other.

As the climate became more stable Mankind evolved, probably in Africa, and rapidly spread all around the planet. One group, handsomer and more resourceful than the rest, arrived at a place that was as fair as anywhere else they'd seen on their travels. The water was sweet and the climate favourable.

"This'll do," their leader declared.

"What shall we call it?" someone asked.

"Yorkshire," he replied, and so it was.

* * *

Ching-ing! Ching-ing! The sound of steel against steel echoed off the far wall of the quarry as Rosie Barraclough attempted to chisel a particularly fine specimen from the limestone wall.

"There!" she declared as it finally broke free. "Who can tell me what these are?"

She handed the splinter of rock to Geoff, who shrugged his shoulders and passed it to me. It was a cluster of crinoids, but I handed it on without saying so. There were six of us in the group, including Rosie, and we all wore yellow helmets and plastic safety glasses. When I read the brochure for evening classes at Heckley High School that plopped on to my doormat, I'd been torn between Geology and Spanish for Beginners. Geology because I was interested and I like to know what I'm looking at when I tramp over the moors and dales; Spanish because it might be useful. I'd decided on Spanish as I walked into the school hall on enrolment night, because I was determined to do more travelling and the learning effort required might keep my brain cells from ossifying. But then I saw Rosie.

She was sitting all alone behind a desk with a label on it that said Practical Geology. I cast a glance at the queue waiting to sign up for Spanish, decided that holidaymakers ought to boycott any country that encourages the ritual torture of animals, and veered towards Geology. Whether it was a wise move or something I'd regret for the rest of my life is open to debate.

"Charlie," I heard her say.

"What, Miss?"

"Any ideas what this is, or have I been wasting my time?"

"It's a fossil."

"Ye-es. But of what?"

I went off dolly birds a long time ago. Rosie was not too many years younger than me and had grey hair, with silver streaks. But it belonged grey. I couldn't imagine it any other colour. Her face was strong and mobile, with a mischievous grin constantly playing around her eyes, and she looked great in jeans.

"Um, an ammonite."

"No, Charlie. You're about 200 million years too late."

"Story of my life."

"Anybody else?"

"Are they crinoids?" Miss Eakin. ventured, and as she looked down at the specimen her hard hat fell forward and dislodged the spectacles, as it had done several times before. There are two Miss Eakins in the class, each a mirror image of the other. Identical glasses, identical anoraks and boots, identical hairstyles. Well, style is hardly the word. Frizzy mess is more like it. They did everything together, as far as we could tell, even to the point of speaking in unison. Asking: "Are they crinoids?" was a great departure from the norm for one of them, a blow for individuality. The other Miss Eakin looked horrified.

"Well done," said Rosie.

The other two members of the class were men. Geoff was a retired building society manager and Tom still worked at something in engineering, he said. Like me, they both enjoyed walking and wanted to know more about what was underfoot. I think the two Miss Eakins only joined because it was an 'ology. There were twelve of us in the class at the beginning of term, but a succession of rainy Wednesdays had washed out most of the fieldwork, so Rosie had gallantly taught theory in the classroom. I didn't mind, still found it interesting, but numbers had dwindled. I'd have been happy if they'd all stayed away. This was the last class of the summer term, and our only foray out into limestone country, to Bethesda quarry, on the southern boundary of the Yorkshire Dales. It was a long way from Heckley, but geology is all about fossils to the amateur, so we'd met an hour earlier than usual and gone looking for them at the bottom of the quarry, beneath the sandstone. And there was a link with the town, Rosie told us: the stone for Heckley Methodist chapel had been donated by the owner of Bethesda quarry.

It was also the last chance I'd have to invite her for a drink.

"Are there any dinosaur bones in here?" Tom asked. If all engineers are like Tom I'm not surprised the industry collapsed.

"No, Tom," Rosie replied without a hint of impatience or dismay. "Down here we are in the Palaeozoic era. The dinosaurs didn't appear until the Triassic period, which would be up there somewhere if it hadn't been eroded away." She waved a hand, still holding the chisel, towards the lip of the quarry.

The worst scenario was that I suggest we all go to the pub for an end-of-term snifter, but it wasn't necessary. As the class started back up the track to where the cars were parked I hung behind, looking for a suitable ledge where I could leave the fossilised crinoids. It wasn't such a fine specimen to be worth keeping, but a future class might appreciate it. I placed it in a niche in the rock wall and sauntered after the others.

Rosie was standing by the boot of her car, collecting our hard hats and spectacles. I placed mine in the box and laid her geologist's hammer, which I'd been carrying, alongside them. None of the others were in earshot, so I said: "Thanks for that, Rosie. It was really interesting and I've enjoyed the course. Do you fancy going for a drink?"

She picked up the hammer, made a knocking motion towards me a couple of times, then said: "An ammonite!"

"Ammonites, crinoids, I was close."

"Only in the dictionary."

"That drink?"

I think she was blushing slightly as she said: "Yes, that's a good idea."

I'd brought Geoff and Tom to the quarry, and Rosie had given a lift to the Misses Eakins. We dropped them off in the school car park, said our goodnights and I helped Rosie carry her stuff back into the geology lab. It was almost dark and the school caretaker was waiting for us, jangling his keys. Ten minutes later Rosie and I were seated in the pub sipping gin and tonics. There's something irresistible about a g and t. I'd gone to the bar feeling quite content and at peace with the world, prepared to order a half of lager for myself, but as soon as Rosie asked for a gin and tonic my salivary glands burst into life and I heard myself say: "That sounds nice. I think I'll join you."

"So what made you become a geology teacher?" I asked, after that first satisfying sip.

"Ooh, that's just what the doctor ordered," she said, lowering her glass and pulling an approving face.

"You must have a different doctor to me."

"I believe in self-medication. Why did I become a geology teacher?"

"Mmm."

"I didn't. I became a geography teacher. Geog's my first subject. Ask me about the rainfall in Namibia, or the climatic factors affecting the rise of the wine industry in Southern Australia."

"None, and it's warm and sunny."

"Well done."

"So how did the geology creep in?"

She shrugged her shoulders. "I needed a second subject, and there's a growing interest in it. It's always held a fascination for me, since I was a little girl. When the other kids received a doll for Christmas, I got a magnifying glass. My dad used to take me and my brother walking along the beach and we'd collect stones and bring them home. Afterwards we'd try to identify them from pictures in books. I suppose that's where it started, although by the same process I could have become an ornithologist or a biologist, meteorologist, just about anything. Dad was a polymath, in his own quiet way, and encouraged us to be the same."

"What did your brother become?"

Rosie lifted her heavy glass and studied the liquid

in it, with its characteristic bloom. "A sailor. He ran away to sea when he was sixteen."

"Ran away?"

"He joined the Merchant Navy. I've never seen him since."

"Your dad sounds a bit like mine," I told her. "He was interested in everything, taught me to ask questions, never to be afraid of making a fool of myself. 'There's always someone wanting to know the same thing but daren't ask,' he used to tell me. Was your dad a teacher, too?"

Rosie gave a tiny involuntary jump, coming back from wherever she'd drifted off to, and smiled as she said: "No, he was a baker. We owned a bakery in South Wales, near a village called Laugharne. Mum was a great fan of Dylan Thomas, who had lived there for a while. That's how we came to know the place."

"So you're Welsh. You don't have the accent."

"No, I'm English. We originated in Gloucestershire and moved to Wales when I was three. And that part of Wales used to be known as Little England. Then... afterwards... we moved to East Anglia. Cromer and a couple of other places."

Afterwards, she'd said, with some emphasis, but I decided not to pry. I wanted to see her again, not learn her life-story. I decided to stay on safe ground. "So it was fresh bread every morning," I stated. "My mouth is watering at the thought of it."

"It was wonderful. We lived over the bakery and awoke to the smell. Dad started work at three in the morning but he'd be finished by noon, so he was always there to meet us from school and that's when we'd go walking on the beach. We looked for fossils and collected various shells and pebbles. He taught me how to identify minerals by doing scratch and hardness tests. Things like that."

I felt envious, and my stomach reminded me that I'd had a canteen pie for lunch and a bowl of cornflakes before I dashed out to the class. OK, so it was a large bowl, and I'd had a sliced banana with honey on the flakes, but I'm a big lad.

"It sounds idyllic," I told her. "So what brought you to Yorkshire?"

"It was, but it couldn't last. Dad... he died, and Mum started to follow the same route as her hero, Dylan Thomas. She hit the bottle. We went from warm, loving, nuclear family to totally dysfunctional in less than three months. I scraped into university and married a fellow student who turned out to be a total waster. Took me twelve years to realise it, unfortunately. I walked out on him and headed north, in search of no-nonsense, northern straightforwardness and hospitality."

"Ha! And did you find it?"

"I'm not sure."

"I'm sorry about the family. I take it you have no children?"

"No. Have you any?"

I looked straight at her, face composed, as I replied: "I imagine so," but I couldn't maintain the look and broke into a grin. "No, no children," I admitted.

"And is there a Mrs Charlie Priest, as in Roman Catholic?"

"That's my line."

"I know. That's what you told me when I asked you your name at enrolment."

"You remembered. I'm flattered." I held her gaze and saw that hint of a blush again. "No, there is no Mrs Priest. Same story as you, except she walked out on me, left me holding the J-cloth."

"She found herself a rich boyfriend," I added, in an attempt to clear myself of any responsibility for the break-up.

"Same again?"

"I'll get them," I said, reaching for my wallet.

"No, it's my turn. G and t?"

"No, just an orange juice, please, with lemonade."

I watched her go to the bar and decided that there was something I liked about Rosie Barraclough, and it wasn't just those slim hips and that handsome face. There was a strange mix of vulnerability and strength in her character, a joy that hid a deep sadness, and I knew for certain that I wanted to play a part in trying to ease that sadness. I never dreamed how wrong I could be; how I would make it a million times worse.

"So what about you, Charlie?" she said as she placed my drink in front of me. "You've learned my life-story, now it's your turn."

When you are a cop, a detective, you learn techniques for getting people to open up and confide in you. You learn all there is about them without giving away a single thing about yourself. Sometimes it's like opening a bottle of ketchup: nothing comes out for a while and then suddenly you're covered in it. In the police station, on the job, that's good, but you find yourself doing it in your private life, too, and that's not good. I had nothing to hide from Rosie, nothing at all, but I don't like talking about myself. If you keep quiet, people give you the benefit of the doubt. Why open your mouth and prove them wrong?

"There's not much to say," I told her. "I've lived in Heckley all my life, went to Heckley Grammar School where I was captain of the football team, then art college, one marriage, met Rosie Barraclough whilst studying geology. I do quite a lot of walking, occasionally paint a large abstract when I'm feeling fraught, and like to do all the normal things that you see in the personal ads. I've a GSH and WLTM an NS for an LTR, or something."

Rosie eyes crinkled as she smiled at me. "Have you ever advertised?"

"No, honest. Have you?"

"I've never been so desperate. I suppose some people are trapped by their circumstances and that's their only chance to meet people."

"I suppose so." I was going to add that night classes were a better way, but decided not to. We talked about our families for a while and I learned that Rosie's mother was still alive, in a nursing home in East Anglia.

"Another?" I asked, pointing at her empty glass, but she shook her head and said she ought to be off. As we walked across the car park I told her that I'd like to see her again. Rosie said she'd look forward to that and we agreed to meet on Saturday night. When you are single it's the weekend evenings that are most difficult to fill. She wrote her phone number on a pay-and-display ticket for me and I put it in a safe place.

"Drink, Chinese, curry, pictures, theatre?" I said. "If

we want to go to the theatre I'll have to get the tickets."
We were standing alongside her car as she held the driver's door open, and a light drizzle had started to fall.

"Not the cinema or the theatre," she replied. "Let's go where we can talk."

"Chinese and a drink?"

"Lovely, and perhaps then I'll learn a little bit more about the enigmatic Charlie Priest."

"I'm afraid there's no more to tell. I'm a very shallow person."

"That I don't believe. I'm still worried about that ammonite."

"The ammonite?"

"The crinoids. You knew perfectly well what they were, so why did you call them an ammonite? Was it to encourage Miss Eakin, which would be kind of you, or was it because you're a control freak, laughing at everybody from behind your sleeve?"

"Damn, you've rumbled me. It was because I was trying to win the heart of Miss Eakin. Either one. The pair of them would have been beyond my wildest fantasy."

"I'll believe you. And you can tell me all about the secret art of the graphic designer. It's a mystery to me what they do."

"A graphic designer? Who said I was a graphic designer?"

"You did, the first night. We were admiring the drawing you did of a trilobite and Tom asked you what you did for a living. I thought you said you were a graphic designer."

"Ah! No. I'm sorry. I didn't think you'd heard that.

It's just a defence mechanism. If I say what I really do people start asking me all sorts of questions, telling me their problems, laying down the law as they see it. It's a lot easier to tell a fib. I always say I'm a graphic designer and that usually silences them."

"So what do you do?"

"I'm a policeman. A detective. I'm sorry if I misled you, it wasn't intentional. You're getting soaked."

I'm not sure if it was the lie or the fact that I was a cop that dismayed Rosie, but something did. Her eyes narrowed and the smile left them. "Oh," was all she said.

"It's an honourable profession." I'd lined myself up to lean forward and give her a peck on the cheek as we said our goodnights, but I didn't get the chance. Rosie slipped into the driver's seat and I said: "I'll ring you."

"Yes," she replied as she pulled the door shut. I gave her a wave and walked over to where my own car was parked. She was embarrassed about being misled, I decided. When I'd plied her with one of Mr Ho's special banquets and her fingers were wrapped around another gin and tonic she'd want to know all about my best cases, of that I was sure. Women always do.

Chapter Two

"Crime pattern analysis, Charlie," Superintendent Gilbert Wood said. "I need figures, not excuses."

"Remind me," I replied. "I've lost the list."

"Percentage increase or decrease in burglary. Percentage increase or decrease in street crime. Percentage increase or decrease in car crime. By this afternoon. I need them for tomorrow."

"Right. It shall be done. Do you want to show that we are a thin blue line manfully struggling against overwhelming odds, or that we are really on top of the job?"

Gilbert looked exasperated. "The truth would be nice, for once. Do you think we could have an accurate picture of what's happening? The idea is to give the public, the newspapers and politicians some inkling of the way trends are heading. It helps formulate government policy, believe it or not. And, as a matter of fact, I'd be quite interested myself."

"The truth is the hardest option,"

"I know, but just bloody do it."

"And it will be meaningless. An informed guess by someone with my experience would give a much clearer picture of the situation."

"Oh no it wouldn't. And when you've done that, get your hair cut. You look like an unemployed violinist."

"Do you know how many mobile phones were stolen in 1982, Gilbert? I'll tell you: none. Not a single one. Or how many cars were stolen in Yorkshire in

1950? You could count them on your fingers. That's at least a ten thousand percent increase. If you don't weight the figures to compensate for other factors, like nobody had a mobile phone a few years ago, the numbers are meaningless. And do you know how much a haircut costs these days? I don't have someone to cut mine, in the kitchen with a tea towel round my neck."

"I'll mention your concerns to the Chief Constable. This afternoon, please?"

"Your wish is my command, mein Fuhrer. I'm sticking round the office if I can, in case the result comes through."

"It will. They gave it what – four hours? – yesterday. They'll give it another couple this morning to make it look respectable and qualify for lunch, and then they'll announce their verdict. It's cut and dried, Charlie, believe me."

"God, I hope so. The longer it takes the less promising it looks. How's young Freddie?"

"On the mend, thanks. They took his appendix out and he sounded cheerful when his mum rang him."

Gilbert's daughter's son had been stricken with appendicitis while on a school trip. "Where is he?"

"In the General. Apparently they'd just set off when he started complaining of stomach pains. One of the teachers recognised the symptoms, thought it might be appendicitis, and they took him straight to Casualty."

"Lucky for young Freddie. OK, I'll get those figures."

I skipped down the stairs, singing a happy tune – "I don't want to set the world on fi-yah," – and burst into the CID office. Big Dave "Sparky" Sparkington was sitting on the corner of a desk with his jacket hooked over his shoulder, like he was ready to be off somewhere, and Pete Goodfellow was tapping away at a keyboard. Everybody else was out making the streets of Heckley safe for children and little old ladies.

"I just want to start... a flame in your heart."

"Blimey, you sound cheerful."

"But I'm always cheerful. Peter, are those figures available?"

"Won't take a second to run them off."

"Good. Deliver them personally to Mr Wood at about ten to five, please. Loosen your tie, roll up your sleeves and splash water on your brow. Make it look as if you've spent all day wrestling with them. You might even crawl in on your hands and knees... No, on second thoughts, forget the crawling."

"Will do."

I turned to Dave. "Where are you going, Sunshine?"

"Sylvan Fields. A burglary last night and it looks as if the phantom knickers thief has struck again."

"Happy going on your own?"

"Yeah, no problem. In spite of its reputation, most of the people who live there are quite decent."

"Blimey, I never thought I'd hear you say that."

"I know. I must be mellowing with age. All the rest are toe-rags, though. Will you ring me if the verdict comes through?"

"You bet."

Off he went and I settled down in my little enclave to attack the pile of paperwork that had accrued. I'd spent an awful lot of the last six weeks in court, at a murder trial, and now the jury was out. Most of the time I'd been hanging around in the corridor, in case

I was needed, with a couple of days in the witness box. Timothy Fletcher had murdered seven people, seven that we knew about, but had died whilst resisting arrest. He fell off Scammonden Bridge on to the M62, at rush hour, under a sixteen-wheeler loaded with Yorkie bars, but nobody was mourning him. The trial had been to decide how involved his girlfriend was in the murders. Was she an innocent dupe, as she claimed, or was she a fully paid-up partner? We went into court convinced that she had been instrumental in luring at least three victims into Fletcher's car, but our chief witness was still traumatised by the attack and we had decided not to expose her to cross-examination. Meanwhile, the prisoner and her legal advisers had had six months to prepare a case and they'd done a good job. Now we weren't so cocky.

I read a policy document about Positive Crime Recording rules but most of it went straight over my head. As I understand it, when somebody comes into the station and says: "I don't want to make a complaint, but..." we've got to record it as a complaint. Normally the desk sergeant would nod gravely, make sympathetic noises, promise to have a word in the appropriate ear, and completely forget the whole thing as soon as the non-complainant walked out through the door. Or, if he deemed it serious enough, he might have that word in somebody's ear. Either way everybody was happy. Now he has to initiate a trail of paperwork longer than Haley's comet. When the villains learn about it they'll have a field day. If every one of them came into the nick and said they didn't want to make a complaint, the whole legal system would grind to a halt. It nearly has already.

I wasn't in the mood for paperwork so I went for a wander. The typists were too busy to chat and the briefing room was deserted. "Where is everybody?" I asked as I drifted into Control.

"Hello Charlie, waiting for the verdict?" the controller replied, turning to face me.

"Mmm. This is the worst bit."

"She'll go down, sure as Christmas. They're all at the hospital. Been a bit of trouble there. Not sure what it's all about, yet."

I looked at him. "At the hospital?"

"That's right. They're not admitted, although one or two of them are contenders for the malingerers ward. We answered a call and they asked for backup. Bit of a riot outside, by the sound of it."

"Is Gareth aware of what's happening?" Gareth Adey is my uniformed counterpart.

"Yeah. He's at headquarters, in a meeting. Said to let him know if it grew serious."

"Is that our serious or his serious?" Gareth has a reputation for magnifying things.

"Ah! Good question. Let's see what I can find out."

He swivelled his chair round to face the console again and started speaking into his mouthpiece. At the second attempt the PS answered.

"What's the position, Paul?"

"Confused. Apparently there's some sort of infection loose in the hospital. They stopped all admissions yesterday afternoon, and this morning they're refusing to release anyone, including the staff. The doors are locked and the only contact is by telephone or the intercom on the door. There's people arriving all the time to pick up patients but the hospital won't discharge them, so they're growing restless, and visitors are arriving all the time too, which doesn't help."

"Any ideas what sort of infection?"

"No."

I said: "Tell him I'll try to contact the hospital manager."

"Mr Priest's with me. He says he'll try to contact the hospital manager. We'll get back to you, out."

But the hospital manager wasn't answering his phone and nobody else was, either. I replaced the handset after ten fruitless minutes, saying: "No doubt all will be revealed in the fullness of time," because that's the nature of infections. They flourish or they wither, but either way, they pull the strings.

I walked across the road to the sandwich shop, bought a cheese and pickle and a curd tart and sauntered back to the office. The phone rang six times. Three were to ask if I'd heard anything; one was a reporter wanting a quote – I gave him You don't need a weatherman to know which way the wind blows – and two were business. Rosie Barraclough didn't ring. I hadn't given her my number but she could have worked it out if she'd been really keen. There again, if she'd been that keen I'd probably have run a mile. I found a tabloid and a magazine in the outer office, made myself a coffee and lunched with my feet on the desk. The magazine was Dave Sparkington's copy of Naked Female Mud Wrestling USA. He takes it for the crossword.

The phone rang for the seventh time. "Priest."

"Hi Charlie. It's that time of year again." It was an inspector from another division who organised the force's contribution to the annual Heckley Gala. Part of the show is an art exhibition, open to all but with a special class for cops. We have a surprising number of respectable watercolourists helping keep law and order on the streets. And one mad abstractionist.

"Oh God," I said. "I haven't anything prepared."

"It's not for three weeks," he told me. "Plenty of time for you to make a few daubs on some hardboard."

"A few daubs!" I exclaimed. "A few daubs! You're talking about fine examples of abstract expressionism."

"That's what I said. Can I put you down for two, as usual?"

"I suppose so."

"Do they have titles?"

"Yes."

"What?"

"Untitled 1 and Untitled 2."

"You're a toff, Chas."

"I know. Have you rung Woodturner Willie yet?"

"No, he's next on my list."

"Ask him to make me two frames for them, please."

"Okie-dokie. How big?"

"Um, oh, about four by three."

"Inches, feet or metres?"

"Feet, numbskull."

"Will do."

I carefully replaced the phone. The pictures might sell for fifty pounds each, which will go to charity. The frames will cost me twenty, the board a tenner and the paint at least that. There's something about business that I haven't grasped, yet.

Eighth time. "Priest."

The voice that answered was one that I'd grown sick of over the last six months, but today it was sweet as music. It was the CPS barrister, from the court. "Not guilty on the first five, Charlie, guilty on the next two and the kidnapping. Twenty years tariff for each. Crack open the champagne."

I didn't leap up with joy, fisting the air like some second-rate sportsman who's done what he's paid to do. I thanked him, told him well done, and slowly replaced the receiver. I was glad nobody was there with me. I buried my hands in my hair and gave an involuntary shudder of satisfaction and relief. Justice had been done and it was over. Over for me and the team, that is. It would never be over for the relatives of the victims, but now perhaps they could start thinking about the future.

I was glad I hadn't been in court, waiting, as those first five Not Guilties were announced, watching the face of the accused. Her spirits would rise imperceptibly with each one, and those of the prosecution team would sink a similar amount. "Was she going to get away with it?" everybody would have been asking as the charges were dismissed, and then came those golden words: "Guilty... Guilty... Guilty," and she would have crumbled. And I wouldn't have liked to see that either, because my feelings towards her might have softened, just a degree, which would have been a betrayal of seven women and a young boy.

I brushed the hair out of my eyes, pulled my shoulders back and took three deep breaths. Gilbert's phone was engaged when I tried to pass on the verdicts, so I went up to see him. A sergeant crossed me on the stairs and shook my hand when I told him the news. "Well done, Charlie, well done."

Gilbert's arm was stretched out, his hand holding the phone as I went in and he looked up at me, fumbling with the handset, having difficulty replacing it. His expression was as bleak as a January dawn, his eyes wide and his mouth hanging open.

"Three life sentences," I announced. "Twenty years tariff."

"Good," he said, half-heartedly, his thoughts a million miles away. "That's good. Well done."

"What is it, Gilbert?" I asked, sitting in the chair opposite him. "You look as if you've seen a ghost."

"Do I? I'm sorry. It's young Freddie, Charlie. He's in the General, you know."

"What's happened to him?"

"Well, nothing, but they won't let his mother in to see him. There's an infection loose and they've quarantined the whole place."

"I've heard about it. They're always having infections in hospitals, Gilbert – it's all those sick people. And the cuts. He'll be all right, mark my words."

But he wasn't listening. "I rang the medical director," he said.

"I couldn't get through when I tried."

"I rang his wife and she gave me his mobile number."

"Don't tell me – he's a lodge member."

"It has its uses. This is in confidence, Charlie. It mustn't go outside these walls, you understand?"

I shrugged my shoulders. If galloping salmonella was rampaging through the corridors and wards of Heckley General I was hardly likely to go shouting it from the rooftops, but it was unfortunate for young Freddie.

"There's a virus loose in the place," he told me.

"What sort of virus?"

"It's Ebola, Charlie. They've got Ebola virus in Heckley General."

There was no need for me or anybody else to shout it from the rooftops, because even as we spoke the news was being disseminated by more efficient means. The nurse who started the scare rang her parents, who recognised the dreaded word Ebola in the midst of her hysterical rantings, and from then on it spread like a bloodstain through the community. At five o'clock it was on the local news, at six the nation heard about it and by twenty past the more daring camera crews started arriving.

A couple of weeks ago there had been a TV special about the 1994 outbreak of Ebola in the Central African Republic, so the public was well clued-up. The Ebola River is a tributary of the Congo, and the people who live along its banks hunt monkeys for food and to sell for medical research. Back in the seventies another virus that the monkeys carry suffered a mutation in its

DNA that gave it the ability to exist in their close relative – Homo sapiens. This virus has an incubation period of several years and is only passed on by the most intimate contact, but it spread stealthily – an invisible cloud of poison that chose its victims all the way from the mud huts of Africa to the marble mansions of the most privileged people in the world. When they started to die it was given a name – AIDS.

Ebola probably has the same origins, but its MO is different. Ebola can be transmitted through the air, like the common cold, and it kills nine out of ten of its victims in fifteen days. There is no cure.

Residents of Heckley who had caravans or bungalows at the coast suddenly decided that now was a good time for a visit. Others decided that an extended weekend away was long overdue and hastily threw a few belongings in the back of the Mondeo. The queue of vehicles leaving town gridlocked with the rush hour traffic trying to get home, anxious to see if the wife and kids were feeling OK, and Heckley ground to a standstill.

I went home, made myself a salad sandwich and watched it on TV. The usual pundits were there, outside the hospital, spouting their limited knowledge at the camera, scaring everybody sugar-less. First symptom was a headache, we were told, then the whites of the eyes turned scarlet as the capillaries burst, followed by bleeding from all the body's orifices.

"I feel like that everyday," I mumbled, fielding a piece of tomato that fell out of my sandwich and reaching for the remote control.

By eight o'clock it was all over. False alarm. "A

patient was admitted who had recently travelled in Africa and showed the early symptoms of Ebola," a hospital spokeswoman told the waiting cameras. "The hospital was quarantined as a precaution, but tests for Ebola have proved negative and the quarantine can now be lifted. This was a routine safeguard and at no time was any member of the public or staff at risk."

Pull the other one. God, what a farce. I went into the garage, cut some hardboard to size and painted it white. In less than three weeks I had to produce a couple of paintings worthy of my not-inconsiderable reputation. Something that "my five-year-old daughter could do," as numerous friends and colleagues would take great delight in pointing out. Would it be a couple of Picassos, or maybe a pair of Modigliani ladies? They always went down well. When I'd finished I thought about phoning Rosie, but it was too late. I'd ring her tomorrow, make arrangements for Saturday. Mr Ho, the proprietor of the Bamboo Curtain, was a friend of mine. One of his special banquets was an event rather than a meal. I was sure Rosie would enjoy it. Before I went to bed I found the bottle of cheap champagne I'd been saving and put it in the fridge.

We didn't make the front page, which was a disappointment for the troops. A Town in Fear was a better headline than The Face of Evil, so the first six pages of the tabloids were filled with graphic descriptions of Ebola symptoms and primary school diagrams of DNA, showing how red triangles could mutate into blue hexagons with deadly results. The broadsheets used the scare to highlight the multi-million dollar trade in living primates, printing hard-hitting articles from their libraries to pad out the pages and demonstrate their concern.

Our PR people had prepared a couple of statements from me – one for if we lost the trial; one for if we won – so I read that I was pleased with the result and hoped that it would be of some comfort for the families of the victims.

"See!" I announced as I went into Gilbert's office for our morning meeting. "Nothing to worry about. When's he coming home?"

"Tomorrow, all being well," he replied, pushing the file he'd been reading to one side. "But it was a worry, Charlie. Did you see that programme on TV about it? If that gets loose it could be the end of the world."

"Nah," I said. "A comet. That's what'll do it, like it did for the dinosaurs, sixty-five million years ago." I've been swatting up on dinosaurs recently.

I opened the champagne in the office and we drank it from our coffee mugs. It was just a little ceremony to mark the closure of the case: a collective sigh of relief and mutual back-slap, expressed in fizzy pop. We'd had a major piss-up the weekend after the arrest, but the job's not over until someone has the key turned on them.

Most of the troops knew what cases they were on with, and I had a couple of others to hand out. Prioritising the work is a big part of my contribution, but it sometimes makes me unpopular with the public. Each detective has at least five or six crimes to deal with at any time. If there's a chance of an arrest in one of them it moves to the front of the queue, if there isn't it goes backwards. So victims sit at home, surrounded by what's left of their scattered belongings, waiting for the handsome crime-fighter to come knocking at the door to detect the villain. But he doesn't come, not for three days, because he knows he has a better chance of finding the youths who screwed the filling station in full view of the CCTV cameras.

One of the DCs approached me, more hesitantly than normal. "Um, can I have a quick word, Boss?" he asked.

"Oh, what do you want, my blue-eyed son?" I asked.

"It's the coffee fund. You're a bit behind."

I delved into my jacket pocket and produced a handful of coins. "How much?"

"That's not enough."

"Go on."

"Twelve pounds."

"Twelve quid! Twelve quid! Just for coffee! It's highway robbery."

"You haven't paid anything for three months."

I found a twenty pound note in my wallet and handed it over, saying: "Make sure you enter it in your book. I think you must have forgotten, the last time."

Dave Sparkington hung back as the team dispersed.

"How did you get on with the knicker thief," I asked.

"Great. We got a description."

"Go on."

"Black lace, open crotch. I'm looking into it."

I exhaled, slowly and deliberately, casting my gaze

towards the ceiling. Sparky likes to tell you things in his own way.

"About fourteen years old," he added. "Short, with fair hair. Wears a grey football shirt. Not sure what it is but it could be something like Leeds United second team Tuesday morning away strip."

"Good. Any other ideas?"

"We've a couple o' names."

"OK. Keep on with it."

He dangled a telephone report sheet in front of me, saying: "They can wait. This came in about five minutes ago while you were upstairs. It's from the General Hospital. They had an admission yesterday afternoon that might be a poisoning. Non-fatal but it could've been. Victim thinks his ex-wife is trying to kill 'im. Thought I'd go along and talk to him but wondered if you wanted to come."

"The hospital?"

"Mmm."

I shook my head vigorously. "Er, no, Dave. I think you can manage that one yourself."

"OK. See if I care. I've had my flu jab. Apparently the ex-wife was runner-up in the Miss Ferodo brake-linings beauty contest."

"On second thoughts," I said, "if it's an attempted murder maybe I should come along. I'll get my coat."

Pete Goodfellow was bent over his keyboard, his typing sounding like a dripping tap. "You're in charge, Pete," I called to him.

"No problem. Where are you going?"

"To the hospital."

"Right. I've an appointment there myself next week, about this knee. It still isn't right. Did I tell you?"

"Yes, Pete, you told us all about it, several times. Have you tried St. John's wort?"

"No. I've tried glucosamine, and cod liver oil capsules, but they haven't been much good. How does St. John's wort work?"

"I don't know but it cured Dave's irritable bowel syndrome, didn't it, Sunshine?"

"No, it gave me it. C'mon, let's go."

We went in my car, with Dave driving. As we pulled out of the station yard he said: "Who is she?"

"Who's who?"

"The woman."

"What woman?"

"The one that's making you so flippin' cheerful."

"What makes you think it's a woman?"

"You mean... it's a man?"

"Er, no. You were right, it's a woman."

He gave a chuckle and looked across at me. "When you die, Charlie, we won't have you cremated or buried. We'll roll you flat and make you into a window."

"Are you suggesting I'm transparent?"

"Only where women are concerned."

"And you'll go before me. Look at you: overweight, sedentary lifestyle. We thin nervous types live to a ripe old age."

"Don't you start, I've enough with Shirley and Sophie lecturing me. But you're right, I need more exercise."

I was quiet for a few seconds. Shirley is Dave's wife, Sophie his daughter and my goddaughter. She's studying at Cambridge, about to start her final year, and breaking Dave's heart. She's tall and beautiful, and had hardly been home this year. Dave was having to come to terms with the apple of his eye being plucked off the tree by someone he didn't know.

"Have you heard from Sophie?" I ventured.

"No. Not for about six weeks. Last we heard she was going to Cap Ferrat with this boyfriend and his parents, she said. They have a place there, apparently."

"It was bound to happen, Dave. And if they've a place over there she can't be doing too bad."

"I don't suppose so. She asked how you were, if you'd found a new girlfriend. Can I tell her about Miss X?"

"No. Tell her that I'm not looking, that she's the only woman for me."

"Uh!" he snorted, and his knuckles tightened on the wheel.

Ten minutes later we were running up the steps into the hospital.

"I assume you were fibbing about the Miss Ferodo bit," I gasped between breaths.

"No, scout's honour," he replied, adding: "Mind you, it was 1945."

The doctor in charge of the patient came to meet us at the front desk. He looked about twenty and smelled like a National Trust gift shop. Dave introduced me and we shook hands.

"Is everything back to normal now?" I asked.

"Just about," he replied, grinning, "but it was interesting for a while."

"Have the Press abandoned you now that there's no story?"

"They have. It was like Downing Street on budget day for a while, out in the car park. They've gone now, thank God, but they might be back when they hear about this."

"Really? So where do we begin?"

"He came in by ambulance," he told us. "Rang for it himself. Must have been quite frightening for the poor chap. They were gathered round him, reading his vital signs and wondering what to do next, when the house-man dealing with him asked if he'd had any illnesses lately. He said he hadn't, all innocent, but he'd just come back from a holiday in Kenya. Could it be something he'd picked up there? And that was that. This nurse – a black girl from Nigeria – said: 'Oh my God, it's Ebola!' and everybody took ten paces backwards."

From the expression on his face it was evident that he was enjoying telling us this. I was more interested in the poisoning but I stayed quiet, content to let the doctor have his five minutes and tell us in his own time.

"How is he now?" Dave asked.

"Ask him yourself. Come on, I'll take you to him."

Dave and I looked at each other and back at the doctor. "You mean..." I began. "You mean... the person we've come to see is the Ebola suspect?"

"He's not a suspect any more. The toxicology results were quite conclusive, but it was quite a relief when they came back. Mind you, the ones with red faces might have preferred a full scale outbreak."

He obviously wasn't one of them. "So what was it?" I asked.

"Warfarin. We pumped him full of vitamin K and gave him a blood transfusion and he's now well on the way to recovery."

"What did it do to him?"

"It causes haemorrhaging, internally and externally. He'd summoned an ambulance because he was having breathing difficulties and then started passing blood. Lives alone, apparently. When he was admitted he was haemorrhaging from his nose and eyes and generally feeling out of sorts. What was happening inside we don't know, but we'll keep him in for a day or two, see how he fares."

"Sounds nasty," I said.

"It was."

"Rat poison?"

"That's right."

"But sometimes used medicinally."

"Yes. It's an anti-clotting agent."

"Had he been prescribed it?"

"He says not."

We'd reached the corridor where the victim's private room was situated, and slowed to a halt outside it. "Could the toxicology report differentiate between the two possible sources?" I asked.

"No, not at the level of testing we have available."

"If it was rat poison, what's the fatal dose?"

"Impossible to say. If the recipient has high blood pressure any dose could be dangerous. Prescribed dose is usually between three and nine milligrams. To be sure of killing someone it would have to be massive."

"How big is massive?"

"Don't quote me, Inspector, but I imagine, oh, thirty milligrams could be rather dodgy for most people. That's what? A couple of tablespoonfuls. It's anybody's guess."

"Would he have died without medical intervention?"

"No doubt about it."

"Right. Thanks for your help, Doc. What's he called?"

"Carl Johnson."

Mr Johnson was sitting up in bed, a drip in his arm supplying him with whatever he needed most. He was gaunt and swarthy, with a bony shoulder poking from the one-size-fits-all hospital pyjamas.

"This is Inspector Priest and I'm DS Sparkington," Dave told him, and the patient reached out with his free arm to shake hands. We found two chairs and sat down beside him.

We asked him to tell us what happened and he started to relate all the gory details, but he had difficulty speaking so I decided that the abbreviated version would do. I poured him a beaker of water and said: "Have you been told what you were poisoned with?"

"Thanks." He took a sip, then: "Warfarin. Rat poison."

"But you're not on warfarin tablets?"

"No. It was her who did it, I'm sure of it."

"Your ex-wife?"

"Estranged. We're only separated."

"Why would she want to poison you?"

"To get her hands on everything, that's why."

"So you think it was an attempt to murder you, not just make you ill?"

"'Course it was an attempt to murder me."

"Any ideas how you took the poison?"

"No. Something I ate, I expect."

"What was your last meal?"

"Curry. Chicken Madras."

"That would disguise the taste of the warfarin. Was it from a takeaway?"

It was. He gave us his house keys and permission to scavenge in his rubbish bins. Dave made a note of his wife's new address and the name of the suspect take-away.

"My money's on Miss Ferodo," he stated as we drove across town.

"Nah," I said. "Mine's on the takeaway."

"How come?"

"Sabotage. Local fish and chip shop fighting back, and fighting dirty." Some cops deal with multi-billion frauds and drug cartels and barons of industry with their fingers in the pie, in Heckley we have takeaway wars.

Johnson's semi on the Barratt estate had all the hall-marks of a home where the woman has walked out: two days' washing up in the sink; dirty towels over the radiator; windows that cut out the light and a smell of stale food permeating everywhere. Otherwise it was pleasant. The furniture was good quality and the decor was freshly applied. Too many ornaments, as usual, and a big wedding photograph standing on the widescreen TV.

Why did he keep that? I wondered. A young version

of Carl Johnson stood proudly next to a bubbly blonde, a grey topper clutched in his hand. I picked up the remote control for the television and flicked round the channels. I couldn't believe what I saw. Were there really, in homes all over the country, people sad enough to be watching that tripe? "Go for a walk!" I wanted to scream at them. "Read a book! Or just look at the sky and wonder at the clouds. Anything but watch this drivel."

"Bad news," Dave announced as he came into the room. "His bin's been emptied. Hey, I like this."

"When it's widescreen," I said, "is the picture just stretched or is there a bit extra stuck on each side?"

"It's stretched. Haven't you seen football on one? The goals look about thirty feet wide."

"No." I pressed the off button and the picture faded. "Let's have a look in the kitchen, then."

The curry tray was in a bucket under the sink, with enough sauce left clinging to the edges for our highly-trained scientists to analyse. We placed it in a plastic bag and labelled it. Beneath the tray we found two empty Foster's cans, so they went into bags, too, along with a mackerel in honey mustard tin and the remnants of a pizza.

Inside the fridge part of his fridge-freezer there was a half-empty tin of Del Monte pineapple rings, my favourites. He hadn't mentioned them but perhaps he'd had a pudding. Something sweet like that goes down well with ice cream after a hot curry. I placed it on the draining board next to the other stuff.

"It's going to cost a fortune to process this lot," I complained. Current charge to put something through the lab was £340 minimum, and Gilbert would not be pleased.

Dave bent over our loot, sniffing at everything. "Any ideas what rat poison smells like?" he asked.

"No. We should have asked the doctor. Let's look in his garage – that might be where it's kept."

There was a Citroen C3 in there, plus enough half-empty tins of emulsion in shades of beige to decorate the set of Desert Song. He had a few DIY tools, nothing excessive, and an assortment of chemicals for dealing with garden pests, but no mysterious crystals in an unmarked jam jar. He kept everything in those plastic containers that stack on top of each other. I found an empty one and commandeered it for the samples. We cast appraising eyes over the car and wandered out into the garden.

He'd done a lot of work in it. There was a kerb around the lawn that was painted white, as was the wall dividing him from his neighbour. The borders were neat and weed-free, but well-stocked with plants, many of which were in full bloom. I'm not good at plants, but these looked the sorts that need a lot of attention. Dave knocked on the neighbour's door, but nobody was home.

"Just a sec," Dave said, back in the kitchen as I started to place the samples in the box. He opened a drawer, decided it was the wrong one and tried another. This time he took a teaspoon from it and reached for the tin of pineapple.

"What are you doing?" I asked.

He dipped the spoon into the juice and transferred it to his mouth. A second later he was spitting furiously into the sink. I turned the cold tap on and told him to wash his mouth out. When he'd finished coughing and retching I said: "Don't you like pineapple?"

"That's it," he declared, wiping his mouth with a handkerchief and nodding towards the tin. "That's where t'poison is."

"Well done," I told him. "I reckon you just saved Gilbert's budget a couple of grand. And if you start bleeding from all your bodily orifices we'll know it isn't Ebola."

He took me back to the station and then went off to the Home Office lab at Wetherton with all the goodies we'd collected. I caught up with the morning's happenings and lunched on a chunky KitKat and a mug of tea. Carl Johnson's wife, who rejoiced in the name of Davina, was in when I rang her number, so I arranged to see her in thirty minutes and went to the bathroom to comb my hair – maybe Sparky hadn't been lying about the Miss Ferodo thing.

Funny thing was I still wasn't sure after I met her. She lived in a first-floor flat in a converted Victorian terrace on the edge of the town centre, only five minutes from the nick. She was about five-two in height with dazzling blonde hair that would have mended a fuse in an emergency. She had her hair lacquer delivered by tanker, like central heating oil, and I could have imagined her lining up with other hopefuls in the Skegness Pier Ballroom, a few years earlier. I could have, but I tried not to.

"Mrs Johnson?" I asked, offering my warrant card

for inspection as she opened the door. She nodded up at me and stepped to one side to let me through.

Rented accommodation, fully furnished. Cheap furniture that a succession of tenants hadn't given a toss about. Dingy curtains; cigarette burns on everything; electricity meter just inside the door, spinning like a windmill. I'd have killed to leave a place like that.

"Are you sure he's alright?" she asked, after gesturing for me to sit down. I'd told her that Carl was in hospital when I telephoned, but didn't say he'd been at the centre of the Ebola panic.

"According to the doctor he'll be fine, but it was touch and go until they discovered what was wrong with him."

"And what is wrong with him?"

"He'd eaten something that disagreed with him."

"What? Like food poisoning?"

"Something like that. Can I ask how long you've been separated?"

"Just coming up to six weeks, but what's that got to do with it?"

"Mr Johnson thinks you may have tampered with his food."

She stared at me for a beat, then jumped to her feet and paced the room. "That's typical!" she declared. "Bloody typical. Everything that goes wrong it's me. He's paranoid, Inspector, bloody paranoid, believe me." She started to say something else, stumbled over the words, then said: "Poison, was it? Poison? Any ideas what?"

I shook my head.

"No? Well I'll tell you how he got it. He did it to

himself, that's what. He's pathetic, feels sorry for himself since he lost his job." She walked over to the window, looked out then turned back to face me. "I'm sorry, I never asked if you wanted a coffee."

"No, I'm fine. When did you last see him?"

"The week after I left him. I'd given him this address, trying to be civilised about it, but he came round every night, promising me the world. It took a week for him to get the message that I wanted shot of him for good."

"Was he on any sort of medication?"

"Medication?"

"Mmm."

"Not from the doctor, but he spent a fortune in health shops. He was into every latest fad there was."

"Any ideas what he was taking?"

"No, I'm sorry."

"What did he do when he worked?"

"He was a sorter at the Post Office."

"And why did he lose his job?"

"The cuts, due to mechanical sorting, or something, but he had a record of bad time-keeping, so they were probably glad to let him go."

"And do you do anything?"

"Yes. I work at Yakuma Electronics, attaching things called FETs to printed circuit boards. It takes me forty-five seconds to do one, and my target is five hundred in a shift."

"Good grief. Aren't you working today?"

"Six this morning until two. I just came in as you rang."

"I'm sorry if I've upset your routine – you're probably

starving. I might want to see you again – will you be working the same hours next week?"

"No. Two till ten next week."

"I've done a few of those myself, Mrs Johnson, so you have my sympathy."

"It pays the rent. I haven't had a penny out of him."

Chapter Three

For most people Friday night is the best night of the week, but lately I'd been finding it a bore. The big case was behind us and settling back into routine was difficult. A high-profile murder opens doors for you, gives you power to cut corners and bypass procedures. When you ask for something to be done, it gets done. You live and breathe the case for twenty-four hours per day, seven days a week, and then it's over. Handshakes all round, have a booze-up with the lads, and it's back to normal duties. Somebody was stealing knickers off washing lines and we might have had an attempted murder by poison. Or maybe it was self-inflicted. Burglary was hovering slightly below its normal level and car theft was slightly down, too. The Assistant Chief Constable (Crime) was pleased with the figures and when he is happy Gilbert is happy, so we have an easy life.

But I miss the excitement. Filling in forms and finding the correct path through the ever-moving maze of regulations that beset the most routine, black-and-white investigation is not my idea of being a cop. It used to be fun. Now, you can find yourself on a fizzer if you don't put sugar in the accused's complimentary cup of tea. You are depriving him of his human rights and subjecting him to unnecessary hardship.

End of moaning – I wouldn't want to do anything else. I hung my jacket in the hall and went through into the kitchen, picking up the mail on the way. I was about to put it all in the bin when the postcard fell from between a World of Reading brochure (any three books on the occult for 99p) and a reminder from BUPA that I wasn't getting any younger. The card showed a yacht marina and a sea front, but as I'd never been to Cap Ferrat I didn't recognise the place. The message read:

Dear Uncle Charles,

Having a great time here in Cap Ferrat. Lots of old people but it's really nice. You'd like it.

Love

Sophie.

The world was ganging up on me, reminding me of my mortality, but I didn't mind. I smiled, pleased that she'd thought of me, and leaned the card against the telephone.

The beef in red wine that I'd bought earlier in Marks and Spencers needed twenty-five minutes in the oven; the vegetables only five minutes in the microwave. I set the oven to 190, switched it on and retrieved Rosie's telephone number from my pocket diary. She answered her phone just as I was beginning to wonder if she was in.

"Hello, Rosie," I said. "It's Charlie Priest, as in Roman Catholic."

"Oh, hello Charlie. How are you?"

"Fine. Top of the world. And you?"

"Not bad."

Hardly the enthusiastic response I'd been hoping for, but I plunged onwards: "Are we still on for tomorrow night? Mr Ho at the Bamboo Curtain is a friend of mine and I can guarantee something special."

"Um, no, Charlie. I'm sorry but I can't make it."

"Oh, that's a disappointment," I told her. "I'd been really looking forward to seeing you. Shall we make it some other time?"

"I'm not sure."

"Well I can't make up your mind for you."

"I know. I apologise for being so wet. I have something to sort out, Charlie. I come with baggage. I'm sorry but maybe we should just leave it."

"At our age, Rosie, we'd've had sad lives if we didn't have any baggage. The secret is to keep it hidden, most of the time. Mine's in the loft, with a dustsheet over it. I don't look at it very often."

"You're lucky – mine won't go away."

"Maybe you should talk about it."

"No, I don't think so."

"OK," I said. "Let's leave it, but the offer's still open. Write my number down in case you change your mind."

I placed Sophie's card back in prime position, leaning against the phone, and returned to the kitchen. The little red light on the oven was still illuminated so I switched it off. I put the steak in red wine and the vegetables back in the fridge and made myself a mug of tea. I couldn't believe that the hesitant, apologetic woman I'd just spoken to was the same confident, humorous teacher of geology that I'd come to know, if only slightly, over the last twelve Wednesday evenings. Perhaps she'd given me the Misses Eakins' number as a huge joke, or maybe there are two Rosie Barracloughs hiding inside that trim figure. I don't know, I'm only a cop.

"It's a report of a post mortem that the RSPCA have done on a dog."

"A dog?" I reached forward and took the proffered sheet from Mr Wood's hand.

"That's right."

"The RSPCA?"

"That's what I said."

"Why has the RSPCA done a post mortem on a dog?"

"Well, Charlie, presumably because they wanted to know how it died. That's the usual reason for having a PM."

I scanned the two sheets of A4, not understanding most of the terminology but the gist of it coming through loud and clear. The poor creature had died an unpleasant death. I skipped the gory bits and jumped to the conclusions. It didn't mention dog-fighting but it stated that the wounds had been caused by more than one other animal, and there were signs of human intervention: namely the crude stitching of some earlier injuries.

"There are some vicious bastards about," I said, handing the report to Gareth Adey.

"Hanging's too good for them, if you ask me," Gilbert stated. He's a Labrador man.

Gareth placed the report back on Gilbert's desk, saying: "I'll ask the community liaison officer to ask around. It could be gypsies, travellers. There's a new bunch of them down on the Triangle."

"For God's sake don't upset them, Gareth, or they'll start quoting Europe at us. I've spoken to the local RSPCA inspector and he thinks it's more organised than they're capable of."

I said: "He's underestimating the travellers if he thinks they're not organised. Halifax prosecuted a gang a couple of years ago for badger baiting and they found maps with badger sets marked on them that went back for a hundred years. They hand them down, along with the caravan and the Royal Doulton crockery."

"Well, spread the word. It's a distasteful business and I'd like to see it stamped out."

"Will do," I said. "Is there anything else?"

"No, I don't think so. Are you on with the poisoning?"

"That's right."

"Keep me informed, please. There is one other thing. It's more in your court, Gareth, but you might have a few ideas, too, Charlie. The annual gala. To be honest, I'm a bit fed up of seeing the dogs jumping over walls and biting someone's arm, and I suspect everyone else is, too. The purpose of our involvement is to win public approval, particularly that of the young public. We need a fresh approach, something that appeals to the kids. Have a think about it, will you?"

We both nodded our understanding of the problem but I fled as Gareth started to voice a few of his ideas.

"Gather round, kiddie-winks," I said as I breezed into the CID office. "Uncle Charlie wants a word with you."

Chairs were turned, newspapers stuffed away, computer cursors clicked on Save.

"Two things," I said. "First of all we've had an outbreak of organised dog-fighting. Keep your eyes and ears open, ask around, you know the form."

"It's gyppos," someone said.

"Possibly. Have a word with any you know, they're not all into it."

"Some were prosecuted in Halifax a couple of years ago."

"That's right, but what happened to them?"

"Fines and probation, but they were never seen again."

"That's why they're called travellers."

"OK," I said, "the second thing is this: it's Heckley gala on bank holiday Monday and, as usual, our uniformed branch will be putting on a display of their skills for the delectation and excitement of the public."

"Lucky public," someone muttered.

"Don't knock it," I said, "or they might ask us to do it. The point is, Mr Wood has realised, after all these years, that a slavering Alsatian pretending to bite someone's arm off does not draw the crowds like it might have done in 1936. We need a new theme for the show; something that might engage the attention of our younger citizens and thereby point them on the path to righteousness."

"You mean something that will scare the shit out of the little bastards?"

"That's what I said, isn't it?"

"I could organise a dog fight," one of them suggested. "There's this bloke I know, down at the pub..."

"By younger citizens, 'ow young are we thinking?" Dave Sparkington asked.

"Not sure. The younger the better, I suppose."

"OK. So how about all the woodentops dressing up as Teletubbies? That should bring 'em in."

"Most of them are the right shape already," someone observed.

"Teletubbies are old hat, it's the Fimbles now," one of my more intellectual DCs informed us, and that opened the floodgates. What had been a sensible, constructive conversation about ways of addressing a pressing social issue degenerated into mockery. I told them I'd pass their contributions to Mr Adey and dragged Sparky down to the car park.

The press were waiting there, swapping stories, flicking their cigarette stubs towards the Super's Rover, seeing who could land one on the roof. The hospital had gone into full defensive mode, issuing a statement saying that the Ebola scare was caused by a non-self-inflicted overdose of rat poison and they'd come flocking back like hyenas to a kill. They switched into professional mode as we emerged from the door and demanded to know how many deaths we'd covered up. I referred them to our press office, saying that a statement was being prepared. At one time I'd have exchanged banter with them, but nowadays anything off-the-cuff or irreverent would be videoed and shown on Look North.

"What's he called?" I asked as we pulled out of the station yard. We were on our way to interview the manager of Grainger's supermarket, where the offending tin of pineapple came from.

"Robshaw."

"Is he expecting us?"

"Yeah, rang him first thing."

"I haven't read the lab report. What does it say?"

"It's on t'back seat. The label had probably been soaked off and then replaced and stuck on with an insoluble glue, such as superglue. The remaining pineapple juice was a saturated solution of war-farin."

"So how did it get in there?"

"While the label was off, two small holes – I think it says one point five millimetres – were drilled in the tin and the juice was probably extracted. After the poison was dissolved in it a syringe may 'ave been used to inject it back into the tin. The holes were then sealed with solder."

"Holes drilled, solder…" I said. "Someone with DIY experience."

"Yeah. The report says it would have been a fiddly job, getting the juice in and out."

"Is that what it said: a fiddly job?"

"Um, no. Requiring patience and determination were the actual words. So what sort of a weekend did you 'ave. You're still in a good mood, I notice."

"Quiet. Caught up with a few jobs that desperately needed doing. Hey! I had a postcard from Sophie."

"Huh. That's more than we've 'ad. What did she say?"

"Just that Cap Ferrat was full of old people and I'd be at home there. Really cheered me up."

"That sound like Sophie. What about Miss X? Did you see her?"

"No. She let me down."

He glanced across at me. "What 'appened?"

"Nothing. I rang her and she said she'd prefer to call the whole thing off."

"Is she in the force?"

"No, just the opposite."

"How do you mean?"

"Well... we were getting along swimmingly until I told her I was a cop. Then her attitude changed."

"So what does this one do for a living?"

"She's a geologist."

"A geologist? Where did you meet her?"

"At a rock concert."

We'd arrived at Grainger's and Dave steered into a space between a Toyota Yaris and a Skoda Fabia. I'm in the market for a new car so I've started noticing these things. I gathered up the paperwork from the back seat and we headed towards the automatic doors of the flagship store in Sir Morton Grainger's ever-growing chain.

We did a detour to the tinned fruit section where I picked up a tin of Del Monte pineapple rings and then introduced ourselves to the customer services manager. Within seconds we were being ushered into the cramped, paper strewn office of Mr Tim Robshaw, Store Manager, as his name badge confirmed.

Handshakes all round, move papers off chairs, sit down. Expansive apologies for the mess. Would we like coffee?

"Is it me you want to interview or one of my staff?" he asked with a grin when we were settled, opening his arms wide in an extravagant gesture to demonstrate that his entire domain was at our disposal.

"You," an unsmiling Dave told him.

Robshaw was a big man, aged about thirty, wearing a short-sleeved shirt and a company tie.

"H-how is he?" he asked, after I'd told him about the tin of pineapple slices and Carl Johnson bleeding from all his bodily orifices. He'd developed a perspiration problem and his face slowly turned to the colour of a tramp's vest as he saw litigation looming large, blighting his prospects of advancement in the Grainger empire. One of those oscillating fans stood on the windowsill and every twenty-two seconds I felt a blast of cool air on my left cheek.

"He could be out today," Dave said, "but it was touch and go."

There were three drawings on the wall, done by an infant who hadn't quite grasped the rules of perspective, or, I suspected, of going to the toilet. Charming, I suppose. Any dad would be proud to put his children's first scribblings on the wall. Nothing wrong with that. But Robshaw had had them framed, complete with non-reflective glass and card mounts, which I thought over the top. Alongside them was a photograph of the man himself, dressed in tennis whites and holding a trophy the size of a cement mixer. Another frame, silver this time, stood on his desk, its back to me, which no doubt held a picture of the aforementioned child. I decided to serve him a big one.

"It was very worrying for him," I said. "And for the staff at the hospital. The symptoms were similar to those for the Ebola virus, and for several hours the hospital was quarantined." Pow! Fifteen love to me.

At the word Ebola he jerked upright as if a small

electric shock had passed through his chair and his mouth fell open.

"Ebola?"

We stayed silent.

"You mean... the outbreak at the General... that's what this is about?"

"'Fraid so."

"Oh my God."

"How long do you keep your security camera tapes, Mr Robshaw?" I asked.

"A week."

"Would there happen to be one looking at the tinned fruit shelves?"

"No. Sorry."

I turned to Dave. "Any point in watching them?" I asked.

He shook his head, knowing that he'd be the one who had to do the watching. "No."

"The pineapple had been tampered with, Mr Robshaw," I said. "Somebody had made a determined effort to contaminate it." Dave produced the label from the offending tin and laid it in front of him and I went on: "We soaked the label off. There's a bar code on it so can you explain what that tells us, please?"

He relaxed when he realised that the offence had been beyond his control and typed the bar code numbers into his computer terminal. The new tin was similar to the one we'd taken from Carl Johnson's fridge, and Robshaw soon confirmed that the price of 432 grams of Del Monte pineapple rings had not changed for six weeks. The offending tin was still with forensics, but Dave had made a note of the numbers printed on the bottom and these were a couple of digits different from those on the new tin.

Robshaw drummed his fingers on the desk and after a few seconds pinned me with his best managerial stare in an attempt to regain the initiative. "Pardon me asking this, Inspector," he said, "but how do I know that this tin came from this store? As you have realised, all prices are indicated at the shelf; we don't use stickers on individual items."

Which saves you money, I thought, and makes it almost impossible for the shopper to check the bill when they get home. I said: "The victim says it came from here and we found a drawer full of your bags at his home."

"But no receipt?"

"No."

He let go with his forearm volley: "So you've no proof?"

I retaliated with a backhand smash. It's my speciality stroke. "He thought he was dying of Ebola. Why would he lie?"

"Good question," he admitted. Forty-thirty to the forces of law and order.

"So what does the code tell you?"

"Right. When I type in the numbers, or a checkout assistant scans it, the terminal is immediately connected to the stock record entry for that particular item." He rotated his flat-screen monitor so we could see the figures. "It identifies the product, retrieves the price and subtracts one unit from the stockholding. Each record entry has a maximum and minimum stock level specified and if necessary an order is automatically initiated. Batch numbers and sell-by dates are also stored, as shown on the base of the tin. That's about it."

"Can you confirm that this batch came to you?"

He turned the screen back to face himself. "Um, yes. 'Fraid so."

"Thank you. So what date did it arrive?"

"Let's have a look. Here we are... July 10th."

"This year?"

"Yes."

Dave coughed and said: "Only ten days ago. Maybe we should look at those videotapes after all."

"I think you'd better," I told him. Turning back to Robshaw I said: "I thought, these days, that you could tell who bought what."

"Not from this program. If a customer holds our loyalty card, certain selected items are recorded and we can use this information to identify their tastes. That's the theory, but for Grainger's stores the system is in its infancy."

Dave said: "Would pineapple slices 'appen to be a selected item?"

"No. It tends to be more specialised lines, such as wine or our cordon bleu ready meals. Then we can target our mailshots and special offers more accurately."

"Thanks for explaining that," I said, making a mental note not to ever buy another ready meal. I didn't want some spotty supermarket analyst dissecting my eating habits. "So, have you sacked anybody in, ooh, the last two months?"

"No. I've never sacked anybody ever, I'm proud to say," he replied. "It's part of the Grainger's ethos that everybody can be usefully employed. It's a question of training and finding an employee's potential. We don't sack people, we redeploy and redevelop them."

"Have you redeployed or redeveloped anybody in the last two months?"

He thought about it before answering. "We do it constantly, but most of them go along with it, accept the need. There was one girl..."

"Go on."

"She was all fingers and thumbs. Kept dropping things on the shop floor. We moved her into the warehouse where she could do less damage, but she handed in her notice after a week."

We asked him for her name and after a phone call he gave it to us.

"So you don't know of anybody who might hold a grudge against the company?"

"No, not at all. Sir Morton might have made a few enemies along the way, but none I know of. Has he been told about all this?"

"Not yet. How often do you see him?"

"We have a monthly meeting but we see his wife more often. She likes to play the secret shopper, sneaking in heavily disguised but all the staff recognise her. There's a daughter-in-law too, who does the same thing, but we're not so sure about her."

We sat in silence for a few seconds until he said: "We'll have to withdraw them all, won't we? And recall them. Oh God, we need this, we really need this," and buried his head in his hands.

"Has anything like it happened here before?" I asked.

Robshaw shuffled in his leather executive chair and

ran a finger under the collar of his shirt. That was the question he hoped we wouldn't ask. He picked up the phone again and asked someone to bring in the complaints book.

"What do you fancy for lunch?" Dave asked as we climbed into his car in the supermarket car park.

"We could have bought something here," I replied.

"And risk being poisoned? No thanks."

"OK. Bacon sandwich in the canteen. The poison in them is slow-acting." I pulled the door shut and reached for the seat belt.

"What did you reckon to him?" Dave said.

"Robshaw? He was helpful, once he realised we weren't after his blood. Not exactly managerial material, I'd've thought, but he'd done well for himself. Credit where it's due."

"He's a twat," Dave stated.

Robshaw's helpfulness extended to furnishing us with a list of the other ten stores in the group, with names and phone numbers, plus Sir Morton Grainger's home number. Not classified information but it saved us about an hour's work.

The complaints book revealed that two weeks earlier a customer had returned some peaches that had turned mouldy in the tin, and ten days before that someone had brought back a tin of blue baked beans. These had been sent to the group's laboratory and found to be contaminated with a harmless food dye. Both customers were placated and the incidents brushed over without involving the local health inspector. There was no investigation into how the tins were breached and they hadn't been saved.

"So what did you think of Sharon?" Dave asked. It was Sharon who delivered the compaints book when Robshaw asked for it. "Personal service," he'd said with a smile as she passed it to him. She was severely dressed in a dark suit which went well with her bobbed hair and dark-rimmed spectacles, but the skirt was short and the heels high and she chose her perfume carefully.

"She's... um, sexy, if you like that sort of thing." She'd sashayed to the door as she left the office and cast a glance backwards as she closed it to confirm that we were looking.

"And we do, don't we?"

"Not arf!"

I was still thinking about Sharon when Dave said: "So what were you saying?"

"About what?" I rubbed the side of my face. "That flippin' fan's given me neuralgia."

"You were telling me about Miss X."

"Miss X? You mean Rosie. She's called Rosie. Rosie Barraclough."

"So where did you really meet her?"

"At the geology class. She was the teacher."

"I'd forgotten about that. How's it going?"

"Fine. Last week was the last one."

"Was it any good?"

"Yes. It was interesting. I enjoyed it."

"Particularly with Rosie in charge."

"Um, yes, she did add to the enjoyment." The 4X4 in front of us had two stickers on the back window:

one for the Liberty and Livelihood jamboree and the other urging us to Buy British Beef. It was a Mitsubishi Shogun.

"So what 'appened."

"Nothing. Last Wednesday was the final night and I invited her to the pub for a drink. We arranged to go to Mr Ho's on Saturday, but when I rang her she'd changed her mind."

"Because you were a policeman, you said."

"Mmm. I'd told someone in the class that I was a graphic designer, and she overheard me. When I told her I was really a cop she went all quiet, as if I'd deceived her."

"I usually say that I'm a cattle inseminator. That keeps 'em quiet. So what are you doing about it?"

I looked across at him. "Doing about it? Nothing. What can I do about it?"

"Charlie!" he gasped. "Won't you ever learn. Women 'ave to be chased. You like her, don't you?"

"Well, she's good fun."

"So ring her again. Say you won't take no for an answer. Faint heart and all that."

"This is the voice of the expert, is it?" I argued. "You married the girl next door which gives you a one hundred percent success record and thereby qualifies you as an authority on the opposite sex."

"Give 'er a ring."

"No means No! Haven't you been listening?"

"Give 'er a ring."

"OK, I'll think about it."

"Good." We were back at the station. "That's you sorted out, now what are we doing about these shops?"

"Bacon buttie first," I replied, "then we'll take half each."

"Just what I'd've done," he said.

"Except that..."

"What?"

"Except that we're assuming only Grainger's are involved. We really ought to look at all the other super-markets, too."

"Sheest!"

In the afternoon I visited the stores in Halifax and Oldfield, and Sparky did three others. Halifax report-ed another tin of mouldy fruit and Sparky discovered two more incidents of blue beans. Puncturing a tin so the contents rotted appeared to be the first MO, fol-lowed by the dye, followed by the warfarin. It was impossible to be precise but it looked as if we had a nutter on the loose and he was on a learning curve. I rang Mr Wood from the car park of Grainger's Oldfield store and arranged a 5 p.m. meeting. Someone was going to die if we didn't act quickly, and the first step in catching the culprit was assessing the size of the problem.

We decided to go public, right from the start. I drew a twenty-mile radius circle on a road map and called it the locus of operations. As soon as we had an incident room organised I'd give it pride of place on the wall. Statements would be issued to local radio stations and the local weekly newspapers, starting with the Heckley Gazette, and tomorrow we would hand-deliver a questionnaire to every supermarket manager within the circle.

"What about the public health people?" somebody asked.

"Tricky," Mr Wood replied. "I'll talk to them in the morning and ask them to bear with us. The supermarkets are probably out of order but I'll ask them to turn a blind eye if it helps the investigation. So far the managers have been most co-operative, haven't they, Charlie?"

"Yep. Very helpful."

"Good. Can I leave it with you?"

"No problem."

"That's my boy. There is one other thing. Another dead dog has been found. There are some photos on my desk and they're horrific. Let's not lose sight of that one, please."

Everybody mumbled their assent and Mr Wood left us to it.

"Three volunteers, please," I said. "One to write the statement, one to liaise with HQ to create the questionnaire and one, maybe two, to list every supermarket in the circle. Then we can get straight on with it in the morning. So far whoever is tampering with the tins is using low-tech means. The warfarin was an escalation and could have led to a fatality. If they get their hands on something like strychnine or arsenic we could be looking for a murderer."

Hands were raised and I delegated the jobs. As the others were leaving Jeff Caton said: "Why does killing dogs pull at the heartstrings more than poisoning some poor soul with rat poison?"

"Because we're a nation of animal lovers," Pete Goodfellow told him. "That's why we have a royal society for animals but only a national society for children. But can anyone explain why dog-fighting is considered less morally defensible than hunting foxes? With the dogs it's one on one, whereas with foxes..."

"Whoah!" I said, holding up a hand. "Let's leave the morality and ethics out of it and stick to the law. We've enough on our plates. C'mon, let's go home."

"Why..." Dave began, looking thoughtful, "why don't you ever see white dog turds these days? That's what I want to know."

"What?" I said.

"White dog turds?" Jeff queried.

"Yeah. White dog turds. Once upon a time dog turds used to be white. Not all of them, just some."

"Gerraway!"

"It's true. They used to be the best ones. When they were dried they floated better than the others."

"Floated? What were you floating them for?"

"We used to have races, on the canal. The white ones always won."

"You had dog turd races on the canal?"

"Yes. Didn't you?"

"No!"

"Charlie did, didn't you?"

"Um, no," I replied. "I had a scale model of the Queen Mary."

"Only a scale model?" Jeff asked.

"It was half-scale," Pete told him.

"Radio-controlled," I said.

"How were these dog turds propelled?" Jeff wondered.

"We threw stones at them."

I said: "Why didn't you make them into little galleons with a cocktail stick and a square of paper?"

"A cocktail stick!" Dave exclaimed. "A cocktail stick! We didn't have cocktail sticks."

"You should have asked. We'd've let you have our used ones."

Jeff said: "If you didn't have cocktail sticks how did you eat your stuffed olives?"

"Stuffed olives!" he exploded. "We didn't have stuffed olives. We had a stuffed cat, to save on the food bill."

Jeff: "Was it on wheels?"

Pete: "Did it catch many mice?"

Dave: "Only stuffed ones."

"Home!" I shouted. "Some of us have a meal to cook. Let's go."

Chapter Four

Altogether we found twenty-one recorded incidents of tampering, all in Grainger's stores, which was a determined effort to make mischief by anybody's standards. It looked as if the early efforts – the dye and the tin-puncturing – had not had the required effect, so more drastic measures had been adopted. But how many suspect tins were standing on the shelves, either in a store or in somebody's larder, was impossible to calculate. There were bound to be some. Grainger's temporarily took tinned pineapple, peaches and baked beans off their shelves and issued a statement offering to replace any that had been purchased from them in the previous three months. It made the headlines locally and was reported in the national press, lost somewhere between news that a Pop Idol contestant had had a boob job and the tomato that spelled out Allah is Great when cut in half.

We were less successful in our attempts to talk to Sir Morton Grainger. He had a personal assistant – male – resident at Dob Hall, the Georgian pile near Hebden Bridge that he called home, who told us that Sir Morton would be passing through on Wednesday afternoon. Mrs Grainger – she held the title of Lady but preferred plain Mrs – was in London, where she had an architect's practice.

We made a list of all the dates but it was meaningless. Things could have been lying around for weeks. As Jeff Caton said, this was the only enquiry he'd ever been on where there was no point in asking: "Where were you on…?" The forensics people started some experiments to see how quickly tinned fruit went mouldy, but we knew it would be of doubtful value.

Wednesday morning Dr Hirst rang me. The name didn't mean anything for a few seconds until he reminded me that I'd seen him at the General after the Ebola scare.

"Sorry, Dr Hirst," I said. "I didn't recognise the name. We're still working on the case but not making much progress."

"I know, I've heard the appeal, but there may have been a development."

"Go on."

"We had an admission through the night with all the symptoms of a severe stroke, but a brain scan was negative. She's very ill – we've put her on a respirator – and in the light of what's been happening I started wondering about botulism poisoning. I've given her a dose of the antitoxin serum and sent a stool sample for analysis, but a full diagnosis may take a day or two."

Twenty minutes later Dave and I were seated in the corridor outside the IC ward with Dr Hirst.

"You work long hours, Doc," Dave told him.

"It's not too bad," he replied with a grin. "They let us use the coffee machine as often as we like. Can I offer you one?"

"No, we'll get out of your way," I said. "So tell us about botulism."

"I suspect you know the general details," he replied. "It's caused by a little blighter called Clostridium

botulinum, which normally lies dormant in the soil."
He paused as a grim-faced man carrying a bunch of
carnations and leading a weepy little girl was taken
into the ward. The door swung silently shut and he
continued: "The bacterium thrives in conditions of low
oxygen, such as in sealed cans, where it produces a
nerve toxin which can be deadly."

"Sounds nasty. What can you tell us about the
patient?"

"Maureen Wall, a fifty-six-year-old widow. Started
feeling ill last night. Blurred vision, slurred speech, difficulty swallowing. She telephoned her daughter in
Ipswich who thought it sounded like a stroke and sent
for an ambulance."

"Is she speaking?" I asked.

"Barely."

"Will she live?"

"She's off the danger list, but it will take a long time
for her to get over the paralysis."

"Do you want me to look for her last meal?"

"It could be a big help."

"No problem. Do we have an address?"

"Right here." He produced a piece of paper.

"And a key?"

"It's with the neighbour."

"Right. I could sign a search authority but it might
be more polite to telephone the daughter."

"I've spoken to her," Dr Hirst said. "She says do
whatever's necessary."

"You're a treasure, Doc. If you ever want a career
change we could use you. If we find something, who
do we leave it with?"

* * *

It was the corned beef. The neighbour wanted to supervise our search but Dave steered her away with threats of having to take intimate body samples "for elimination purposes" if she stepped one inch over the threshold. It was a tiny kitchen in what I believe is called a maisonette, designed for older couples or singletons. There was a group of them, each block containing four homes, situated around an overgrown patch of lawn with cherry trees, long past their best.

I opened the refrigerator door and immediately saw the remains of the corned beef on a saucer, covered with cling film. In a swing bin under the sink we found the tin. Dave sniffed at it, said he couldn't smell anything, but I declined the opportunity. He turned the tin in his fingers, holding it by the edges, and gestured for me to look. In the middle of the O of Corned was a tiny hole. When you looked inside you could see how the metal was displaced. This hole had been made with a nail or something like a drawing pin, not drilled.

"Brilliant," I said. "You and the doctor could crack this one between you and I could go home." We bagged the evidence and dropped it off at the hospital's toxicology lab.

In the car on the way back to the station I said: "It's good to be out on the streets again, Dave, making enquiries. Sitting behind a desk was getting me down."

"Serves you right for joining." What he meant was that promotion above the rank of sergeant always took you one more step away from the sharp end, where the real policing was done.

"True," I agreed.

After a silence Dave said: "It's great to see you more relaxed, Charlie. We were worried about you after the last job."

"I was worried about myself. I thought I'd gone mad."

"Yeah, well, it was a tough 'un. The rest of us were feeling edgy, too."

"I know. Everybody in the team felt a personal involvement, but I don't think I handled it as well as most of you."

"It was your head that was on the block, Charlie. I don't know 'ow you stood the pressure."

"Well it's behind us now, and I learned a lot from it. From now on I'm going with the flow. It's tough luck on Mr Johnson and Mrs Wall, and I'll do everything in my power to give them justice, but it's their problem, not mine. I hesitate to admit it, but I'm enjoying this case."

"You might not if someone dies," Dave cautioned.

"Yeah, well, let's say a little prayer that it doesn't come to that."

"Amen. So why do you think he's suddenly started using poison?"

We were going through the town centre but it was still early and not many shoppers were about. Two girls and a youth were standing outside the side door of the HSBC bank, shivering in the cool morning air and drawing on cigarettes as if their lives depended on it. The last remaining greengrocer in Heckley was loading his outdoor display with fruit and veg. Hand-written signs showed the prices of carrots, apples and oranges. I started to laugh.

"What's so funny?"

"Nothing."

"Well something's tickling you."

"It's nothing."

Now Dave was laughing. "It doesn't look like nothing."

I found a tissue and blew my nose. "Do you remember when I was in digs at Chapeltown?" I said.

"At Mrs Stalin's? I remember." Dave had been a PC and I was a rookie sergeant.

"Well, there was this youth lived next door. Had a car with a straight-through exhaust. An Avenger or an Allegro, some rubbish like that. A Morris Ital, I think that was it. Anyway, every morning at eleven minutes past seven he'd slam the door and rev the engine like he was starting a grand prix, ruining my beauty sleep, especially if I'd just come off nights."

"That sounds like Chapeltown," Dave said.

"So, this fine sunny morning I was coming down Roundhay Road on my bike at the end of the shift when I saw this great big cooking apple lying in the gutter. I stopped and picked it up. It was the biggest, greenest, shiniest apple I'd ever seen. I got off my bike at Mrs Stalin's and I was wondering what to do with the apple. It was a cooker, but not big enough to make a pie with. And then I saw Laddo's car, and knew that in exactly thirty-one minutes he'd be revving the damned thing enough to wake the dead. And me. So I jumped over the fence and stuffed the apple up his exhaust pipe."

Dave chuckled and gave me a disbelieving look. "What 'appened."

"Nothing. I fell asleep and never heard a thing, and next morning the car was as noisy as ever."

"So why are you confessing after all these years?"

"You asked me why the person tampering with the tins had turned to poison. Because he wasn't getting any feedback from his other activities, that's why. He planted the tins with the dye, at great personal risk, but never heard anything more about them. It was one big anti-climax, so he upped the ante. Now he's in the papers, reading about his handiwork. For months it was eating my heart out not knowing what happened to that apple. My next stunt was going to be a bomb wired to his ignition but fortunately my promotion came through first."

"You sneaky so-and-so. Sir Morton this afternoon?"

"Yep."

"Am I invited?"

"You bet."

Dob Hall was built by a merchant adventurer who made his fortune out of wool in the eighteenth century, according to the local history society. Less charitable authorities suggested that slaves, guns and opium may have made a contribution to the family's wealth. Sir Morton's father, also a Sir Morton, had switched from blanket manufacturing into the grocery business when he realised that the duvet would do to blanket sales what the steam engine did to sail-making. When a shrinking army caused his lucrative military contracts to dry up he opened his first supermarket.

Originally the family had been called Grossbach, but the great-grandfather changed this to Grainger at a time when a foreign-sounding name was not good for a family business. The Saxe Coburg Gothas became the Windsors for similar reasons.

I knew all this because I'd asked Pete Goodfellow to do some research, and his findings were neatly typed and left on my desk. He'd resumed his normal duties, looking for the knicker thief and following up on burglaries, so I scrawled a message on the bottom of the sheet and placed it back on his desk. I put: That's great, Pete. It looks as if Sir M. inherited the family business. See if you can discover any disgruntled siblings hovering in the wings.

At five minutes to three Dave steered us into the imposing gateway of Dob Hall and spoke into the security system. A lone hot hatchback was standing outside them with a young female reporter from the Heckley Gazette dozing behind the wheel. She jerked awake as we stopped and climbed out of her car.

I wound my window down, shouting to her: "What time does the Gazette go to bed, love?"

"Anytime now. It's Inspector Priest, isn't it?"

"Never heard of him, but if you contact our press office you might just get a scoop."

She thanked me with a big smile and started to stab a number into her cell phone. If not a scoop at least she'd be up there with the tabloids when the news of the poisoned corned beef broke. The gates opened and we drove forward. The personal assistant met us at the front door and we were ushered into a side room, lined with books, and invited to sit down.

"Sir Morton will be down shortly," he told us. My idea of a personal assistant didn't run close to this one. He was about thirty and of a type that women find attractive, if you can believe the deodorant adverts:

dark-haired and designer stubble. Yasser Arafat has a lot to answer for.

He turned to leave, but before he could I said: "I get the impression that Sir Morton is just passing through."

"Yes."

"It sounds a hectic schedule. Any idea where he's going or how long he will be away for?"

"I'm sure Sir Morton will be able to tell you that himself," he replied, scowling at me from beneath bushy eyebrows, and left.

"Good try," Dave said.

"The soul of discretion."

"Think he's gay?"

"It's possible. Is it relevant?"

"It's possible."

In the middle of the room was an antique table with a shine on it that took a hundred years of sore knuckles to produce, and on the table was a perspex box, keeping the dust off the model it held. I stood up and walked over to inspect it.

"It's this house, I think," I told Dave.

He came to join me. It was beautifully made, with delicate stonework and tall chimneys, and an ornate, tiled roof that must have taken hours to construct. Tiny figures were grouped at the front around a model car and others were neatly parked nearby. Trees like the ones I'd seen on model railway layouts were dotted around the grounds, and at the back ancient met modern. There was a huge extension, bigger than the floor plan of the original building but only one storey high, with two more cars – a Rolls Royce and a little yellow coupe – parked outside. His and hers, at a guess. It was all metal and glass, one part being a swimming pool and the rest of it what looked like office space.

"Like it?" said voice behind us like the crack of a whip. We turned and introduced ourselves to Sir Morton Grainger, multimillionaire and supermarket supremo.

When we'd shaken hands I said: "Is it this place?"

"That's right," he replied. "My wife made the model to help get the improvements past the planning people."

"Did it work?"

"Oh yes, it's all up and running. Been so for nearly five years."

He was about five feet seven tall and dressed in what I believe is called County: hacking jacket; fawn slacks; heather-mix shirt and woven tie. His hair was fair and crinkly and the broken veins on his cheeks indicated an outdoor man who enjoys a drop or two. A hunting man, at a guess, with a military background.

He gestured for us to sit down and I noticed that his brogues were shiny enough for him to shave by in the absence of a mirror, or perhaps use to signal a passing plane were he ever unfortunate enough to be ship-wrecked. There's no substitute for breeding, I reluc-tantly admitted to myself, drawing my grubby footwear under the chair, out of sight.

"Thanks for seeing us, Sir Morton," I began, "and I apologise for you hearing about this business some-what indirectly. We did try to contact you but you lead a busy life."

"The price of success, Inspector. Constantly trying to keep ahead of the game. Actually, I'm glad you're here. Any chance of you doing something about the press – they're camped outside the bloody gates?"

"There was just one there when we arrived," I told him, "and we've sent her on her way."

"Oh, that's good. Thank you. So how is the man who was poisoned?"

"He's recovering, but there's been another."

"Oh dear. It's a nasty business. Is he alright?"

"It's a woman, but we're told she'll recover. This time it appears to be a tin of corned beef that's caused the problem. I'm afraid you'll have to widen the scope of the call-back."

"Bloody hell! That's all we need. So how much nearer are you to catching the person responsible?"

"No nearer at all, but we'd like to ask you a few questions."

"Right. So fire away, but make it quick, I've a train to catch."

"Will do. First of all I'd like to say that all your managers have been very co-operative. These days, what with all the red tape, political correctness and civil rights that we are beset with, it would have been easy for any one of them to obstruct the enquiry, but they didn't and we're grateful. I believe you're just passing through."

"That's right. You're lucky to catch me. I'm on my way to play in a pro-am at St Andrew's. Charity do on the Old Course. Won't be back until Monday."

Golf, not hunting. Near enough, though. I said: "Sounds fun. In that case, as we won't be able to contact you, it would be helpful if you could issue an instruction to your managers to keep up with the co-operation."

"No problem, Inspector. I'll put Sebastian onto it straight away."

"Smashing. Thanks for that. Now, if we can ask you a few questions pertinent to the enquiry..."

He'd always tried to play fair, he told us, and as far as he knew had no business enemies. Some of the stores were built on greenfield sites and opposition, both local and from organised groups, had been vocal, but the applications had gone through. Supermarkets were what people wanted. He hadn't cancelled any big contracts causing companies to go bust, and he'd received no threats or demands for money.

"You will," I told him, "but most will be from cranks, opportunists. It's important that any that arrive are sent straight to us with the minimum of handling."

He said that he understood and he would include that in the message to his managers. When he started looking at his watch we stood up to leave. We shook hands again and as he walked us to the door I said: "Your wife's an architect, I believe."

"That's right. She's a partner in a practice."

"In London?"

"Head office is in London, but she works from home most of the time."

"Oh. Did she design the extension?" I tried to think of a grander word than extension, but couldn't.

"The leisure and office complex? That's right. With her own fair hands."

"She must be a clever lady."

"Yes, she is."

But there was no pride in his voice as he said it.

* * *

"So what do you think?" I asked as we drove out through the gate.

"He's a twat."

"Another one! But a rich twat, wouldn't you say?"

"And that."

"With no enemies."

"If you believe that you'll stand for the drop o' York."

"He seemed concerned about the victims."

"The only thing he's concerned about is his profits."

"And his golf handicap?"

"Aye, and I bet he cheats at that."

"Is your ulcer playing up?"

"It could be. Did you ring her?"

"Who?"

"Who! Who do you think? Rosie."

"No, I didn't."

He snorted disdainfully and concentrated on driving. A woman was negotiating her way across the High Street with a baby buggy and Dave held up the traffic for her. She smiled a thank you and tipped buggy and youngster it contained violently backwards to mount the kerb. A Reward poster fastened to a lighting column caught my eye. I twisted in my seat as we accelerated away and saw that it was for a lost cat. Approaching the turn-off for the nick I said: "Have you got the address of that girl in your notebook? The one who was relocated by Robshaw. It was somewhere in the Sylvan Fields."

"Yeah. Want to go see her?"

"We might as well. She may give us a different perspective on the cosy world of Grainger's super-stores."

Sylvan Fields is a rambling estate on the edge of Heckley, although it might be more accurate to say that Heckley is a small industrial and market town on the edge of the Sylvan Fields estate. Most of the houses date from the between-the-wars era, built for heroes, what was left of them, in a wave of compassion and social engineering. All went well for a couple of gener-ations, but by the seventies the decline was well under way and accelerating. Nobody knows what the mech-anism is, although thousands of theses have been writ-ten on the subject. Greater freedom, less respect for authority, prosperity, poverty, lower morals, break-down of family life? Who can say? Alcohol and drugs, the advent of the motor car? Rock and roll and the Pill?

How about Y-fronts? Perhaps the decline in stan-dards and increased tendency for violence, particularly amongst young men, was brought about by something as simple as the introduction and widespread use of snug-fitting underwear, causing the testes to overheat with the subsequent over-production of testosterone. Thinking about it, I could not recall a single case of a burglar or mugger being described by witnesses as wearing a kilt.

Dave passed me his notebook and I found the address. "28, Windermere Drive," I told him. "Know where it is?"

"No problem."

"Anywhere near where you lived?"

"No, we were at the rough end. Shirley lived in the next street, Buttermere Drive."

I didn't speak as Dave negotiated the estate, avoiding the bricks that strewed the road and the various wheeled devices dotted about the place like exhibits in a sculpture park: old prams, shopping trolleys and a couple of burnt-out cars. A dog chased out of a gateway at our car, then changed its mind and trotted back whence it came. There was a community centre on a corner that I'd seen a picture of in the Heckley Gazette when a local councillor cut the tape, its walls already sprayed with graffiti. Jeb and Shaz believed in advertising their feelings for each other.

I think Dave sensed what I was thinking, so he said: "There are some nice people live here, Charlie. They're not all yobs, y'know."

"I know that, Dave."

The litter thinned out and the houses changed colour. The council has a segregation policy, lumping most of the problem tenants at one end of the estate, together with the single mums, divorcees and rent-evaders. The best tenants, the ones who've had the foresight and wherewithal to buy their homes, are on the north side. Now the gardens were tidy, the hedges trimmed or replaced by brickwork, and the houses painted in individual styles. Burglar alarms adorned walls instead of satellite dishes. Dave turned into Windermere Drive and we looked for house numbers.

The girl was called Rebecca. She was born north of the tracks but was heading south, fast. It must be heart-breaking for parents to bring up a child to be polite, speak in sentences and take an interest in the world outside, only to see all their hard work swept aside by street culture as the kid reaches puberty.

Rebecca was eating Pringles, watching television, as her mother showed us through into the front room. The house was spotless but cluttered in a familiar way. They just didn't make them big enough for a growing family. She was dumpy and pasty-faced, with a mouth that permanently drooped at the corners.

"Two gentlemen to see you, Becky," her mother said. "About when you worked at Grainger's. It's about this food scare."

Becky's gaze switched from the TV to me and back again as she felt for her mouth with another Pringle. Her mother invited us to sit down and asked if we'd like a cup of tea.

"No thanks," Dave said, "but can we have the TV off, please." In a fantasy story Becky's glare would have turned him to stone.

"How long did you work at Grainger's, Becky?" Dave asked.

Realising, probably for the first time ever, that pressing the red button caused the moving images to go away, Becky turned on the settee to face her interrogator. "'Bout six months," she replied.

"Did you like working there?"

"No."

"What was the problem?"

"It wa' borin'"

"Have you seen anything on telly about the scare we're having?"

"A bit."

"Did you ever see anything suspicious while you were at Grainger's?"

"Suspicious? Like what?" Her mouth re-formed into a snarl, as if she thought the question ridiculous.

"Like anybody tampering with food. Tinned food in particular."

"No."

"Nothing that you can remember?"

"No."

"Are you sure?"

"I've said so, 'aven't I?"

"Becky!" her mother admonished.

"Are you looking for another job?" I asked.

She turned to me and I felt the chill of her disdain. "There is nowt," she stated.

"But you're looking?"

"I'm trying to get my 'ead together."

"I understand you were moved from the store floor into the warehouse," Dave said.

Becky's expression changed quickly, from a brief flash of embarrassment, through glee and back to bored stiff again, like a shaft of light through a crack in a wall.

"That cow had me moved," she said.

"Becky!"

"Well she is."

"Which cow would that be, Becky?"

"Mrs Brown. Sharon stuck-up Brown cow."

Her mother said: "Becky, will you try to be polite to the gentlemen."

"It's OK," I told her with a grin. "We get much worse."

"Why did she have you moved?" Dave asked.

"I dropped things."

Her mother coughed. "Becky's always had this problem," she explained. "She's all fingers and thumbs, keeps dropping things."

"What did you drop?" Dave asked.

The look of glee returned and lingered this time. "Jars of things."

"What sort of things?"

"Beetroot. Pickled onions. Things like that."

"Big jars?" Dave asked. Now he was smiling.

"Yer. Right big jars."

I stood up and stretched, rotating my shoulders a couple of times. "Could we have a word in the kitchen, please?" I said to Becky's mum, and moved towards the door.

The sun shone in through the window and there was a pleasing smell coming from the oven. "That cup of tea would be most welcome," I said. She clicked the switch on the kettle and it rumbled into life.

"Sugar and milk?"

"No, just black. Has Becky always been a problem?"

She nodded and turned away from me, and I heard her sniff a couple of times.

"We learned that Becky had left under a bit of a cloud," I said, "and we've been looking for someone with a grudge. It's obviously not your daughter but we thought she might have some ideas, give us an insider's view of the company. DC Sparkington will tease it out of her if she's seen anything."

Her mother poured the tea and handed me a mug.

"Thank you. Is Becky looking for another job?"

"There isn't anything," her mother replied. "She goes to the job centre – sometimes I take her – but the only jobs she could do are in catering. And what with her little problem..."

"It sounds difficult."

"It is. We thought she'd be all right at Grainger's, but we were wrong. Now she doesn't seem bothered. Trouble is, there's no incentive for someone like her. She was on minimum wage, which wasn't too bad for a girl with Becky's qualifications, and most welcome, believe me, but she sees other girls on the estate who are much better off. Girls who went to school with her and are living the life of Riley, getting benefits and the rent paid because they've got kiddies."

She had a moan about the injustices of the system and we agreed that it was an insoluble problem. Try to do something about it and the children were the ones who paid the price. Dave came through, edging his bulk into the kitchen and rolling his eyes as he saw the mug of tea in my hand. Voices from the other room indicated that the TV was back on. We said thank you and she asked how the poisoned man was.

"He'll live," I told her.

"Back to t'nick?" Dave asked as he started the engine.

"Yes please, driver. What did you learn?"

"Aha!" he responded. "Wouldn't you like to know."

"OK. I'll just sit here patiently waiting for a moment when you might find it convenient to fill me in."

"Right. Get this: Becky reckons that all-hands Robshaw is screwing old-cow Mrs Brown."

"Gerraway! All-hands Robshaw. Is she saying that he belongs to the touchy-feely school of management training?"

"Can't leave the girls alone, it would seem.."

"And presumably Mrs Brown is the bespectacled lady called Sharon who brought in the complaints book?"

"Head of human resources, based at the Heckley branch."

"You did well."

"There's a bit more. Becky left because she was being bullied. It was OK on the shop floor but started when she was moved to the warehouse. Mrs Brown knew about it but didn't do anything."

After a while I said: "Poor kid. What do you reckon's wrong with her?"

"Don't know. When we went in, after a few seconds, I had this flash that she was Down's syndrome. Then I realised that she wasn't, just – what do we say these days? – has learning difficulties."

"Hmm. I went through the same process."

"Makes me realise how lucky we've been with our two."

"I bet. Have you heard from Sophie yet?"

His shake of the head and ensuing silence were more eloquent than words and I knew I was treading a minefield, so I changed the subject.

"What have you got against Grainger – Sir Morton?" I asked him. "You didn't exactly take to him when we met."

"Huh!"

"Go on."

"I'll tell you in the office."

But he didn't have the chance to tell me. There was a note on my desk from Pete Goodfellow and another saying that Mr Wood wanted to see me ASAP. Pete had done his homework about Sir Morton, as requested. He was a Foreign and Commonwealth Office man, not army, and had held a junior position at some God-forsaken outpost in the Pacific until hurriedly promoted when his boss drowned while snorkelling. He was stationed in Fiji, and when the Queen, on a tour of the more distant corners of the Commonwealth, unexpectedly changed her itinerary to visit her loyal subjects in Tuvalu, Junior Consul Grainger had filled the breach and ensured that everything went along swimmingly. His reward was promotion and promise of a KCMG, whatever that meant. Grainger's older brother had inherited the burgeoning family business, but he was killed while racing a vintage grand prix car in Belgium and the whole lot passed to Morton, or Sir Morton as he became on leaving the FCO.

A line from Dylan's "Idiot Wind" flashed through my mind: And when she died it all came to me, I can't help it if I'm lucky. I walked through into the main office and passed the note to Dave.

"Tuvalu?" he said, after considering the note for nearly a minute.

"Yep."

"Wear the fox hat?"

"It's in the Pacific."

"Thanks. That pins it down. Fancy a pint tonight?"

"Good idea. Gilbert wants me, I'll be upstairs."

Gilbert wasn't alone. A tall man with a navy blue sweater and the resigned expression of a long-term political prisoner was sitting in my chair, nursing a coffee. Gilbert introduced me and confirmed what I'd already deduced by reading the logo on the man's epaulettes: he was an RSPCA inspector.

We shook hands briefly, but then I turned back to Mr Wood, saying: "How's young Freddie?"

Gilbert brightened and shuffled in his seat. "He's fine, thanks, Charlie. As good as new. This morning I had the public health people on to me, about the botulism. I told them it was the result of criminal activity, not a natural outbreak, and that seemed to satisfy them for the moment. Does that sound right?"

"Yes, that's fair enough."

"Good. Now, John here was telling me about the apparent increase in dog fighting. He believes there's an organised ring, and they're into badger baiting, too."

And for the next hour Inspector John regaled us with horror stories about Man's inhumanity to his fellow creatures. The natural world is red in tooth and claw, as we all know, but Man, with his gift of imagination and insatiable desire for excitement, adds a new dimension to the game. I wasn't unsympathetic, and doing unspeakable things to animals is only a small step away from repeating the practise against human beings. It was chicken for tea, in lemon sauce, but I didn't enjoy it.

"This is a pleasant surprise," I said, stooping to give Shirley, Dave's wife, a peck on the cheek. When we go for a midweek drink Dave and I walk to the pub and Shirley usually collects us towards closing time.

"Wouldn't let me out on my own," he complained. "Said you were a bad influence."

I got the drinks, with a packet of crisps for myself, and we made ourselves comfortable at a corner table. "We've got to concentrate on the dog fighting," I said after the first sip of my pint. "There was an RSPCA inspector with the boss and he reckons it's widespread. And badger baiting. Gilbert's promised to divert resources in that direction, whatever that means."

"Send a panda down the lane once a shift," Dave replied.

"Yeah, but it would be good PR if we made a few arrests, and that's what it's all about, these days."

"Why do they do it?" Shirley asked, adding: "They must be sick," to answer her own question.

"Has Dave told you all about our visit to Dob Hall?" I said, changing the subject. "You'd've loved it. Talk about how the other half live."

"No, he never tells me anything."

"That's not true," he protested, and extricated himself from blame by describing in intricate detail the precise geography of the hall, as gathered from studying the scale model.

"It sounds rather grand," Shirley agreed without enthusiasm, adjusting the position of her glass so it was dead central on the beer mat and then slipping her jacket off her shoulders. Dave reached across and helped arrange it on the back of her chair.

"You never finished telling me why you're so fond of Sir Morton," I said, and Dave made a grunting noise and picked up his pint.

When it was firmly back on the table I said: "So?"

He looked uncomfortable, glancing at Shirley, at his

pint and back to Shirley. "I was going to tell Charlie about your mum," he said to her.

Shirley reached for her glass, turned it in her fingers and replaced it. "If you want," she said. "It can't hurt Mum now."

Something had happened but I didn't know what. I opened my mouth to say that if it was personal I was happy to be kept in the dark, but before I could find the right words Dave started speaking. "Shirley's mum was done for shoplifting," he said, "six months before she died."

"Oh, I didn't know. She died... what? About a year ago?"

"It will be twelve months on the 18th of August," Shirley said. "The day before my birthday."

"She'd bought a trolley full o' shopping at Grainger's Halifax branch," Dave continued, "including a toothbrush in a plastic tube. It fell through the wire of the trolley a couple of times so she must have put it in her pocket. She was stopped outside and hauled off to the manager's office. They have no discretion, they always call the police and prosecute."

"Discretion requires making a decision," I said.

"Exactly. So, at the age of seventy-two, and never having been as much as a day behind with a payment for anything, she finds herself summoned to Halifax nick for an official caution."

"God, Dave, why didn't you say?"

"It's all right. I had a word and she didn't have to attend. But that's when the decline started and she was dead in six months."

"Like Lady Barnet," I said.

"Who?"

"Lady Isobel Barnet," Shirley replied for me. "Something similar happened to her, a long time ago. Mum wasn't the first and she won't be the last."

We had another drink and decided that was enough. Dave went to the loo and I followed him. There was one person already in there, shaking the drops off. When he'd gone, without washing his hands, I pushed open the doors to the two cubicles with my toe to prove they were empty.

"You realise," I said, "that this makes you a suspect. You have a motive."

"Yeah, I know. Me and a few hundred others."

"Jeez, you're right."

Shirley was waiting in the car for us. "Dave says you've had a postcard from Sophie," she said, brightly.

"That's right, last Thursday, I think it was. Said she was having a good time and that I'd like it in Cap Ferrat because everybody was old."

Shirley laughed. "Good old Sophie, tactful as ever."

"It wouldn't hurt her to send a card home," Dave grumbled. "If she doesn't send you one on your birthday she's in big trouble."

"She's young," Shirley explained. "She's probably in love. Leave her alone."

"Huh!" he snorted.

When I was at art school I remember my dad coming out with a maxim that was prevalent at the time: send your sons to university but keep your daughters away. I'd a feeling that Dave had heard the same maxim.

Chapter Five

Thursday I gave a talk to a mixed bunch of police officers attending a conference on major crimes at the staff college in Bramshill, Hampshire. I drove down for the day and on the car radio I heard that there'd been another case of contaminated food in Heckley and the police were investigating.

"Tut tut, whatever next?" I said to myself. Staff college had booked me over a year ago, so I'd had plenty of time to prepare my lecture. There were delegates there from all over the UK and Thursday was serial killer day. A forensic psychologist explained how his techniques could narrow down the field and indicate which way an enquiry should progress; my job was to demonstrate how this should not be allowed to hijack the investigation. Forensic, in my book, means "for use in a court of law." Drawing dots on a map is very interesting, but forensic it is not. At lunch I sat with an inspector from Newcastle, a chief inspector from Exeter and a captain in the RCMP who had wandered into the wrong dining room. We had a back-slapping time and came away with his card in our pockets and invitations to visit, any time we wanted.

The lecture room was still empty when I returned, prior to my session. Several of the delegates had left their morning newspapers on the desks, and I saw that the botulism scare had made the front pages of them all, with the warfarin story being resurrected to reinforce the impact. We were between wars, so all the familiar faces of TV and tabloid journalism had donned their designer parkas and headed north again, smelling a story. An outbreak of one deadly disease is unfortunate, two outbreaks in the same small town smacks of outside forces at work. They named the usual bogeymen and railed about the lack of readiness of the authorities. At the very least a madman was on the loose, and somebody would die soon if he wasn't caught. If they discovered that the officer leading the enquiry was swanning it at the staff college they'd have a field day. No doubt HQ would hold a press conference, probably at that very moment, and the nation would be reassured that coincidences do happen and the outbreaks had been contained. Meanwhile, purely as a precaution, if anybody did happen to have a tin of pineapple or corned beef on their shelves they should place it in a bucket of water and surround it with sandbags. Alternatively, they could return it to their nearest branch of Grainger's.

"How did it go?" Dave asked, next morning, when I came down from Gilbert's prayer meeting.

"How did what go?"

"The talk, Dumbo."

"Oh," I said, dismissively, "you know how it is. Boring speakers, nobody interested in what you say. Complete waste of time."

"So you won't be going to any more?"

"We-ell, you know how I hate to disappoint people. According to Gilbert I missed all the fun."

"Big-hearted Charlie. Yeah, you got out of it quite nicely. It's kids' stuff this morning compared to yesterday. It was like the fall of Saigon in the car park. There was even a TV crew from France. No doubt a few more of our delicacies will be taken off their shelves."

"No doubt. Did you find anything else?"

"Not much. Two more tins of corned beef found at the Huddersfield store and a tin of peaches at Oldfield."

"All with puncture holes?"

"That's right. They're at Weatherton now."

"Well done. It's worth a try but dozens of people could have handled them."

"Nuh uh. Not necessarily so. They're loaded on to the shelves twelve at a time in a cardboard tray, and up to then all the handling has been mechanical. The person whose delicate fingers punctured the tin could be the first one to touch it. We're in with a chance."

"Hey, that's brilliant. Meanwhile, it wouldn't hurt to cherchez la femme. I've a feeling that's what this is all about. Let's start by bringing Mrs Sharon Brown down to size." I found the number for Heckley Grainger's and dialled it. "Could I speak to Mrs Brown, please?"

"Sorry, but Mrs Brown is off work for a few days."

"Oh. When will she be back?"

"Tuesday. Can I put you through to her secretary?"

"No, it's a personal call. I'll ring her on Tuesday." I replaced the receiver and turned to Dave, saying: "She has a secretary."

"Might be worth having a word with her."

"True. I'll put Pete on to it, preferably away from the office. He can charm the ducks off the water."

We weren't following leads or pursuing a clearly defined course of action. We were, frankly, floundering. The culprit might be a nutcase loner, living in a tower block, or a bitter housewife with a grudge, or it might be an insider conducting a personal vendetta. We'd re-situated CCTV cameras to cover the first two possibilities, and for the third one all we could do was gather information about the principle characters, listen to gossip and go where it led. That way, when the break came, we'd be prepared.

Dave said: "Pete doesn't charm them off the water, he talks them off it."

"But he gets them talking back, too. Much better than I can."

"If they can get a quack in. He's done a chart for you."

"Good. I like charts. Charts make it look as if we're doing something. Where is he?"

"Probably in the briefing room. He's taken a shine to the new probationer. I'll fetch the chart."

It was a map, and he'd done a good job. All the findings were marked on it, colour coded to indicate peaches, pineapple or corned beef, with different shapes for punctured tins, the coloured dye and the warfarin.

"Well, this should impress the ACC," I said. "I'm not sure if it will progress the investigation, but the ACC will have an orgasm." I spanned the spaces between incidents with my fingers, making mental adjustments for distance, numbers of cases and degree of seriousness, remembering the talk I'd heard the day before and adding a few touches of my own.

"He lives there," I declared, stabbing a finger at the centre of gravity of the case. "I've done a course on this and it never fails."

"Let's have a look," Dave said. He considered the location for a few seconds before adding: "Well that should make it easy. According to your course he lives in Heckley nick."

Have a day off and the paperwork accrues. Nobody does it for you and the problems don't go away. The troops had plenty to be on with so I listened to what they had to say, made a few suggestions and sent them on their way. We'd opened an incident room at the nick for the Grainger's job and I pinned Pete's chart on the wall next to the map with the twenty-mile radius that I'd drawn. His contribution looked more professional so I unpinned my map and stuffed it in a drawer. I'd ask Pete to add the radius to his map.

Back in my own office I answered a few letters, including one to a local councillor who persistently complained about harassment of young people for skateboarding in the mall car park. We'd captured the problem on video and the mall management were receiving equally vociferous complaints about damage to parked vehicles, but the councillor would not listen. Not even when we told him about the needles being left all over the place. He also complained about the older youths in souped-up cars who congregated in one of the town-centre car parks late at night, about the lack of amenities for our budding basketball players and about the speed bumps on Fellside Road. He lives on Fellside Road. He has a regular column in the Gazette and he uses it to beat the police. Our community affairs officer had talked to him, explained the problems, told him what limited powers we had, but he wouldn't listen and now he was coming through to me. There's nothing wins votes like a fearless campaigner, and he had nothing to fear because we'd long ago stopped dangling our critics from the ceiling and administering the bastinado. I politely told him that, much as I sympathised with him about the children from the comprehensive dropping litter outside his sweet shop, it was not my intention to take any action, and in future I was only prepared to correspond with him through his solicitor.

I was basking in the warm glow of indignation gratified and gathering my strength for an assault on the staff development reports, thirteen months overdue, when the phone interrupted me. It was the front desk.

"Lady thinks she may have seen the knicker thief, Charlie. I'll put her through."

I waited a few seconds then said: "Detective Inspector Priest here. How can I help you?"

"Oh, hello. I think I may have seen this... person who's stealing underwear from washing lines."

"That's music to my ears, Madam. First of all, can I ask you your name, please?"

She was called Mrs Mavis Lewis and had been reading the Heckley Gazette as her smalls went through the rinse cycle when she happened to see an article about the thefts from washing lines. To be accurate, they were her daughter's smalls. Miss Lewis was a nurse at the White Rose clinic, just outside town, and changed her underwear twice a day. Every Friday Mrs Lewis did a big wash and, weather permitting, hung her daughter's frillies on the line to dry. Last week a shower interrupted the process and as she unpegged them she became aware of a youth standing in the garden that backed on to her garden, in the shadow of the overgrown privet hedge. He appeared to be watching her, but when she looked again he'd disappeared.

"This was last Friday?" I asked, and she confirmed that it was.

"And you're doing a wash now?"

"Yes. They've just finished spinning."

"Are you going to hang them outside?"

"I wasn't thinking of, it looks like rain again."

I glanced out of the window and banks of clouds glowered back at me. "I know. What time did you see the youth?"

"It would be sometime after one o'clock. The lunchtime concert had just started."

"The lunchtime concert?"

"On Radio 3."

I was impressed. Radio 3 listeners don't make up a significant percentage of our clients. They don't make up a significant percentage of the BBC's clients. If the thief knew her routine there was a chance that he'd come back today, and if he did, we could nab him.

"If I sent a couple of officers over would you be happy to hang the washing out, Mrs Lewis?" I asked.

"Yes. No problem."

"OK. Don't do anything just yet and I'll be with you in about twenty minutes to see how the land lies."

I contacted Dave and two other DCs and told them to come back to the station, then drove to Mrs Lewis's home. It was a semi, built back in the Thirties when houses had decent gardens but tiny kitchens. I drove round the block a couple of times, learning the street names, and parked a few doors away.

She was a pleasant woman, overweight and jolly,

and not at all troubled by the attentions of the knicker thief. Her husband was there, sitting in an easy chair with a pair of headphones on. He had a bushy beard and wore brown brogues and a tweed jacket with leather patches on the elbows. Men who wear their shoes and jacket in the house make me lose sleep at night. I can't help thinking that they're prepared for a quick getaway. He removed the 'phones and stood up to shake hands.

"Don't let me interrupt the concert," I said.

"Tchaikovsky," he replied with a sniff. "Music for lifts."

Ah well, that was one of my favourite composers demolished. Mrs Lewis took me through into the kitchen, from where I could survey the garden. The rain had blown over but the next lot wasn't far away. There was a shed halfway down the garden, which would make a good observation post, and the neighbour had a greenhouse filled with tomato plants.

"Do you think your neighbours would let us use their greenhouse?" I asked, and I was assured that she wouldn't mind, so I rang the station and told Dave and the other two to come over, and arranged for a panda to stand by a couple of streets away. Then I asked Mrs Lewis to hang out the washing.

I sat on a step-ladder in the kitchen, Dave took the shed and the others lay doggo in the greenhouse. We stayed like that for three hours, as Miss Lewis's underwear came under more scrutiny than the Turin shroud. It hung from two lines like a set of teeth from some fabulous beast until the occasional gust of wind disturbed the image.

Dave rang me on my mobile at frequent intervals. "They're big, aren't they?" he observed.

"Affirmative. Have you seen anything?"

"No, only some porn magazines."

"I meant down the garden," I said, squashing my ear with the phone and praying that Mrs Lewis, standing next to me, didn't have hypersensitive hearing. She was wearing an anorak and trainers, and carrying a stout walking stick, determined to join in the chase should the need arise.

At four o'clock the phone rang again, but this time it was Heckley nick. "Have you had your mobile off, Charlie?" a smug sounding controller asked.

"No. Why."

"We've been trying to contact you all afternoon."

"Well it's switched on, and Dave's rung me several times without any problems. What did you want?"

"Ah well, there's no harm done. Just to report that uniformed branch have arrested a twelve-year-old youth on suspicion of theft of undergarments from washing lines. They took him home and his mother let them into his bedroom, which he kept locked. They found a regular lingerie department in there, apparently, and they're bringing him in."

"You what?" I hissed.

"You heard. The lads in the panda you had standing by nabbed him. He walked round the corner but when he saw them he turned turtle and started running. Unfortunately for him we had Yorkshire's four hundred metres champion on the case, so it was no contest. You can bring your boys in, now, Charlie. It's all under control."

Dave's comment was unrepeatable, Mrs Lewis

was delighted and the two in the greenhouse were incensed. They'd had a break from watching CCTV videos and eaten a few tomatoes, but the neighbour didn't believe in using insecticides and they were covered in mosquito bites.

As the four of us trudged into the nick a grinning desk sergeant held up two bulging plastic bags, saying: "Want to see some saucy items, chaps? We've got something for all tastes here."

On the stairs we crossed Gareth Adey, no doubt coming back from regaling Mr Wood with news of his boys' success. "Hello Charlie," he gushed. "Had a busy afternoon?"

We were in the office, drinking tea, when my power of speech returned. "Well they can do all the sodding paperwork," I declared.

"Adey'll never let us forget this," Dave said.

"In that case, we'd better get one back at him."

"Like what?"

"I don't know. Let's go home."

"It's Saturday tomorrow."

"True."

"It's a great weather forecast – fancy going for a jog with the others?"

"Good idea. Bring your kit."

"Have you rung her yet?"

"Who?"

"You know who."

"Umm, yes, but she wasn't in."

I had a big fillet of cod for tea, done under the grill with melted cheese on top, accompanied by new potatoes and petits pois. For pudding it was semolina and chopped banana. When you live alone there's a temptation to neglect yourself, eat junk food, but I try to take care. You are what you eat, as the bluebottle said to the dung beetle.

I rang Rosie afterwards, to undo the lie I'd told Sparky, and she wasn't in, just like I'd said. Except, when I put the phone down, I wished she had been in. I had a long soak in the bath and watched a video of Band of Brothers that one of the crew had loaned me. In under three weeks I had to produce two paintings for the show, but I had no ideas what to make them. I spent an hour looking at art books – Paul Klee, Picasso and Kandinsky – wishing I had their flair and originality. Whatever I produced, it would only be a pale imitation.

It was late when I rang Rosie again, but now I was resolved to speak to her. Sophie's postcard still lay alongside my phone, and I doodled on it as the ringing tone warbled in my ear, filling-in the loops of her writing with red Biro. I switched to a blue pen as the phone in Rosie's house played its shrill monotonous music to the empty room, and replaced the receiver with mixed emotions. I was disappointed she wasn't there but now I knew how my paintings would look. I went into the garage and painted one piece of board bright blue and the other yellow. Reading in bed is an art I've never mastered, but it was only poetry. I took the New Oxford Book of English Verse and Philip Smith's 100 Best-Loved Poems to bed with me.

Seven of us had a Saturday morning jog: five doing an easy four miles and two hard men galloping round the six-mile route. It was a bright sunny morning filled with the promise of a hot day. I'd gone in early and had an hour at the staff development reports before the others arrived. My intention was to stay on, after a shower, and finish them off, but someone suggested a pint in the Bailiwick and the temptation was too great. Then I saw the menu and smelled the cooking and decided to have lunch there, too. I went home feeling quite replete and mellow.

The boards I'd painted were four feet by three. I took a watercolour pad and drew squares on it twelve inches by nine, which was one-sixteenth the size of the boards, and wrote pieces of verse, gleaned from the poetry books, across them in loopy, joined up writing, as if they were snatches of a letter. I wrote:

How do I love thee? Let me count the ways.
I love thee to the depth and breadth and height
My soul can reach, when feeling out of sight

and:

Remember me when I am gone away,
Gone far away into the silent land;
When you can no more hold me by the hand,
Nor I half turn to go yet turning stay

I did it all again, but this time I started writing one word into the first line and continued off the edge of the frame, to make them appear to be random pages of prose rather than pieces of verse. Then I filled in all the loops with different coloured fibre-tipped pens, so they looked like love letters someone had received and carelessly doodled all over, perhaps while speaking on the phone to another lover. I gave one letter some Mickey Mouse ears and made another into a Smiley face. Nobody at the show would recognise the hidden story behind the paintings, but perhaps Lizzie Browning and Chrissie Rossetti would have approved.

The next step was to transfer the writing on to the painted boards, but at many times the size, and this would be time-consuming. The enamel on the boards was dry but not hard, so I decided it would be better to leave them for another day. I made a mug of tea, found a couple of custard creams and fell asleep with the football on the telly.

I was awake again, planning the evening menu, when the phone rang.

"Charlie Priest."

"Hello Uncle Charles. It's me."

"Sophie!" One of those exploding birthday cakes went off inside me, with a great bang and a puff of smoke, and six dancing girls in silver lame costumes high-kicked down the hallway. "How are you?" I picked up the phone and slid down the wall to sit on the floor.

"I'm fine. How are you?"

"Brilliant. Where are you speaking from?"

"I'm on a train. I've tried ringing home but nobody's in. Could you possibly pick me up at the station, please?"

"No problem. What time do you arrive?"

"Ten to seven in Leeds, but I'm not sure about the connection to Heckley."

I looked at my watch and did a quick calculation. "Don't bother hanging about for the connection, I'll pick you up in Leeds."

"Are you sure?"

"Positive."

We chatted for a few minutes until I said I'd better be on my way. My instinct was to ring Dave and Shirley to tell them that their beloved daughter was coming home, but it occurred to me that Dave might insist on collecting her himself, depriving me of that pleasure, so I didn't. It would be all the more of a surprise when I produced her on their doorstep. I had a quick shower and teeth-clean, changed my clothes and set off for the station.

They'd made some changes there. The tunnel under the lines was gone, replaced by a bridge that linked the platforms. I was early, but by the time I'd worked out which platform she would arrive at the train was due in. I stood near the ticket barrier, watching as the bridge disgorged gaggles of travellers who flashed their tickets to the disinterested clerk, wondering how much Sophie had changed since I last saw her.

As soon as she appeared at the top of the stairs my legs turned to spaghetti. She was wearing a short skirt, high heels and a blouse with a high collar. Mandarin, I believe it's called. A bag hung over her shoulder with a leather jacket looped through it, and she turned slightly sideways as she came down the steps, feeling for each one, as if afraid she might topple over. Lovely Sophie hadn't quite mastered the art of walking in four-inch stilettos. She saw me and waved.

"You look sensational," I said, pecking her on the

cheek. She was wearing Mitsouko, by Guerlain. The only perfume I recognise and one that brought back memories that I didn't need. Not then or at any other time.

"You don't look bad yourself, Uncle Charles," she replied.

I just stared at her, happy as a sandboy, and said: "Huh!"

"I've been reading about you in the papers."

"It's not true. I never touched her." She wouldn't let me take her bag as we wandered out of the concourse into the gloom of the evening. In the car I said: "Hungry?"

"Mmm, a bit." She drew her bare legs under the seat and tipped her knees in my direction.

"Nice suntan," I said.

"Thank you."

"Cap Ferrat?"

"That's right."

"With all the old folks. Will a pizza be OK?"

"Lovely!"

"Right. I'll show you that sophistication exists outside the hallowed groves of Oxbridge."

It was only a short drive to Park Square, where Terence Conran has one of his restaurants. The furnishings are art deco, the waiters and waitresses look as if they come from central casting and the pizzas are the only ones I've ever had that I could honestly say I'd enjoyed. Sophie beamed her approval, and that was good enough for me. We had a glass of wine each and she told me about Cap Ferrat and Cambridge over our quattro staggioni and pepperoni with black olives.

Her blouse was made from a heavy silk material, embroidered with dragons and pagodas, and when I admired it she said it was a present from China. The pearls for buttons were in pairs, close together, and the high collar and her piled-up hair emphasised her height. Halfway through the meal, after she'd called me Uncle Charles for the tenth time, I raised a disapproving finger and said: "A ground rule."

"What?" she asked, suddenly serious.

"Well, now that you're almost qualified as a... whatever it is you're almost qualified as, I think you ought to start calling me Charlie. I know I'm old, but Uncle Charles really rubs it in. All these people think I'm a sugar daddy out with my girlfriend, and it would really destroy my credibility if they heard you call me Uncle Charles, so could you please indulge in an old man's whim and call me Charlie? Please?"

"Oh, OK then," she said, "Charlie it is," and kicked me on the shin.

I winced, and she said: "Was that your leg?"

I nodded confirmation between the waves of pain.

"Sorry, I thought it was the table," Sophie giggled.

I took a sip of wine, grimacing as I said: "Purely for anaesthetic purposes," and replaced my glass next to hers. She'd left a smear of lipstick on its rim. I'd never known her wear lipstick before.

"That was a lovely meal," she said, as we crossed the road outside an hour later. "Thank you. I'm glad Dad wasn't in."

"So am I. It's a nice place. Conran has them all over but that's the only one I've ever eaten at."

As we stepped on to the pavement I swapped sides

and placed my hand in the small of her back as I crossed behind her. She took my left arm in hers and hugged it, resting her head on my shoulder, like Suze Rotolo on the cover of Freewheelin'. I felt like a teenager, didn't want the evening to end.

In the car Sophie retrieved her phone, pressed a button and held it to her ear.

"No reply," she said after a few seconds. As we approached Heckley she tried again, with the same results.

"Do you have a key?" I asked, and she said she hadn't.

After another try she said: "We could always go to your house for a coffee."

Why didn't I think of that? "Sounds a good idea," I agreed, switching lanes to head away from her home.

I filled the kettle, plugged it in, switched it on. Milk from the fridge, sugar from the cupboard, biscuits in the tin. Cups, saucers, plates. Was that it? No. Spoons. We needed spoons. Spoons from the cutlery drawer. I placed them all on the table, where I normally breakfasted, and turned to rest against the work surface as the kettle hissed and grumbled into life. Sophie was leaning on the doorframe, watching. She came over and stood before me, her head bowed. I'd a feeling that she was about to say something portentous. I reached forward, taking hold of her elbows and said: "What's the problem, Sophie?"

"There's no problem," she replied, looking up into my face. She'd slipped the shoes off and was back to her normal height, which was still tall. "Except..."

"Except? Except what?"

"Except, I've lied to you. Don't be mad at me, Uncle Charles."

"Charlie."

"Sorry."

"When did you lie?"

"Just now, in the car. And earlier. I didn't try to ring Dad, because I don't want to go home. I want to stay here with you, just for tonight."

I ran my fingertips up her arms and held her by the shoulders. "Why, Sophie? Why are you doing this to me?" My voice sounded like it was coming from a well at the far end of a tunnel.

"Because… I don't know. I wanted someone to talk to. Someone I loved, and I love you." She slipped her arms around my neck and I pulled her close. I leaned my forehead against hers, squashing her nose with mine, until we both turned our faces a fraction to bring our lips into that perfect, bewitching angle with each other's.

Chapter Six

I brushed my lips across Sophie's, then lifted my face and kissed her on the forehead. I pecked her on the cheek and on her neck, and reached behind my head to find her hands and unlink her fingers.

"This isn't what I want, Sophie," I told her, shaking my head. "I can't. I'm sorry, but I can't."

She looked up into my face, bewildered and hurt. "Why not? Don't you love me?"

"Of course I love you. I love you more than life, but I don't want to start something we – I – couldn't stop."

"I don't understand."

"Neither do I." The kettle came to the boil and I broke away, turning my back, grateful for the interruption, not wanting to face her. I spooned instant coffee into mugs, poured on the water, added milk and stirred them for longer than necessary. "Let's sit where it's more comfortable," I said, leading the way into the front room.

We sat on the settee, Sophie at one end, me at the other. Her head was bowed and I was aware that I'd probably just paid her the biggest humiliation in the repertoire. She was embarrassed and confused. This was not the way it was meant to happen. I shuffled sideways until I was next to her and placed my arm across her shoulders. She snuggled closer, her head on my shoulder.

"I'm tremendously flattered, Sophie," I told her, my voice a hoarse whisper. "I know it's the greatest compliment you could pay me and that it wasn't something you'd decided lightly, and I'll never forget it. But it would spoil everything, don't you see? Apart from us, I'd be betraying your parents. OK, I could possibly cope with that. Then there's the fact that I'm your godfather, and that's supposed to give me responsibilities, but I could live with that, too. But it would spoil things between us – you and me – and I'd find that unbearable. You'd turn against me, sometime in the future, when you were in a different frame of mind and whatever it was that brought you here was forgotten. And for what? One night in bed together? We mean more than that to each other, don't we?"

"I'm sorry."

"Nothing to be sorry about, nothing at all, but maybe you should tell me what's behind it all, why you want to snog with old Uncle Charlie when there's all these handsome young bloods at Cambridge falling over themselves to go out with you."

"Huh!" was all she said.

We sat like that for a while, then sipped our coffee. "Tell me about Cap Ferrat," I said, replacing my mug on the low table.

"It was fun," she replied, smiling.

"Thanks for the card. What's the boyfriend called?"

She bit her lip and glanced at me. "Promise not to laugh."

"Scout's honour."

"He's called Digby."

"Digby? That's a fine name."

"You're laughing at me."

"No I'm not, but it might raise a few eyebrows the

first time your dad takes him down to the Mechanics'
Institute for a Sunday lunchtime pint."

"I won't let him go to the 'stute for a lunchtime pint."

"You'll have to, it's a tradition. So is this one serious?"

"Yes."

"I have to know a bit more about him before I give
my approval. It's one of a godfather's duties, did you
know?"

"Is it? What do you want to know?"

"Is he a good bloke? Does he deserve you?"

Sophie giggled for the first time that evening. "He
doesn't have any tattoos or body piercing, if that's
what you mean."

"And does he deserve you?"

"I think so. He's asked me to marry him."

"Really! And what did you say?"

"I said that I'd think about it and tell him on
Monday."

"And what have you decided?"

"I'll tell him that I'd be proud to be his wife, if he'll
still have me."

I had to think about that. Eventually I said: "I admit
I'm a bit slow about these things, Sophie, but if you're
going to accept Digby's proposal on Monday why did
you want to spend tonight with me? I don't understand."

She rested her head on my shoulder again and I
took her hand in mine. "Have you ever fancied
Mum?" she asked with all the subtlety of a rampaging
cocker spaniel.

"Erm, your mum?" I asked, hesitation colouring my
reply with guilt. "Well, er, she's an attractive woman.

And she makes cracking apple pies, but unfortunately your dad found her first." I stood up and walked over to the CD player. Livin' La Vida Loca seemed appropriate. "What made you ask that?"

"I asked her if she fancied you and she blushed."

"You what!"

"I asked her if she'd ever fancied you. We had a long talk before I went to uni." The first bars of salsa invaded the room and her head nodded to the rhythm. "Ricky Martin, I bought you this."

"I know you did."

"Do you play it much?"

"All the time. I thought you and your dad had a long talk."

"Fibber. I bet this is the first time. We did, but he just said he'd come and duff up anybody who gave me aggro. You said much the same thing. Mum said that she loved Dad and wouldn't want to be married to anybody else, but she was young when she married and she'd known him all her life. Sometimes, she said, she wished she'd had a bit of a fling. Can I tell you a secret, Uncle Charles?"

"I think we're well into secret-keeping territory, Sophie."

"Well, once, when I was young, I imagined that you and Mum had been lovers and that you were my real dad. I thought it was ever so romantic." I heaved a big sigh and shook my head, not believing what I was hearing. "So," she went on, "I asked Mum if she'd marry you if anything happened to Dad."

"And what did your mum say?"

"She told me to mind my own business. But she was blushing as she said it."

"I think you've been reading too many... um, Penelope Teapots."

"Who's Penelope Teapot?"

"No idea." I took her hand in mine again. "Is that what this was supposed to be, Sophie? A bit of a fling?"

"Are you mad at me?"

"No, of course not. I'm flattered, but I'm still mystified, when you have all those handsome young fellows at your beck and call."

She leaned on me again and I embraced her, my face in her hair, breathing in that old familiar perfume. After a while she said: "Digby's not my first boyfriend, Uncle Charles."

"Good. There you are, then. You've had your fling."

"I went out with a boy from Bristol when I was in my first year. Then I started going out with Digby."

"So you've known him a long time. What – two years?"

"No, nearly a year. I wish you still knew Annabelle. I could talk to Annabelle."

"Annabelle's long gone, I'm afraid." Except it was her perfume Sophie was wearing and it felt like only yesterday that I'd almost drowned in its headiness. "Can't you talk to your mum?"

"Not about this."

"I don't know what to say."

"Do men always enjoy sex, Uncle Charles?"

"Well, um, usually," I mumbled, taken aback. Sophie inherited her dad's forthrightness as well as his height. "Not always, but usually." Ricky Martin was urging someone to be careful with my heart in case you break it. "Is… is that what the problem is?" I ventured, and I felt her nod her head against my shoulder.

I sat in silence for several minutes, practising opening lines and abandoning them. It was Sophie herself who broke the ice. "I enjoy it, but…" That's all she said.

"But it's not worth all the fuss," I suggested, and felt her nod again. "So you thought it might be different with an older man? Someone more experienced?" Another nod. "Well, it might have been, but I doubt it. Sometimes you have to learn about a person. Sometimes you have to be married to them before you can really relax and enjoy it. When you're young, a young man, that is, you tend to be impatient, not as considerate as you ought to be. Talk to Digby, I'm sure he'll understand. The important thing is not to worry about it: don't develop any hang-ups and don't believe everything you read in Cosmopolitan. If you love each other the sex bit is just a bonus. You're a lovely lady, Sophie, and I suspect you're just too much for young Digby, but he'll settle down once he realises that you're not going to run away from him."

"Am I being stupid?" I heard her whisper.

"No, you're not being stupid. You'll be OK, just don't expect perfection every time." I decided that sex therapist was not my calling and changed the subject. "What's Digby's second name."

"Merriman-Flint."

"'Struth! With a hyphen?"

"Yes."

"Blimey. So will you be Sophie Merriman-Flint or Sophie Sparkington-Merriman-Flint?"

"Sophie Jennifer Sparkington-Merriman-Flint," she replied.

"Of course. It suits you." I held her for a while, swaying gently to the music, then said: "Do you love him, Sophie? Really love him?"

She turned to face me and I was alarmed to see tears welling up in her eyes. I pulled her back into my arms and hugged her tight, but the tears turned into full-scale weeping.

"What is it, Sophie?" I whispered. "What's the problem? I'm sure it's not as bad as it seems. We'll work it out."

"I'm pregnant, Uncle Charles," she sobbed. "I'm having a baby."

"Oh Sophie, Sophie." I wanted to say I was sorry, rocking her back and forth, then decided it might not be appropriate. Every thought that came into my head sounded more fatuous than the one before. "How... how..." I began, stumbling for words.

"The usual way," she sniffed with a tearful smile. "Clever clogs, know-it-all Sophie has gone and got herself pregnant. It's right what they say: It's always the nice girls that get banged up."

"I meant... how long have you known?"

"Since Friday morning."

"And how... how long...?"

"How far gone am I? About four weeks."

"That's not long. Are you sure?"

"Positive."

I wiped her cheek with my fingertips. "So what are you going to do?"

"Have a baby, I expect. Not what I'd planned but I'm growing used to the idea."

"Does Digby know?"

"No. You're the only person I've told. I don't know what Digby will say. Maybe he'll be mad at me, not want to see me again. I'm scared, Uncle Charles, really scared."

I gave her an extra squeeze. "He won't be mad at you," I assured her. "If he's the sort of person I would expect you to go with he won't be mad at you. He'll be surprised, confused, for about twenty seconds. Then he'll be the happiest man in the world, believe me."

"What if he isn't? What if he doesn't want me?"

"In that case, you come back to me and we'll run away together, to somewhere where your dad would never find us."

"Like where?"

"Antarctica, but I'm sure it won't come to that."

"That would be nice. I do love you, Uncle Charles."

"And I you. So when will you tell him?"

"Tomorrow, and when he gets over the shock I'll ask him if the offer still stands."

"It will, I'm sure. Then there's the little matter of your parents."

"I know. I'll tell them about the engagement first, if there is one, let them get used to that, then take it from there. There's no hurry, not for a while."

"Your dad will be disappointed."

"That's true, but only until he's a granddad, then he'll be as soppy as ever."

"No, I meant about having a son-in-law called Digby."

"Mmm, that is a problem." She chuckled and sniffed at the same time and I found a tissue for her in my pocket. "But there are compensations."

"Compensations?"

"Yes. His family own half of Shropshire."

"Ha ha! Good for you. Which half?"

"That's what Dad will say."

There was thunder in the distance through the night. Just before dawn it trundled off the hills and away down the valley like a powerful army, content to have reminded us of its presence. I spent the night on the settee, listening, until with a final rumble the storm shook its fist at the town before skulking off and I fell asleep.

Sophie slept through the dawn chorus and through the noises of the people next door hitching their caravan to the Volvo, dad shouting orders to everyone, before they went off for a day's fun queuing on the bypass. I had some Frosties and a cup of tea, and at ten to nine took a tray upstairs.

I knocked at my own bedroom door and asked if I could come in. A sleepy voice granted me permission.

Sophie was sitting up, the duvet drawn up under her armpits. Holding the tray on the fingertips of one hand I pulled the drawstring for the curtains to open them slightly, letting the morning sunshine spill into the room. Her hair had fallen on to her shoulders and it shone like spun gold where the sunlight caught it. She yawned and made noises of contentment, stretching her arms and smiling at me.

I said: "Orange juice, coffee, Frosties and toast. Will there be anything else, Ma'am?"

"Ooh, thank you. I like this hotel. No, that should be everything. I wasn't asleep, just dreaming."

"Did the thunder disturb you?"

"Thunder? No, did it thunder?"

"Just a little. Flattened two houses down the street and blew the roof off next door."

"Well, I didn't hear it."

I placed the tray on her lap and dropped another pillow behind her head. "Don't be all day," I told her. "There's a faint chance that your dad might call."

"Is that why you told me to bring my shoes and bag upstairs?"

"Yes." She laughed and called me silly, but I told her that there was nothing silly about self-preservation.

I turned to go, but she said: "Uncle Charles."

"Mmm." I stopped and leaned on the doorjamb, my hand on the handle.

"About last night."

"What about it?"

"I'm glad we… you know… that we didn't."

"Good. So am I."

"But somehow, it feels as if… as if it was still a bit special. I feel… closer to you, if you know what I mean. I was upset when I decided to come to see you, all mixed up. You were the only person I could think of. Thank you for looking after me. I love you, I really do. You're my best friend."

"Yes, Sophie," I replied. "I know what you mean, and I love you more than ever. That's not always the case, the morning after, believe me. Now eat your breakfast. I want you downstairs in ten minutes."

As I crossed the landing I heard her call: "Can I have a shower, please."

"Yes!" I yelled back.

I drove her down to Cambridge and we breakfasted at a Little Chef on the A1. Sophie said she was determined to get her degree, even with a baby to look after. If Digby stayed on for his masters it shouldn't be a problem. Near Cambridge we stopped again and had a chat sitting in a car park outside a greasy-spoon. I warned her that her mother's birthday was looming large and that she'd be in big trouble if she forgot to send a card. She said that might be a good time to introduce them to Digby and announce their engagement. We said our goodbyes, swore our undying love, and I told her that I'd always be there for her.

"And don't forget to send me an invite," I said as I started the engine for the last few miles.

"You're top of the list, Uncle Charles."

"Thank you."

"Shall we make it and friend?"

"No, I don't think so. Which way?"

"Follow the ring road. Is there anybody?"

"Not really. I thought there might be, but suddenly she doesn't want to know."

"Why's that?"

"I don't know."

"What's she called?"

"Rosie."

"She's a fool. When she knows you better she'll

change her mind." Sophie reached out and touched my face. "Your hair's long."

I tilted my head to trap her fingers between my cheek and shoulder. "It needs cutting."

"I like it long. It suits you."

"Thanks. I don't think Rosie will ever have the chance to know me better."

"In that case you'll have to work at it, won't you? And then we can all be happy."

"Are you happy, Sophie?"

There was the slightest hesitation before she said: "Yes, I am."

"Then I'm happy too," I told her.

I hadn't tried to put a face on Digby, but he wasn't quite what I expected. He was an inch shorter than Sophie but broad-shouldered, with sandy hair and a rugby player's nose. The rugby image was reinforced by the county shirt he was wearing, and I suspected that he'd earned it, not bought it at JJB Sports. He was clearly devoted to Sophie and his face lit up like an herbaceous border as he hugged her. He shook my hand, then asked Sophie how her parents were.

"They're fine," she replied, lying with a facility that would have been the envy of most of the villains I meet. "Uncle Charles came round and insisted on driving me back."

"That's really nice of you," he told me.

"My pleasure," I replied. "We see so little of Sophie these days."

They gave me afternoon tea and Digby said he was studying computer sciences and had been offered a job with Intel in Dublin. I liked him, and thought Sophie's dad would, too, once he'd cleared the Digby hurdle.

"Look after her," I told him as we shook hands again, standing on the pavement next to my car.

"I will," he promised, and I believed him.

Sophie gave me a peck on the cheek as she hugged me and I rubbed the small of her back in a non-avuncular way. "Don't forget to talk to Rosie," she said, matter of fact, as much for Digby's benefit as mine, I suspected. Round the corner I stopped and sorted through my CDs for the long drive north. "Desire" would do for starters:

> I married Isis on the fifth day of May
> But I could not hold on to her for very long.
> So I cut off my hair and I rode straight away
> For the wild unknown country where I could not go wrong.

Hooray for 24-7 supermarkets. It was early evening as I hit Heckley, so I called in Grainger's and did a medium shop. The place was manned by schoolgirls, earning money for riding lessons and the latest Pop Idol CD, but I wasn't complaining. I had a calorie-counter's sweet-and-sour chicken for tea, followed by sticky toffee pudding and custard, all done in the microwave. Very tasty. As weekends go this one had been pretty serendipitous. OK, be honest, it was one of the most serendipitous weekends of my life. I was on a roll, so I decided to push it. I found my diary and dialled Rosie's number. She picked up the phone after the first ring.

"Um, hello Rosie," I said, slightly off guard. "It's

Charlie Priest." This time I didn't add the as in Roman Catholic.

"Hello Charlie. How are you?"

"I'm splendid. Fine, thanks. And you?"

"Oh, I'm all right."

"Are you sure?"

"Yes, I'm fine."

"You don't sound it."

"Well I am."

"Good. So how about that drink sometime?"

"I don't think so, Charlie. I thought I made that clear the last time we spoke."

"Rosie," I began, "I'm not very good at this sort of thing, and I don't want to be a nuisance, but I thought we were getting on reasonably well, and then, I don't know, you suddenly became distant. Did I say something I shouldn't have, or offend you in any way?"

"No, of course not, Charlie. It's just that... I don't want to become involved."

"Going out for a Chinese is hardly becoming involved."

"I know. I tried to tell you, on the phone. I come with baggage."

"To hell with baggage, Rosie. I don't give a toss about baggage. We were doing fine until I said that I was a cop. That's when your attitude changed. Now, I don't think you're a master criminal – a Mafia godmother or head of an international drugs cartel – so what's it all about?"

She was silent for a while and I expected her to come back and tell me to mind my own, but eventually she said: "You're right, Charlie. It is to do with you being a detective. I'm involved in a legal procedure and I've been advised not to speak to any policemen, that's all."

"What, by a solicitor?"

"Not exactly."

"Then by whom?"

"By a TV production company. First Call TV."

"And why don't they want you talking to any policemen?"

"Because they say you'll try to influence me. We're taking out an action against the police, and they say you'll apply pressure for me to drop it."

"Oh, I see. Well, no I don't see. If you had a case, Rosie, we'd probably help you. There are procedures for this sort of thing. Do you want to tell me what it's about?"

"It's about my father. I'm trying to clear his name and they're helping. They want to do a documentary about his case."

Alarm bells started clanging when I realised that journalists were involved. For Rosie's sake, not the police's. As with politicians, there are some good ones. And there's probably life on Mars, too.

"What did your father do?" I asked.

"He didn't do anything," she protested, her voice beginning to crack. "It's what he had done to him."

"I'm sorry," I said. "I guess I'm conditioned to adopt an attitude. I've been in the job too long. What did they do to your father?"

"They hanged him, Charlie," she sobbed. "They hanged him for a murder he didn't commit."

* * *

I did a quick calculation. The last people to be hanged in the UK were two hapless souls in Lancashire, back in 1964. Rosie would have been a little girl, a baby, then. I tried to think of names but they wouldn't come, and Rosie's mother may have changed hers after the event. Capital punishment doesn't punish just the accused. A vast cone of misery extends out from under the gallows, enveloping everyone involved with the whole rotten process, including the victim's family. Their expectations that a life for a life would ease the burden always proved to have been a hollow promise.

"Rosie," I began. "We can't leave it like this, and I'm not happy with you being involved with a TV company. They want a story, that's all, and they don't care who gets hurt. I'm coming round to see you. I'll be ringing your doorbell in about fifteen minutes. If you don't want to let me in, fair enough, but I'll be there."

"I don't know..."

"Fifteen minutes." There was a long silence as I waited for her to either reply or replace her handset, but before she could my brain reminded me of a simple fact. I said: "There's just one thing. You told me in the pub that you live on Old Run Road. It's a long road and I don't know the number. I could ring the station and ask someone to consult the electoral roll, but it would be easier for you to tell me."

After an even longer silence she said: "Two hundred and twelve. It's number two hundred and twelve."

* * *

On the way over I called in a filling station and bought a bunch of flowers. Pink carnations. Outside her house I wondered if they were appropriate, but decided to risk it. She lived in a small bungalow with a neat garden and her Fiesta was parked on the drive. Its presence confirmed that I was in the right place and something in my stomach did a little fandango at the thought of seeing her again.

Rosie was watching for me and opened the door as I extended my hand towards the bell push. I thrust the flowers at her, saying: "Last bunch in the bucket, I'm afraid, but they look OK."

"Flowers," she said, with obvious pleasure as she took them from me. "It's a long time since anyone bought me flowers."

We had tea in china cups, with home-made carrot cake. Rosie was bare-footed, wearing red jeans and a baggy V-necked sweater, with no jewellery or make-up. That strange mixture of confidence and vulnerability struck me again and I had to remind myself that this wasn't a date: I was here in the role of friend, adviser and confidant. But her toenails were painted scarlet and the sweater clung to her and although one shoulder was poking out of it I couldn't see a bra strap. When she lifted the teapot and looked at me I nodded a "Yes please" and she leaned forward to fill my cup.

I said: "First of all, Rosie, I'm not here as a policeman. I'm here as your friend. I don't know anything about the case and if you don't want to tell me I'll understand, but I must warn you about any involvement with television. You want to prove your father innocent; they want a story. They have a documentary to produce. I don't know what your father is supposed to have done or if he is innocent or guilty, but just suppose – just suppose – that he is guilty. The crew won't go home saying: 'Oh well, we lost that one.' No, they'll put a spin on it so that they become the heroes of the plot: they proved your dad was a villain and the public will get their half-hour of entertainment. Your feelings will be cast aside like... like... I don't know, yesterday's tea bags."

She sat back in her easy chair, white-faced, pulled the sweater on to her shoulder and sniffed.

I went on: "That's all I want to say, Rosie. Be careful, because the chances are you'll get hurt. If you want the case re-opening there are other ways of doing it. Safer ways."

The picture over the mantel was an interpretation of Malham Cove, semi-abstract but still quite distinctive. Very appropriate for a geologist. I stood up to inspect it more closely and Rosie asked if I liked it.

"Yes, it's good. Puts my own efforts to shame, I'm afraid."

"Oh, I'd forgotten you were an artist," she said.

"Mmm." I turned and sat down again. "I used to be an art student. That's where I learned to draw." I smiled at her. "Then it was either graphic design or the police, and the police won."

Rosie returned the smile. "More tea?"

"Ooh, go on then."

"They're small cups." She poured for both of us, then said: "It may be too late to stop the TV people."

"If they're on to a story it will be impossible to stop them. Have you signed a contract or anything?"

"Not a contract, as such. A request for an exhumation. They've applied to the coroner's office for a warrant to have my father's body exhumed, and for something called… what is it… a faculty of the diocese, or something?"

"I think that's just permission from the Church of England to do work on their land," I said. "What are the grounds for conducting the exhumation?"

"Because of the availability of DNA profiling. And they said that there are new techniques that can show if statements have been interfered with."

"ESDA," I said. "It's called ESDA."

It was nearly dark outside. Rosie drew the curtains and switched on the light. It was a pleasant room, small and minimally furnished, with plain walls and the odd splash of colour from a painting or poster. There were candles in the hearth and she was halfway through Pride and Prejudice. I looked but I couldn't see a television. Maybe it's at the foot of her bed, I thought.

I finished my tea slowly, watching her above the rim of the cup. She drew her legs under her and gazed at a spot somewhere to the left of the fireplace, her brow furrowed. Eventually she said: "I was in the school play. Eleven years old. We were doing A Midsummer Night's Dream and I was Mustard Seed. It wasn't much of a part but I put my heart and soul into it. We had a rehearsal after school but I forgot to tell my parents. Dad came to collect me, as he often did, but I wasn't ready to leave, so he walked back home alone."

I slowly replaced my cup and saucer on the low table and waited for her to continue. "The girl was called Glynis. Glynis Evelyn Williams, aged thirteen.

Lived three doors away from us. When she didn't arrive home from school a search party went out to look for her. They found her body on the hillside. She'd been strangled. Not raped or anything, just strangled. There was blood under her fingernails, group B, less than ten percent of the population. They tested all the men in the village and a week later arrested my father and charged him with murder. He made a full confession, they said, and hanged himself in his cell later that night. He plaited strips of material from his shirt into a rope and hanged himself. The police took great delight in telling Mum that it would have been a slow death, but only what he deserved."

"Have you seen the confession?"

"No, not yet."

I didn't know what else to say. Rosie's loyalty towards her father was only what I expected, but she was very young at the time, living a childhood that was close to perfection. I could imagine the scenario. Her father got himself into a situation with a girl from the village, a girl that he knew, and ended up with a dead body on his hands. We stand on our soapboxes and rail at the guilty party, then say a secret prayer that begins with the words: "There but for..." She was heading for more heartbreak, of that I was certain. All I could try to do was prepare her for it, ease the blow when it fell.

"Apparently you have something called noble cause corruption," she said. "The producer told me that a signed statement could easily be faked, especially when otherwise you wouldn't have enough evidence. It was dictated by my father, the police claim, and written down by the investigating detective. Why would it be done like that when he was perfectly capable of writing it himself?"

"I don't know," I replied. "That's just how it was. Probably to save time because most of our clients have difficulty spelling MUFC." Normal procedure was to ask the suspect to sign the statement directly below the last line of writing, but many an old-time bobby wasn't averse to asking for a signature at the bottom of the page, then adding a few words of his own.

"There's fitting up," I told her, "and there's this thing called noble cause corruption. We know fitting up goes off because there have been cases of it proven in the West Midlands and in the Met, but I've been in the job a long time and I've never met a policeman who would willingly fit up an innocent person just to improve the clear-up figures. Noble cause corruption is slightly different. Let's say we've arrested someone for rape, or persistent burglary. You know he did it, he's done it before and he'll do it again, but the evidence is circumstantial and he's on legal aid and you're not allowed to reveal his previous convictions to the court. You want him off the streets, so there's a temptation to take steps to strengthen your case. It happens, I'm sure. I've no proof but I've had my suspicions once or twice." And Charlie Priest could lie for England, I reminded myself. "What I'm saying is... even if the statement is faked, it doesn't prove anything. It might help show that he was wrongly charged, but that's not the same as innocent. Do you know if the autopsy samples have been saved?"

"You mean the blood?"

"Yes, the fingernail scrapings."

"Apparently they're stored in a lab in Chepstow."

"It's got to be the DNA, then. That's your only chance."

She thought about what I'd said, curled up in the easy chair, sitting on her feet. Wrongly charged or insufficient evidence wasn't good enough. We couldn't bring her father back from the dead and it hadn't occurred to her, until I spelt it out, that neither of these would clear his name.

"Where is your father buried?" I asked.

She continued to stare at the carpet until my voice registered and she looked at me with a start. "Sorry..." she said. "What was that?"

"I was wondering if your father was buried in the village."

She shook her head. "No. The local vicar wouldn't allow it. Or maybe he daren't. Feelings were high. The day after Dad was arrested the first stone came through the window. After that we had police protection, if you could call it that. Eventually we moved into lodgings in Cardiff but the news leaked out wherever we went. After the inquest Mum contacted the vicar at Uley, in Gloucestershire, where they were married, and he allowed Dad to be buried there. We moved around a bit and eventually settled in Cromer. Things were better for a while, but they caught up with us."

"It must have been dreadful," I said. "Dreadful."

"Yes, it was."

I thanked her for the tea and hoped I hadn't resurrected too many bad feelings. She told me that they'd never been laid to rest and thanked me for the flowers. At the door she said: "You think he did it, don't you?"

I shook my head. "Someone did it, Rosie."

"It wasn't my father. If you'd ever met him you'd understand that."

I wanted to say that hundreds of paedophile vicars and priests and teachers and youth workers were able to indulge in their vile practices undetected because that was exactly what everybody said about them, but I didn't. Instead I gave her a bleak smile and turned to go.

"The producer said you'd close ranks, defend your own. Is that what you're doing, Charlie? Closing ranks."

I spun round to face her again and saw that she was close to tears. "I don't give a shit about closing ranks, Rosie," I declared. "If there's any way in which I can help you, I will. I just don't want you to be hurt any more."

"Will you? I'd desperately like to believe that."

"It's the truth, Rosie. I'll see what I can do."

Chapter Seven

"I'll see what I can do." How many times does the average detective say that in his working week? And "Leave it with me." They make "The cheque is in the post" sound like an extract from the Sermon on the Mount. I drove home with the weight of the case pressing on me like I was carrying a rucksack filled with wet cement. The joys of my encounter with Sophie had fled like sparrows away from a cat. And next morning I had to face her dad.

"Good weekend?" he asked as he breezed into my office.

"OK. And you?"

"Not bad. Tidied up the garden. Nearly rang to see if you fancied a walk on Sunday, but Shirley made me mow the lawn."

"Good for her."

"Did you watch the grand prix?"

"No. Who won?"

"Schumacher again. It was rubbish. But hey, guess what. Sophie rang last night. She sends her love. She's bringing this boyfriend fellow up next week so Shirl's in a right panic. You'll never guess what he's called."

"Um, no."

"Digby!"

"Digby?"

"That's what she said. Don't think she's having us on."

"It's a fine name. What have you on today?"

"Watching CCTV film, unless you have anything in mind. I was thinking that maybe we should have another visit to Dob Hall while the boss is away. Maybe talk to the desirable Sebastian or even Mrs Grainger, if she's there."

"What good would that do?"

He shrugged his shoulders. "I don't know. Shake the bastards out of their complacency, do some stirring, something like that."

"We can't just go over and cause trouble. Carry on with the CCTV, please Dave, and tell Jeff to come in, will you?"

"Oh, OK." He lifted his bulk out of the chair and sloped off back into the main office.

He was right, though. This morning would be a good opportunity to talk to Sebastian while Sir Morton was away in Scotland, thrashing a defenceless ball round – what did he say? – the Old Course. I'm not a golfing man. Don't like the trousers. I presumed that St Andrews saved the New Course for major tournaments. We still needed a talk with sexy Sharon, too, Grainger's head of human resources, but she wouldn't be back until tomorrow.

And that thought made something click in my brain. Is it being so suspicious that makes me a good detective, or is it the dirty mind? I logged on to the Internet and clicked on Favorites, then Google. When I asked for St Andrews it came up with nearly half a million entries in a tenth of a second. The fourth one down was the chickadee I needed.

Hell's teeth! It cost £105 for a round of the Old Course; God knows what it would cost on the new one. Presumably that included a free set of clubs, but I wasn't certain. I wrote down the number, had a quick look round the site and logged off.

"I wonder if you could help me?" I said to the charming young lady with the voice as clear as a babbling burn who answered the phone. "A friend of mine was playing the Old Course in a pro-am competition over the weekend, for charity. He's tapped me for a contribution and I'm just making out a cheque, but I can't remember the name of the charity. I don't suppose you'd know, would you?" More lies, but sometimes it's necessary.

"The Old Course, did you say, sir?"

"That's what he told me."

"There was no pro-am competition on the Old Course this weekend. Friday until Sunday it was the Highland Malt tournament. What is your friend called?"

"Sir Morton Grainger." Now I was glad about the subterfuge. If word got to him that he was being asked after, he couldn't trace it back to me.

"One moment, please..." I heard the rattle of a keyboard. "No, nobody of that name was playing. Is he a member here?"

"I don't know."

"Let's see then... No, I'm afraid we have no Mr Grainger, Sir Morton or otherwise. You must have made a mistake."

"It sounds like it. He probably said the Belfry. Thanks for trying."

"You're welcome."

So, I thought, Sir Morton tells pork pies. I clicked the

cradle and fumbled one-handed for my diary. A breathless Rosie answered just as I was about to abandon the call.

"It's Charlie," I said. "Do you still have contact with any of your schoolfriends from back when... you know, when it happened?"

"No, none at all. We moved away, as I told you, but I was persona non grata in any case."

"Right. What was your school called?" I asked for the spelling and wrote it down. "And can you remember the names of any of your classmates?" Jeff Caton poked his head round the door while I was speaking and I gestured for him to take a seat. "That's fine, Rosie," I said. "Let me know if First Call contact you again, if you will."

She promised she would and I kicked my chair back away from the desk and rocked back on two legs. "That was a friend of mine called Rosie Barraclough," I told Jeff. "Thirty years ago her father signed a confession to strangling a thirteen-year-old girl and then hanged himself whilst in police custody. A TV company is making a documentary about the case, trying to prove he was fitted up, and Rosie, of course, would like to prove his innocence."

"First Call?"

"Mmm."

"They do true crime programmes on Channel 5, usually slanted to show what a bunch of incompetents we are."

"I think they're using her, spinning her a line. They've already conned her into signing a request for her father's exhumation, to obtain DNA samples and, of course, to make some moody TV. No doubt they'll do the exhumation at night and organise a rain machine and lots of dry ice. If I make it right with Mr Wood will you do some leg-work for me?"

"I'd love to, and it's got to be more interesting than poisoned corned beef. The question is, did he do it?"

"What do you think?"

"I'd say she's heading for a fall. If it were my father I'd settle for the uncertainty and believe what I wanted to believe."

"Me too, but maybe we can break that fall. If we only beat First Call to the truth it would be something."

"OK, where do I start?"

Contacts are a major resource for any policeman, both inside and outside the force. A phone call to some anonymous officer in another part of the country will be treated with civility and evoke promises of help, but he's a busy man and his superintendent has a bigger pull on his time than you have. But if you've had a pint together and are on first-names you can usually generate a little enthusiasm for your case. When I gave the talk at Bramshill I distinctly heard a Welsh accent to one of the questions. I found the course notes and thumbed through them. He was called Bryan Pinter, a DCI in Powys.

"Hello Bryan," I heard myself saying, three minutes later. "It's Charlie Priest. I met you at Bramshill last Thursday." He remembered me, he said, and had enjoyed the course. My talk had been most interesting. "I need a name," I told him. "I'm resurrecting a case from the seventies down in South Dyfed and want to talk to someone about it. Do you know anybody there who might help me?"

Ten minutes later it was: "Hello Derek. I've just been talking to Bryan Pinter... he sends his regards, by the way... yes, he's fine... and he suggests that you are the man I need to give me some help."

I loaded things so that it sounded as if I were trying to take the steam out of First Call's expose. If they were going to beat us around the head with a false confession perhaps we could hold our hands up to it before the show was broadcast and pre-empt their swaggering. I didn't say that the accused's daughter was a friend of mine and I wanted to prove his innocence even more that First Call did. Rosie was right: when the enemy is marching over the drawbridge with a mean look on his countenance there is a strong temptation to close ranks.

Dave came in. "I've got square eyes," he complained. "It's a waste of time."

"Any more cases reported?" I asked.

"No. Looks as if the worst is over. They've either died, moved or stopped doing it."

"Fair enough. So why don't you go to a couple of the stores and talk to the security people. I know that they've been told to contact us if they see anything suspicious, but you know what they're like. Have a word with them."

"If you want. I was still thinking that maybe we should talk to Sebastian and Mrs Grainger, while the cat's away."

"No," I said. "I'd rather you talked to security."

He gave me a hangdog look, said: "OK," and turned to leave.

"Close the door, please," I told him.

When he'd gone I picked up the phone and dialled. "Is that Sebastian?" I asked the voice that answered, certain that it was. "This is Detective Inspector Priest from Heckley CID. I'd like to come over and have a word with you, and also with Mrs Grainger, if she's available."

Sebastian met me at the door and suggested that I follow him. He picked up a tray laden with Thermos, cups and a plate of biscuits from a sideboard in the hallway and set off at a fair pace into the bowels of Dob Hall with me trotting obediently behind.

"Sir Morton's away playing golf, isn't he?" I called to his back.

"So I am led to understand," he replied.

"Does he play much golf?"

"A fair amount."

"I enjoy a round myself. Which club is he a member of?" The corridor we were following ended at a glass wall and beyond it was the leisure and office complex.

"I don't know. Mrs Grainger said she will see you by the pool."

"How long have you worked for the Graingers?"

"Eight years."

The white light of fluorescence replaced the gloom of the hall, ozone was in the air and pot plants stretched towards the high roof. It was all glass and aluminium and fabricated wooden beams. A figure in a black costume was doing an expert crawl down the length of the pool.

Sebastian placed the tray on a hardwood table and invited me to take a seat. "Coffee or orange juice, Sir?" he asked.

"Oh, um, coffee, please," I replied and he poured me a cup.

"Help yourself to biscuits, and Mrs Grainger will be with you in a moment."

He sasheyed away and stood at the end of the pool as the swimmer approached. When he caught her eye he gestured in my direction and she gave me a wave. Sebastian turned to leave and the swimmer pushed off and did two lengths without surfacing for air.

She climbed out of the pool, sleek as an otter, wrapped herself in a huge black and white striped robe and came over to meet me.

"Hi, I'm Debra Grainger," she said in an American accent, extending a hand.

I stood up, saying: "DI Charlie Priest." I wasn't sure whether to shake her hand or kiss it but settled for a shake. "You swim like a fish."

"Yeah, well, I've been swimming since before I could walk."

"Obviously not in this country."

"Ha! No. How's the coffee?"

"Fine. Just fine. Can I…?"

"It's OK, I'll help myself. Will you excuse me for a few seconds while I put on some clothes, then you can tell me what it's all about?"

I nodded my acquiescence and she carried her coffee away with her. I walked over to the glass side of the building and looked out. There'd been a mist earlier on but the sun had burned it away and the temperature was rising. At the other side of the valley the fell-side rose like a wall, still in the shade, with what I thought was Stoodley Pike projecting upwards from the highest point. Victorian Man's attempt to dominate the landscape. I looked at the cloudless sky and wanted to be out there.

"Admiring the view?" she called to me as she came back from the changing room.

I turned to face her. She was now wearing a jogging suit and trainers with her hair held back by a headband. I'd have said she was four or five inches taller than Grainger and a good twenty years younger.

"Yes," I said, truthfully.

"More coffee?"

"No, that was fine, thank you."

"Let's go where it's more comfortable."

We went through into the office part of the leisure and office complex and emerged in one of those offices you normally only see in the colour supplements, before the people have been allowed in. There were three workstations with flat screen VDUs, each with a fancy keyboard and mouse but not a cable in sight. The VDUs were off and nobody was working in there. In one corner there was an old-fashioned drawing board with wires and a setsquare, which I found strangely reassuring.

"I understand you designed all this," I said as we passed through.

"That's right. Like it?"

The glass wall was either tinted or it had dimmed to

exclude the glare of the sun. The light level was bright and shadowless but I couldn't see any fittings.

"I'm not an expert, but it looks superb to me. Anybody would be delighted to work in these conditions."

"Why, thank you. That was the intention." Her office was adjoining. It was quite small, just a desk and a telephone, with two easy chairs. She beckoned me to sit down.

"I noticed the drawing board in the corner," I remarked. "Do you still hanker for the feel of a pencil?"

"Yes, I do. There was something therapeutic about standing at a board for hours at a time. Now we use it when we have work experience kids in. We show them how to draw an object in isometric and third angle projection and then let them loose on the computer, using CAD. They enjoy it."

"Did your company design the stores?" It was a leading question. The Grainger's stores had attracted wide criticism for being barren, depressing blots on the landscape. Hence most of the opposition to them.

She smiled. "No. We were invited to tender, but that's as far as marital loyalty got us. When it comes to financial matters Mort has a skin like a rhino. So, how can I help you, Inspector?"

"You're already helping me," I replied. "Frankly, we're making no progress with the case, are no nearer to discovering who is contaminating items, so I'm just collecting background information, familiarising myself with the situation. Only Grainger's stores appear to be involved so we're wondering if it's a grudge that someone holds against Sir Morton, or even yourself."

She looked suitably puzzled, said she couldn't think of anybody, but Mort was a businessman and although he tried not to, it was inevitable that he'd stepped on a few toes on his way up.

"Any names spring to mind?" I asked, but she shook her head. She rarely became involved with the business.

"How long have you been married?"

"Is that relevant, Inspector?"

"You're an attractive lady. Any old boyfriends still carrying a torch for you?"

"I see. Twelve years. Mort's been married before but his first wife did quite well for herself, married a judge and lived happily ever after."

"Any children?"

"Mort has a married son. He sees him occasionally, when he wants money."

"Ah yes," I said. "I've been told that his daughter-in-law sometimes works as a secret shopper for Sir Morton. Is that so?"

"No. Not officially. Mort wouldn't countenance such a thing. She uses the stores and then comes complaining to him about the service, or whatever. He ignores her, but politely."

"Actually," I began, "I've been told that you sometimes pose as a secret shopper. You wear a disguise and..."

She threw back her head and laughed. "Good God, Inspector, who have you been talking to?"

I smiled at her. "Anybody who'll give me the time of day."

"I shop at Grainger's. Is that a surprise? I wear

normal, off-the-peg clothes. Do they expect me to shop in a cocktail dress?"

"OK, I'm convinced. I'll cross out secret shopper. Can you give me the son's address, please?"

"No problem."

"Thanks. I believe that Sir Morton is away playing golf somewhere."

"That's right, in Scotland."

"If you don't mind me being personal, how do you know he hasn't spent a weekend of passion in the arms of one of his checkout girls?"

"Because I know Mort, Inspector, and I can assure you that he'll find nothing with one of his checkout girls that he couldn't find at home, with interest. This whole thing is putting him under tremendous pressure, what with all the call-backs and the press constantly harassing him. He deserves his weekend away from it all."

It was a convincing reply, but she'd taken the question in her stride, almost as if expecting it. "When I said checkout girl," I explained, "I didn't necessarily mean literally. I was referring to the entire female sex."

"And my answer is the same, with interest."

"Right. And what about you? Any skeletons in your cupboards?"

"I love Mort, Inspector, and he loves me. We trust each other and neither of us is playing fast and loose with anyone else. All this has been a terrible strain on him and we'll both be grateful if you can find the perpetrator."

"OK. Thanks for being so frank with me, Mrs Grainger, and thanks for the coffee. I wonder if it will be possible for me to have a quick word with Sebastian?"

"Sebastian? No, Inspector. I'm afraid he's taken the rest of the day off."

The valley traps the heat and the temperature was rising. The forecasters had promised the hottest day of the summer and it wasn't letting them down. Heading through town I dived into a parking place and walked to the sandwich shop, my jacket slung over my shoulder. A woman in leggings and an FCUK T-shirt coming in the opposite direction put on an unexpected burst of speed to beat me through the door. She had a face like bag of potatoes and a perspiration problem. I felt like asking her why she had fuck emblazoned across her bosom, but she would only have whined that it stood for French Connection United Kingdom and accuse me of having a dirty mind.

Bollocks, I thought. It's just another nail in the coffin of civilization. Another tiny smidgeon of indecency to inure us against the collapse of public taste. Sex sells; selling makes money; money is God; amen. At that very moment some shit-brained graduate down in Soho or Docklands was no doubt wondering if the world was ready for an advertising campaign built around the English monarch who tried to stop the tide coming in – King Cnut. It was only a matter of time. I asked for a chicken tikka, in a soft roll, and followed the woman out into the sunshine.

So what did that make me? I turned my head and watched my reflection in the shop windows: package in one hand; jacket dangling from the other; long legs striding out. Charlie Priest, lawman. Two nights earlier I hadn't gone to bed with my goddaughter, hadn't made love to her, and I was glad. There'd be no awkward silences when we next met, no avoiding being left alone with each other and no embarrassed looks across the table when we all went out together. We wouldn't have to measure our words every time we spoke, to avoid imaginary or accidental innuendos. I gave myself a wink and almost collided with a bus stop.

I picked up the phone, put it down again, walked over to the window. The sunlight bounced off the station's windows and back-lit the building opposite. Down in the street people wandered about in skimpy tops and shorts. I can never understand how they change their clothes so quickly as soon as the sun comes out. I stared at the phone for a long moment, then picked it up and dialled.

How did Mrs Grainger know that Sebastian had taken the rest of the day off? Perhaps he was going to, but he could still have been lurking about somewhere. She was quite certain that he'd already gone. Didn't she want me to talk to him? Mr Wood answered the phone almost immediately.

"It's Charlie, Gilbert," I said. "I wouldn't mind taking the afternoon off."

"Fair enough," he replied. "Is it work or play?"

"A bit of both."

"No need to book it then."

"Cheers."

And that invigorated me. The sun was shining, the outdoors beckoned and I had a free afternoon. I dialled another number.

"Technical support," a voice confirmed.

"It's DI Priest," I told it. "I want to borrow something."

At home I changed into shorts and boots and put a few items in a rucksack. An hour after speaking to Gilbert I was sitting in the pay-and-display car park in Hebden Bridge, trying to be patient as a young woman loaded two infants and all their paraphernalia into a VW Golf. She gave me a hesitant wave as she drove away and I claimed the spot.

I slung the gear over my shoulders and headed out of town, over the River Calder, the canal and the railway line. The signal was green and I like watching trains, but I'd a stiff walk ahead of me so I pressed on. A notice on a lamppost caught my eye, like the wanted poster I'd seen in Heckley, and further on I saw another. I crossed the road to read it. Claudius the cat had gone missing and its five-year-old owner was grieving. Small reward offered.

The slope starts almost immediately, giving you little time to raise your metabolism, and I was soon puffing. The shade of the trees that cling to the valley side was welcome, but it was the hottest part of the day and I could feel sweat trickling down my spine. Fat bees busied themselves amongst the Himalayan balsam that lined the road and a peacock butterfly flew ahead of me, its wings flickering with colour in the dappled sunshine. If you could see Stoodley Pike from Dob Hall, you didn't have to be Isaac Newton to know that you'd be able to see Dob Hall from Stoodley Pike. I'd been there plenty of times in the past, usually making a decent circular walk of it, but today I took the more direct route, straight up Pinnacle Lane. In ten minutes I'd left the last house behind and soon broke out of the shelter of the trees.

I'd borrowed a telescope from technical support. "What's it for?" I was asked.

"Um, watching someone."

"Is this an approved operation?"

"Off course it is."

"Right. Do you prefer straight or angled?"

"I haven't a clue. Something you just look through."

"We'll make it straight, then. Any idea what magnification?"

"You tell me."

"How far away are they?"

"About a mile, perhaps a little over."

"Daylight or darkness?"

"Daylight. This afternoon."

"Nice and bright then. OK, I'll fit the 40x eyepiece but put a 20x in with it in case you find that too difficult to hold. You'll need a tripod, too."

"Great. Any chance of someone bringing it over?"

So in my rucksack I had an Opticron 50mm telescope, as favoured by birdwatchers, and a Vivitar tripod was slung over my shoulder.

The track gains about five hundred feet in a quarter of a mile, which is a stiff climb. I'd brought a bottle of water but didn't need it just yet. The path levelled out and then it was a straight blast towards the summit.

It's hard to imagine the euphoria that swept the nation after Wellington's victory at Waterloo. It must have been like VE Day, the Falkland and Gulf War celebrations and the Millennium all swept into one great orgy of triumphalism. Honours were piled upon the man, and this part of the kingdom showed its gratitude by subscribing towards a monument, now known as Stoodley Pike. It fell down after forty years but they built another one and used a better concrete mix the second time. The hint of a breeze on the exposed moor was welcome, then it was another climb for the last half mile.

They picked a good spot for it, with views of the kingdom in all directions. To the west and east stretched the plains of Lancashire and York, their boundaries lost in the haze, while to the south the moors lay folded and rumpled all the way down into Derbyshire, like a duvet on an unmade bed. But I was interested in the opposite direction, across the Calder valley. It was in full sun, basking in the uncharacteristic heat wave, and I wondered if property prices depended on which side of the valley you were situated. A field down below was set out with jumps as if a gymkhana was expected, and traffic was stationary all the way into Todmorden.

There's a viewing gallery about twenty feet up the tower, accessed by a spiral staircase. For part of the way you are in total darkness, groping for the steps with your feet while trailing a guiding hand on the wall. The tripod slipped off my shoulder and nearly tripped me, but after a few seconds we were stepping out into the sunshine again. I walked round the gallery, taking in the view, but it wasn't much better than at ground level, and the balustrade was at an awkward height, so I felt my way back down the stairs and set up the telescope on a flat rock at the edge of the escarpment.

I scanned the far side of the valley with my binoculars but couldn't locate Dob Hall. Back to first principles. How did I get there this morning? Find the road, follow it along, turn right after the pub. Ah! There it was. I'd been underestimating the power of the binoculars, moving too far. The Hall was in a wooded area but the trees had been cleared from the front to open up the view. I wondered how they won permission for that, but was grateful at the same time. The front of the house was visible, with a lawn to one side and the garage block to the other. The office and leisure complex was at the rear, out of sight. I scanned around, looking for prominent landmarks, then turned to the telescope.

It was harder than I expected but eventually we mastered it and the Georgian facade of Dob Hall with its elegant entrance portico swam into view. There were two cars parked in front of the house and a single sun lounger sat on the lawn. Keeping one eye closed was irritating after a few minutes so I used the binoculars. I don't know what I expected or hoped to see. Sebastian prowling around the premises, proving Debra Grainger had lied? The woman herself skinny-dipping in the fish pond? I don't know, but it was a good excuse for an afternoon out of the office, and I'd settle for that.

I ate the chicken tikka sandwich and drank some of the water. A steady procession of walkers stopped at the Pike before giving me a friendly wave and moving on. They were mainly grey-haired couples, no doubt with matching anoraks stuffed in their 'sacks. I reminded myself that it was Monday afternoon but for them it was just another day. Perhaps there would be life outside the police force, after all.

I was doing a sweep with the bins when a movement caught my attention. A figure, no doubt Mrs Grainger, was spreading a towel on the sun lounger. She placed something on the little table that stood alongside, carefully tucked in the ends of the towel and arranged her elegant limbs to take advantage of the sun's rays. She was wearing a one-piece white swimsuit. I smiled to myself, wondered if what I was doing was perverted, and turned to the telescope.

It was a better view, much better, but at that magnification, even with a tripod, it's difficult holding the picture steady. And maybe my hand was shaking just a little. Somehow, it didn't seem real. It was like watching her on TV, starring in an Andy Warhol film where nothing happens for eight hours. I stood up, did a few stretching exercises and watched a train crawl down the valley towards Mytholmroyd, Halifax and the rest of the world.

I was back at the telescope, wondering whether to try the 20x eyepiece, when the action started. Mrs Grainger had turned over to cook her back when a pair of black-trousered legs appeared alongside her and their owner lowered a tray onto the little table. She turned her head away from him in an eloquent gesture, but he wasn't to be rebuffed. He stood looking at her for a few seconds, as if saying something, then sat next to her on the edge of the lounger and placed his hand in the small of her back. She leapt to her feet, snatching up the towel, and I knocked the telescope out of focus.

It must have been nearly a minute before I found the garden again, this time with the binoculars. Sebastian, if it was he, was stretched out on the sun bed, hands behind his head. He sat up, reached for something off the tray and appeared to down it in one gulp before resuming the horizontal position. Well, well, well, I thought. What was all that about?

He stayed there for another five minutes before storming off into the house. I packed the gear and set off back down the hill. There's a rather nice teashop in town, and a piece of apple pie, with cream and a pot of tea, would round off the perfect day just nicely.

Chapter Eight

Derek Johnstone from South Dyfed rang me that evening, one second after I'd dipped a number six squirrel hair brush into a tin of black enamel. I dropped the brush and raced into the house to answer the phone.

"Sorry to ring you at home, Charlie," he began, "but I'm taking tomorrow off."

"A great idea, Derek," I said. "Wouldn't mind taking advantage of this weather myself."

"Well, actually, it's for my aunt's funeral."

"Oh, I am sorry."

"That's all right. She was ninety-one and would insist on riding her bike."

"Oh. Right."

"I've managed to have a look at the files for the case you mentioned and I've put some of the relevant stuff in the post. Frankly, Charlie, it all looks cut and dried. At least on the face of it. Witnesses saw Abraham Barraclough following the girl, the blood group matched, he had scratch marks on his neck and he made a full confession."

Abraham Barraclough. That was the first time I'd heard his name, and Rosie had evidently reverted to her maiden name after her divorce. Good for her. I said: "Witnesses. Who saw him?"

"Several adults and children. There's a bit of a headland between the village and the school. The road and footpath follow the coastline round it, but some of the kids take a shortcut over the hill. The girl – Glynis

Evelyn Williams – was seen to take the shortcut, and Abraham Barraclough was seen outside the school, hanging around. Later, they found her body up there."

I knew about the blood under Glynis's fingernails, presumably causing the scratch marks. It sounded like the clincher. I wasn't prepared for this interview, didn't know which way to take it.

"You said: 'Cut and dried, on the face of it.' What did you mean by that?"

"Ah!" he replied. "That's one small blot on the landscape. I thought you might like to talk to the investigating officer who took the statement, one Chief Inspector Henry Bernard Ratcliffe, so I looked him up."

"Go on."

"Apparently he was pensioned off on, um, ill health about two years after this case."

The way he pronounced the words gave them added meaning. "You mean it wasn't ill health?" I said.

"This was back in seventy-six, Charlie, when ill health was a convenient way of sidelining somebody with minimum fuss."

"So what did he do?"

"Not sure. I've mentioned it to a couple of the lads who were around then and they think he was involved in the death of a vagrant in Swansea. Apparently he had rather strong views on things and didn't care where he aired them."

"That's interesting, Derek, I'm very grateful for all the trouble you've taken. Is this Henry Bernard Ratcliffe still alive, do you know?"

"Pensions will tell you that."

"So they will. You're a treasure."

* * *

He lived at Crest View, Tarporley Road, Chester, I learned next morning when our pensions department rang me back. I bit my lip, dithered awhile and dialled the number.

"Matron," came the reply. Not what I'd expected.

"Oh, er, good morning," I blustered. "My name is, er, Priest and I'm trying to locate an old colleague. I was given this number but was expecting it to be his home."

"It may very well be," Matron replied. "This is the Crest View Hospice. What is your colleague's name?"

"Ratcliffe. Henry Bernard Ratcliffe."

"Yes, we do have Mr Ratcliffe staying with us. Do you want me to try to find him for you?"

"Um, not for the moment, please. Can you tell me what's wrong with him?"

"No, Mr Priest. I'm not at liberty to discuss a patient's medical details."

"Of course not," I agreed in my most understanding tone. "I shouldn't have asked. Fact is, Matron, I'm a police officer, as was Mr Ratcliffe, and some questions have arisen about one of his cases. Would it be possible for me to come and discuss it with him?" I struggled to find the correct expression for having all his marbles and settled for: "Will he know what I'm talking about?"

"Oh yes, Mr Priest. Chief Inspector Ratcliffe has all his mental faculties. It's his body that's letting him down. I'm sure he'll be delighted to see an old colleague."

I wasn't so sure, but three hours and seventy-eight

miles later I was turning the two handles on the door of Crest View Hospice. They put two handles on the door to stop the inmates escaping. When I haven't the wit to get round that one I'd rather be out of it. Unless… unless the idea is that if you take both hands off the Zimmer frame you fall to the floor. I shuddered and pushed the door open.

It was an old building, probably built in the thirties, but the inside was shiny-clean and smelled of furniture polish and boiling vegetables. It was nearly lunchtime and one or two patients were already seated at a long table that I could see through an open door. I knocked on the Matron's door, also open, and she looked up and smiled.

"Mr Ratcliffe is sitting outside," she told me after the introductions. "I told him he had a visitor coming." She led me through a lounge dotted with easy chairs, mostly unoccupied, and down a short corridor. An impossibly tall, thin man coming the opposite way stood to one side and snapped me an impeccable military salute. He was wearing a red beret with a feather cockade in the front. I smiled and gave him a rather sloppy one back, like President Reagan used to.

"Major Warburton," Matron explained as we walked along.

The husk of what had once been Detective Chief Inspector Ratcliffe was hunched in a wheelchair in the corner of a courtyard, catching the sun. Matron pointed to him and then left me, as if she didn't want to be there, but I suppose she had work to do. He was wearing a shirt buttoned to the neck, a straw trilby and grey trousers that hung over his bony knees. A walking stick leaned against one of them.

"Hello, Henry," I said, pulling a plastic chair nearer to him. "I'm DI Charlie Priest, from Heckley, and I'd like to ask you a few questions."

"You and the others," he replied, not offering a handshake.

I didn't know what he meant but filed the comment for later use. I nodded towards his legs, saying: "I'm sorry to see you like this, Henry, it must be hard for you."

"Aye, well…" His voice was clear, with a touch of gravel in it.

"I want to talk to you about a job you did in South Wales, back in seventy-three."

"Glynis Evelyn Williams. That's who you mean, isn't it?"

"That's right. Questions are being asked about the result. How well do you remember it?"

"There's nothing wrong with my memory. Abraham Barraclough did it and when I stand in front of St Peter – which won't be long, now – and he asks me what I did with my life I'll tell him that I'm the one who nailed Barraclough. He'd've got life, been out now, if he hadn't hung himself. Good riddance, I say."

"He had scratch marks on his neck, I believe."

"He had, and his blood group matched. Group B, eight percent of the population. And then there was the confession."

"Were any pictures taken of the scratches?"

"No. Why did we need pictures? And they'd nearly faded away by the time we caught him."

"Did the pathologist look at them?"

"Not that I know of."

"How did you catch him?"

"He gave himself up. We were taking blood samples of everybody in the village and he knew the net was tightening, so he walked into the station and said he'd done it."

"And you believed him? Every murder attracts nutters who confess."

"He had the scratch marks. He was dead by the time we matched the blood group, but the coroner was happy."

"You took the confession, I believe."

"That's right."

"Were the words yours or his?"

"I... helped him. He just kept saying that he'd done it, didn't want to go into details. He saw her and wanted her, he said. She struggled and he suddenly realised what he was doing, but she was dead by then. She had blue knickers. Pale blue, not dark ones. Not navy blue like most of the other schoolgirls. He kept going on about them. That's about it."

"Was he right about the knickers?"

"Of course he was right about the knickers. Have you seen a picture of her?"

"Of Glynis? No I haven't."

"She was lovely. Lovely. Long blonde hair. A daughter any parent would be proud of, and that monster snuffed her out for his own gratification. What did you say your name was?"

"Charlie. Charlie Priest. Why didn't you let him write his own statement, he was an intelligent man?"

"Intelligent! You call that intelligent!"

"Tell me."

"He was a commie. Didn't you know that, Charlie? A commie bastard. Every dispute there was he was in the thick of it. Council meetings, championing all the down-and-outs; on the picket line with the miners the year before. Gave them cheap bread, he did. I'd have given them bullets, not bread. Shot them all, that's what they deserved, and what happened? They brought the government down, that's what. Democracy! You call that democracy!"

"When I said I wanted to talk to you," I began, "you said something about the others. What others?"

"Huh! Television people. They've written to me three times, asking me to contact them. The Post Office forwarded the letters here but I haven't replied. Why can't they let sleeping dogs lie?"

"That's why I'm here, Henry. I want to find out the truth before they do."

"You know the truth. It's staring you in the face. Abe Barraclough strangled poor little Glynis Williams and then hung himself in his cell. End of story."

"They're going to dig him up. Dig him up so they can compare his DNA with that found under Glynis's fingernails. That'll prove things one way or the other."

"Good!" he snapped, leaning forward as if about to rise from the chair. "Good! And then maybe them and you will leave me alone to die in peace."

I lifted my hands in a gesture that said I was happy with his reply, and sat back to enjoy the sun, hoping to lower his guard and encourage him to tell me more. I wasn't disappointed.

"Paedophiles," he ranted, after a few seconds. "That's what they are. Paedophiles. And all you all want to do is defend them. Who defends the poor kiddies? Tell me that. Who defends the victims?" I sat forward again and he grabbed my arm. "And asylum seekers," he rambled. "Bringing diseases with them. Aids and TB. Why do we let them in? They make a mess of their own countries and come here, and what do they do? Have loads of kids, draining the Health Service; try to make this place like the one they've left. So why do they come, all the Pakis and niggers? Because we're too soft, that's why. Send 'em all back, that's what we should do. Go into any town and what do you see? Beggars, making more than you and me ever did, sponging on society. Scum, that's what they are: scum."

I prised his fingers off my arm. "Is that what the vagrant in Swansea was, Henry? Was he scum, too?"

"He was…" He grabbed the stick and his hands shook as he leaned on it. "He was… a parasite. Took our money under false pretences."

"What did you do? Give him a good kicking?"

"Natural causes, that's what the inquest decided. He died of natural causes."

"Oh, so you only pissed on his sleeping bag and let him freeze to death."

"He deserved everything he got."

"And you got early retirement on a full pension, on the grounds of ill health."

He nailed me with his rheumy eyes and said: "Aye, well, they got the date of that a bit wrong, didn't they?"

Major Warburton saw me and half rose from his

chair as I strode through the lounge, but I just kept going. I'd had my fill of old soldiers for one day.

Pete Goodfellow was sitting at my desk when I arrived back at the nick, busy with my paperwork. My In basket was empty and he'd arranged everything into four neat piles.

"Wow, that looks efficient," I said as I walked into my office.

"Hi Chas," he replied, starting to rise from my chair. "Had a good day?"

"You stay there," I told him, sitting in the visitor's place, "and keep up the good work. I've been to see the investigating officer in the South Wales job."

"Learn anything?"

I told him all about my little talk with Henry Bernard Ratcliffe. When I finished Pete said: "So you think he'd be capable of fixing the confession."

"I think he'd be capable of fixing the confession, the evidence and the coroner, Pete. Even allowing for the state of his health he's a bundle of fun. What about you? Did you find anything for me?"

"Mmm," he replied, pushing a sheet from the telephone pad my way. "One of the names that Rosie gave you who was in the dead girl's class. Still lives in the village. There's a telephone number, too."

"Hey, that's great," I said. "I'll ring her tonight."

Dave returned from wherever he'd been and joined us. He was wearing a short-sleeved shirt with little pictures of Abbott and Costello all over it and his nose and cheeks were the colour of tomato soup.

"Before I forget," he began, "the brass band's

playing in a competition at Leeds Town Hall on Friday. Fancy coming along to support the boys?"

"Er, no Dave. Count me out, please," I replied.

"It's always a good night out."

"No, I've a few things to do."

"Pete's coming, aren't you?"

"Try stopping me," he said.

"I can't make it."

"Fair enough. So where've you been skiving off these last two days."

"Conducting investigations," I told him. "You look as if you've been sitting in a beer garden all day."

"Someone's got to keep their eye on the ball. I've been thinking about Sebastian at Dob Hall. We should have a talk to him. And Mrs Grainger. I have my suspicions about them."

"Ah," I replied, unable to disguise my unease. "Fact is, Dave, I had a word with her yesterday. You'd gone out but I decided you were right: we should talk to her while Sir Morton was away. I didn't catch Sebastian, though."

"Right," he said. "Right." But his expression was at odds with the words. He looked as if I'd eaten his last custard cream. I thanked Pete and he left us.

"Sit down," I told Dave, "and I'll fill you in."

When I finished he nodded knowingly and said: "So I'm right. All is not well there."

"That's the way it looks. "

"You reckon Sebastian tried it on with her?"

"Mmm."

"And you saw all this through the telescope?"

"Yep. And that's not all. There's a son and a

daughter-in-law who live nearby. We ought to talk to them as soon as possible."

"Don't change the subject. You spent all yesterday afternoon up at Stoodley Pike spying on Mrs Grainger as she lay topless on a sunbed?"

"Not quite, she was wearing a one-piece costume."

"You're turning into a dirty old man, you know that?"

"You could be right. It was rather fun."

"Remind me to keep you away from my wife and daughter. Where do they live?"

"Who?"

"The son and daughter-in-law."

"Heptonstall."

"Let's go see them, then."

"I'm supposed to say that."

Three churches appears excessive in a village the size of Heptonstall, but the Victorian parish church was built to replace its 15th century predecessor after its roof was blown off. For some reason they left the old church standing, so you could argue that they only count as one. Mopping up any Nonconformists is the Methodist chapel, where John Wesley preached. Corduroy and worsted paid for them, blood, sweat and religious fervour did the rest. Sylvia Plath is buried in the churchyard.

A steep cobbled lane leads up to the village, high on a windswept hill. The place had a renaissance in the Sixties, inspired by Plath and her husband, Ted Hughes, when it attracted a community of poets and painters, some good, most indifferent. After one winter most of them left.

"What are they called?" Dave asked as the road levelled and I eased off the accelerator.

"Julian and Abigail."

They lived in three wool-maker's cottages knocked into one, on the far side of the village. It was three stories high, with a row of windows all along the top floor to allow light into the rooms where the work was done. That's what the books say, but it could have been to save lifting blocks of Yorkshire stone all the way up there. Builders were a canny lot even in those days. We parked alongside an elderly Volvo 340 and Dave pressed the bell. The thud-thud-thud of a drum machine or a big engine shook the ground beneath our feet.

Abigail Grainger answered the door. She had black hair that reached halfway down her back and was wearing a tie-dyed kaftan and beads. For a moment I was back at art college, bottle of cider in my hand, asking if this was where the party was. Dave checked her identity and introduced us.

"Is Mr Grainger in?" he asked.

"Please come in," she said with a smile. "Yes, but he's busy for the moment." The noise was louder now, and had resolved into a dum dum da-dum, dum dum da-dum, dum dum da-dum, repeated endlessly. She led us into a white-walled sitting room with a bare wooden floor and Habitat furniture and invited us to take a seat. There was a large painting on the wall, consisting of a single smear of red paint on a white background. People knock abstract expressionism, but paintings like that are difficult to do. The best way is to put the canvas on the floor at the bottom of a tower and drop the paint on it from the top. The skill is in hitting the canvas. You get one go and there's no touching up. This one didn't quite work, because the artist had tried to improve the initial splash, and you can't do that.

"Can I ask what it's about, Inspector?" she asked, addressing Dave and speaking artificially loud to overcome the background noise.

He didn't correct her. "It's about the food contamination at the Grainger's stores," he told her. "Just routine enquiries. Can I ask what Mr Grainger does for a living?"

"I'd have thought that was obvious," she replied with another smile, wafting a hand through the air.

"He's a drummer, a musician?" Dave tried.

"A rhythmologist," she replied.

"A... rhythmologist?"

"Yes, otherwise known as a drum therapist. He has a client with him at the moment, but he'll soon be through. We're all held together by vibrations, Inspector. All matter can be reduced to a waveform. The seasons, menstrual cycles, lunar cycles, circadian rhythms, alpha and beta waves... when these get out of synch with each other the problems start. Drum therapy helps find the common harmonics and bring them back into synchronism. It's a wonderful technique."

The intensity of the noise had increased. Now it was dum dum DA-DUM, dum dum DA-DUM, dum dum DA-DUM and there appeared to be two drummers at work.

"I see," Dave lied.

I jumped in to the rescue and pointed at the painting. "Are you the artist, Mrs Grainger?"

"No," she replied, looking down and adjusting the kaftan over her knees. "I'm not so talented. I have a gift but it's a very small one."

"And what's that?"

"Auras, Constable," she replied, looking at me. "I see auras."

"I wouldn't call that a small gift."

"A gift, a curse, I'm never sure what it is."

We weren't sure either, so we kept quiet. Drum therapy and seeing auras can kill a conversation as surely as accountancy and fitting tyres.

Mrs Grainger fidgeted, smiled and looked slightly embarrassed. "Would you... would you like me to describe your auras?" she asked.

Now it was our turn to fidget and look embarrassed. "Um, yes, please, if it doesn't hurt," Dave replied.

"Or cost," I added.

"On the house," she laughed. "Well, as soon as I opened the door I saw it. Your auras are different, very different, but they blend together perfectly. It's what I was saying about vibrations. You are a team, and it shows." She turned to face me. "Your aura is largely blue," she said, "with some green transitions. You are the rock of the team. Some might describe you as a plodder, but that's what gets the work done. I'm being honest. You don't mind, do you?"

"Um, no," I told her.

"And you, Inspector," she went on, turning to Dave, "yours is much more complicated. I see oranges and yellows, the colours of inspiration and flair. You take the sideways view, see past the obvious and right into the heart of a problem. And into the hearts of people. Your intuition and the constable's dedication make you a formidable team."

Dave stretched forward to lean on his knees and stare down at the floor. When he looked up his face was a mask. "I'm impressed," he said through clenched teeth, nodding his approval. "I'm really impressed. You've got us to a T."

I stood up and wandered over to the window. As I was looking out, admiring the shadows on the cottage opposite and taking deep breaths, the drumming stopped and the relief reminded me of the time I had an abscess lanced. Behind me I heard Mrs Grainger ask if we'd like a glass of water. When she left the room I turned round and resumed my seat. Dave gave me a big, self-satisfied smile.

I pointed at the painting. "Tell her you like it," I whispered.

She came back carrying a tray with three tumblers of iced water. Dave was standing in front of the painting, about a foot from it.

"What do you think?" she asked, placing the tumblers on a low table.

"Hmm, I like it," Dave replied.

"Good. What do you like about it?"

"Oh, er, it's very, um, very, um, red," he replied.

"You're so perceptive," she told him. "The artist – he's an old friend of ours – mixes his own colours. He says that's the reddest red in the world."

"Is it true," I asked, desperate to bring the conversation under control, "that you sometimes act as a secret shopper for Sir Morton?"

"No," she replied with a smile. "Who on earth told you that?"

"Oh, it just came out in conversation."

"I shop at Grainger's, of course I do, and sometimes I read the auras of the staff. If I see something I don't like I write to Morton and tell him, but that's all. Dishonesty, untrustworthiness, laziness, they all show in the aura, but he doesn't believe me."

Floorboards creaked somewhere and we heard voices. "That's Julian," Mrs Grainger said, standing up again. "I'll tell him you're here." When she returned we were both sipping our water.

"How's the water?"

"Very refreshing," I replied. "Just what we need on a day like this."

"We bring it from a spring we found, on Moss Crop hill. We think it's wonderful."

I gulped down the mouthful I'd taken and wondered about sheep excrement. "Have you had it tested?" I enquired.

"It has a good aura," she assured us. "If I've interpreted it properly there are lots of GFRs in it."

"GFRs?"

"Good free radicals. It's been in the ground for millions of years, so all the bad free radicals have been taken up. There's nothing in it to combine with the body's free radicals and oxidise them."

"That's good." I placed my tumbler on the table, nearly crashing it into Dave's as he did the same. Her husband and a thin man appeared outside the window, talking earnestly. They shook hands four-handed and Julian turned to come back in.

He was wearing jeans and a Save the Planet T-shirt with sweat patches under his arms and on his chest, as if he'd just finished a marathon. He was balding on top but his ponytail clung on in defiance of the passing years. I jumped up and did the introductions, properly, but his wife didn't appear to notice the switching of the ranks.

He turned to her for a moment, his face alive with as much fervour as the people who once thronged the churches along the road. "What did you think?" he asked her.

"It was wild," she assured him. "You were really emping. I could feel it."

"We were, weren't we? I think we'll move on to the tom-toms next session." He turned to us. "Sorry about that, Inspector. Just discussing my last client. Has Abi told you what I do?"

"Yes, she has," I replied. "And all about our auras."

"Ha ha! She's very gifted. I keep telling her that she should exploit it more, but she won't listen. Now, how can I help you?"

I told him why we were there and asked him if he had any ideas about who might be contaminating the food. What did he know about Sir Morton's business dealings and had he heard of any grudges or threats against his father?

Julian Grainger shook his head and looked puzzled. He agreed that his dad must have trod on a few toes over the years, but basically he was a decent man and always tried to do the right thing.

"I'm interested in ethical trading, Inspector," he told us, "and I've had many a long discussion with Dad about it. He always listens and tries to take on board what I say. It isn't always possible because if he doesn't make a profit he goes out of business, and that doesn't help anybody, but he does what he can. We're getting him there, slowly, aren't we, Abi?"

Abi nodded enthusiastically. I suspected she emptied the swing bin with equal enthusiasm. After reading its aura, of course.

"How would you describe your relationship with Sir Morton?"

He grimaced before answering and took a drink from the glass of water he'd brought in with him. "OK, I'll be honest, Inspector. We don't always see eye to eye. We've had our differences. I'm a disappointment to him, I suppose. Can't see the Queen ever telling me to rise, Sir Julian, can you?" – Abigail giggled at this – "but blood's thicker than water, isn't it? and at the end of the day we're always there for each other."

"Are you financially dependant on him?"

"No. He bought this place for us and we regard it as a wedding present. It's worth a bit now, but we got it for peanuts. He's given us the odd interest-free loan, but I cost him a lot less than most sons who have a stinking rich dad, I'm sure of that." He paused, then said: "Am I a suspect, Inspector?"

"Everybody's a suspect," I admitted, glad that he'd asked. It cleared the air, made it easier to ask personal questions, such as: "How do you get on with your stepmother?"

"Debra? OK, I suppose. How does anybody get on with a stepmother who is only four years older than they are?"

"How often do you see her?"

"Her birthday, Dad's birthday, Abi's birthday, my birthday and Christmas. We all go out for a meal and it's all very civilized. Plus I might pop in, once or twice a year if I'm passing. That's it."

"Why doesn't she use her title? She's Lady Grainger, isn't she?"

"She claims it's because she's a republican, but it's really because it makes her anonymous. My mother, Dad's first wife, is Lady Alice Grainger. Being a mere Lady Grainger doesn't appeal to her. It's inverted snobbery."

"Do you like her?"

"She's dad's trophy wife. Miss Florida Oranges. If he's happy, I'm happy for him."

"I asked if you like her?"

He looked uncomfortable, opening his mouth to speak then deciding not to. Eventually he said: "I was nineteen when Dad first brought her home. At university. I came home for a few days but Dad had to go away on business, which left us alone together in the house. Miss Florida Oranges did the calculations and decided that a rich man's son four years her junior might be a more attractive proposition than the rich man himself who was twenty-two years her senior. She wasn't my type and I'd just met Abigail. I stuck around for three days then hotfooted it back to Nottingham, fast as I could. Next thing I knew Dad had married her in America."

I looked across at Abigail who appeared to have lost her enthusiasm as she was reminded of the three missing days. Julian hadn't hotfooted it back to her quite as quickly as she would have liked.

"Tell him about the baby," she said, her mouth a thin line.

Julian scowled at her and flapped a hand in a what's the point gesture.

"What baby?" I asked.

"Oh, it's something and nothing."

"Go on."

"Well, when they married Dad told us he was going to be a father again. He was as chuffed as a peacock. We all were. It was a joy to see him. And then… nothing happened."

"She lost it?"

"Or there never was one. A phantom pregnancy. She's neurotic, so we wouldn't put it past her to have imagined the whole thing."

"But you're not sure?"

"No."

"Has your dad included you in his will, do you know?"

"No idea."

"Are you bothered?"

"What will be… will be." He grinned at the feeble pun.

"So the answer to my question is no, you don't like her."

"She's trailer trash, Inspector. Trailer trash."

I left the car in second gear and let it roll at its own speed down the hill, the steering wheel swinging from side to side as the tyres felt their way around the cobbles.

"Twats?" I suggested, looking across at Dave.

"They'd give twats a bad name. A pair of friggin'

zonkoes if you ask me. If they're right in their heads I know where there's a big house full."

"I have to say, Dave, that you handled your promotion well."

"I did, didn't I," he replied, beaming a smile at me. "But it's not as easy as it looks."

"They certainly did a fair assassination job on the other Mrs Grainger."

"Your friend Debra? What did you think of her?"

"Who? Debra?"

"Mmm."

"I thought she was rather nice. Talented, attractive, a good aura. I was impressed, could understand what the little man sees in her."

"You're a sucker for a pretty face."

"I know. Do you think they might be behind the contaminations?"

"The fools on the hill? No, it's not their style. They'd settle for sticking pins in a corn dolly."

The paintbrush I dropped the evening before was ruined, and they're not cheap. I found another and cut the thick skin off the top of the paint. After a few trials on a piece of scrap wood I started writing the words of Elizabeth Barrett Browning's most famous poem across the blue board. How do I love thee? Let me count the ways…

It was laborious work and I soon tired of it, and started having doubts about the whole project. Maybe it wasn't the great idea I'd thought it was. Never mind. I'd complete one to see if it worked, and if not I'd just have to copy a couple of Picasso's. I wrote the words in big looping letters, as if done by giant fountain pen, with plenty of circles and ovals for me to fill in with colour afterwards. Red, green and yellow.

When the board was covered in writing I stood back to assess the work. The blue was a little too dark, but might look better when the bright colours were on it. I'd underpaint them in white to make them brighter, and broaden the downstrokes of the letters. A thought struck me. The idea was that it would look as if someone had doodled carelessly all over a love letter, but if I drew a line down the middle of all the ovals and put a bit of fuzz at the top of them, they'd look like ladies' whatsits. Front bottoms. Then the recipient of the letter wouldn't appear careless about the sender, he'd be obsessed, with only one thing on his mind.

If I did the whole thing about ten feet square it could be a contender for the Turner prize. Then I thought about the previous winners and the prize money. It was only twenty thousand, and I didn't need it that bad. Picasso was obsessed with ladies' whatsits in his dotage. His late sketches were covered in them. It's where artists go when they run out of ideas. Not just painters. Writers, sculptors, songwriters, the whole lot of them. I'd stick with my bright colours.

I carefully washed the brush and went into the house. I made myself a mug of tea, put stew and dumplings in the microwave and rang the number in South Wales that Pete had given me.

A man answered the phone.

"Oh, hello," I said. "Sorry to disturb you. My name is Detective Inspector Priest from Heckley CID, up in Yorkshire, and I'd like to speak to Mrs Dunphy."

"What's it about?" he demanded.

"I believe she knew Glynis Williams, the girl who was…"

"Why don't you fuck off and leave us alone!" he shouted at me and the line went dead.

The microwave pinged to say my meal was cooked, so I put it on number one to keep warm and rang the number again.

"What?" he snapped.

"Please listen to what I have to say, Mr Dunphy," I said. "I'm a detective in Yorkshire and certain issues have arisen about the murder of Glynis Williams. I need to talk to your wife. Now I can either drive all the way down there and perhaps interview her at your local police station, or preferably we can sort things out on the telephone."

"How do I know you're what you say you are? They said they were from the police."

"Who's they?"

"Journalists. From the TV."

"Is this recently?"

"Last week, and the week before."

They'd tried to contact Ratcliffe and now they were after Mrs Dunphy. I was one step behind them all the time.

"Right," I said. "Here's what you do. Ring your local nick and ask them for the number of Heckley police station, in Yorkshire. I'm at home, so ask Heckley for DI Priest's home number. I'll have to ring them to tell them to release it to you. Then you ring me."

"That's OK, I believe you," he replied. "The wife's here. I'll put her on. Sorry I swore at you."

"I've heard worse. Thanks a lot."

Mary Dunphy had the first decent Welsh accent I'd heard but it was attractive and she spoke clearly. I envisaged her in the big skirt and hat, with lace petticoats, playing the harp. Racial stereotypes. I could get the sack for that if the thought-police were watching. After the introductions I said: "How well did you know Glynis?"

"We were in the same class at school, and she lived just across the road."

"Were you friends?"

"Not really. We had different interests, and she always seemed more grown up than the rest of us."

"Was she a pretty girl?"

"Pretty? No, she wasn't pretty. She was a big girl, tall and heavily built, but she wasn't pretty."

So much for Ratcliffe's description of her. "Did you know the Barraclough family?" I asked.

"Oh yes. They lived just down from Glynis, on the corner. They had a bakery, so everybody knew them."

"What was Mr Barraclough like?"

"He was a big man, with a bushy beard. We all thought he was nice, until... you know."

"Did you see much of him?"

"Yes, he was about all the time. Always had a kind word or something funny to say. He was a Pied Piper sort of character. When you went to the shop he'd always try to find a broken gingerbread man to pop in with your order, that sort of thing. The kids used to follow him around."

I couldn't resist asking: "Did you know his daughter?"

"Rosie? Yes, I knew Rosie. She was younger than me. Cleverest girl in the school, and the prettiest. We envied her living in the bread shop, and having a dad like that. I often wonder what happened to her."

"Was there ever any talk of Mr Barraclough behaving improperly towards any of your schoolfriends? Did you ever have any reasons to distrust him?"

"No, I never heard of anything like that, until…"

"Until what, Mrs Dunphy?"

"Well, until afterwards. Like I said, he was friendly with all the children. Nowadays, what with all you read in the papers, that makes you suspicious, doesn't it?"

"I'm afraid it does, Mrs Dunphy. We live in a sad world. Did you believe it when they said he'd killed Glynis?"

"Well, he confessed, didn't he? He wouldn't have confessed if he hadn't done it, would he?"

"I suppose not, but up to then, before he confessed, did you consider he might be the murderer?"

"No, he was the last man I'd have thought of."

"Thank you. Is there anything else you can tell me that might be relevant?"

There was a long silence before she said: "No, I don't think so," but in the background I heard her husband say: "Tell him."

"Tell me what?" I asked.

"Oh, I don't know…"

"Go on," I urged her. "Now you'll have to tell me."

"It's just that… I don't like speaking ill of the dead."

I thought it was going to be some revelation about Abraham Barraclough so I braced myself for bad news and said: "It can't hurt them now, Mrs Dunphy."

"No, but it can hurt her family. They still live in the village."

I heaved a silent sigh of relief. "Tell me what you know," I said.

"Well, let's just say that Glynis was what you might call an immoral person."

"Immoral!" I heard her husband scoff in the background. "That's putting it mildly!"

"Put him on," I told her. There was a mumbled exchange of words and a scraping noise before his voice greeted me again.

"Tell me what you know about her, please," I said.

"Well, Inspector, let's just say that she did it for friends and she had no enemies. Glynis might have only been thirteen but she was a tart, and no mistake. The school had a rugby team, and when they did well she would reward them in her own special way. When they lost she commiserated with them. They didn't mind, it was all the same to them."

"Sex," I said. "You're talking about sex?"

"Well I'm not talking about her giving them a pep talk. I reckon every lad in South Dyfed lost his cherry to Glynis Evelyn Williams."

I pondered on his words. In court, her reputation could have made the difference between a murder rap and manslaughter. "Have you spoken to the TV people at all?" I asked.

"No, I told them where to go."

"I'd be grateful if you kept it that way."

I thanked them and rang off. By rugby he no doubt meant the union code, so now I had fifteen possible suspects. The dumplings were done a treat but the tea was cold so I switched the kettle on again. Knowing Glynis's reputation, ninety-nine men out of a hundred would have claimed that she led them on, but what was it that Ratcliffe had said? "He saw her and wanted her," that was it. And: "He suddenly realised what he was doing." Nothing there about her leading him on, no blame laid on the girl, but were the words in the confession Barraclough's words or Ratcliffe's?

I didn't know. Holy Mother of Mary, I didn't have a clue.

The warm weather held and the office looked more like a holiday camp than a dedicated crime-fighting establishment. Shades and summer shirts were the order of the day. Dave came in and asked what I was doing so I told him all about the Abe Barraclough case. He's my best mate and I don't like having secrets from him. Well, not many.

"Blimey," he said. "That's a bummer."

"You can say that again."

"Well, it explains your odd behaviour. Last week you were all smiles, this week you've been like a wet Sunday in Filey."

"Thanks. Any more tampering cases come to light?"

"No, but I've got a photo for you." He dashed out and came back holding a still from a videotape. "Thought you might like this one for your collection, although you might not recognise her with her clothes on."

It was taken from the CCTV cameras at the entrance of a supermarket and showed a tall woman in a long dark coat, wearing sunglasses and a headscarf. She looked like a Hollywood star out shopping. Incognito, but not too incognito.

"Mrs Grainger?" I said.

"The security man at the Heckley store gave it to me. He thinks it's her, in mystery shopper mode."

"It looks like her, all right. Why the long coat? And gloves. Look, she's wearing gloves."

"It's raining hard," Dave explained. "Look behind her – someone's closing an umbrella and the pavement's shiny,"

"Mmm, I suppose so." There was a number printed in the bottom left hand corner. "Is that the date?" I asked.

"Yeah. Third o' May, 2.33 p.m."

"Right, thanks. I'll put it on my bedroom wall with all those I took of her with the zoom camera I borrowed from technical."

"Otherwise," Dave said, "it's all gone off the boil. I think we should stir things up a bit."

"Where do you suggest we start?"

"Well, we haven't done anything about the delightful Sharon's weekend of passion with Sir Morton, have we?"

"If that's what it was."

"It will 'ave been, believe me."

"'Spect you're right. I wonder if she calls him Sir Morton in bed?"

"Oh! Sir Morton!" Dave shrieked.

"Sounds like a song. Let's go see her, then." I stood up, tucked my shirt in and unhooked my jacket from behind the door.

Dave said: "Oh, before I forget. You're invited to lunch on Sunday."

"Super. I'll look forward to that." Dave's wife, Shirley, cooks the best Yorkshire puddings east of the Appalachians.

"Yeah, Sophie's coming up, bringing this boyfriend with her. It must be serious."

"Sophie!" I exclaimed.

"Mmm. My daughter, your goddaughter, remember?"

"Yes. I meant, um, Sunday. I might not be able to make it on, um, Sunday."

"Why not?"

"Er, Wales. I might go to South Wales with Rosie."

"Fair enough, but the invite's there. Bring Rosie along if you want."

"Right. I'll mention it to her."

The telephone saved me from further embarrassment. I listened, replaced the receiver and hung my coat back on the door.

"Sharon's off for this morning," I said. "Gareth Adey's in a meeting with the ACC and the knicker thief is waiting downstairs for an official reprimand. He wants me to do it, so I'll see you later."

He was twelve years old, sitting on a chair in the foyer with his feet not reaching the floor. Hair plastered down, grey trousers and a school blazer, fear oozing from his well-scrubbed pores. His father sat next to him.

"Interview room?" I said as I breezed past the front desk, and the sergeant flapped a hand in their general direction. Take any one, business is slack.

"I've interviewed murderers in this room," I said

when we were seated, after the introductions, "and now I've had to drop an urgent case to talk to you." The boy, Robin, glanced up at the tape recorder on the wall. "We're not recording this talk," I told him, "but I hope you'll remember it."

"There was a meeting," I went on, "to decide what to do with you. Six people who'd never met you, deciding on your future. How does that make you feel?"

He shrugged his shoulders.

"How do you think that makes your dad feel?"

Another shrug. "Answer the Inspector," his father told him.

"Not very happy," Robin admitted in a whisper.

"That's right. Not very happy. Disappointed. They decided to give you a reprimand. That means that you admit the offence and it doesn't mean that you've got away with it. Do you understand?"

He nodded. "Yes."

His dad nudged him. "Yes, Inspector."

"Yes, Inspector."

"Good, so tell me. Robin, why were you stealing items of underwear from washing lines?"

It was all a joke, a display of bravado. Several boys from school had dared each other to see who could collect the most. After a bit of probing it looked as if there was a hint of bullying behind it.

"I don't suppose you want to tell me the names of the other boys?" I said.

He didn't reply, gazing down at the table.

"OK, in that case I won't ask you. But let me tell you this: When there's a serious crime the first thing we do is interview what we call the usual suspects. We have a register with all their names on. If your name is on that we can call on you any time we need to, day or night, for the rest of your life. An offence like this should warrant putting you on the list. Is that what you want?"

"No, Sir."

"Good. As you're so young we've decided not to put you on it, this time. Now, how do you feel about apologising to the people you stole from?"

He looked from me to his father and back to me again. The fear had turned to terror. Probation service run a scheme called the victim/offender unit, where certain selected villains are challenged to meet the people they stole from to apologise and offer reparation. I explained the scheme to Robin and his father and Robin reluctantly agreed to cooperate. I asked him to wait outside while I chatted to his dad.

"I'll have a word with probation," I said, "to see if he's suitable. With there being sexual overtones it might not be wise to disclose Robin's identity."

"I don't think sex comes into it," his father said. "He doesn't bother about girls at all. His testicles haven't dropped yet."

"Fair enough, but I think we've given him something to think about."

"You certainly have. Does this mean he has a criminal record?"

"No, a reprimand is what we used to call a caution but it's not a conviction, although by accepting it he has admitted his guilt. We'll have his name on file until he's eighteen, but there's no need for him to disclose it to any future employer. These other boys. Do you think you could ask him for their names, and let me know? I didn't want to push him into a corner. Grassing up his friends and all that wouldn't be good for his self-esteem, but telling you might not be such a big deal."

"No problem. And thanks again."

We left the room and I escorted them off the premises. Prompted by his father, Robin apologised and thanked me. "I don't want to see you in here again," I told him, "unless you're wearing the uniform."

The office was empty when I went back upstairs, so I stuffed my wallet into my back pocket and went walkabout in town. Inspector Adey, resplendent in white shirt, short sleeved and with epaulettes, was coming out of the HMV shop, carrying one of their bags as I crossed the road. It must have been a short meeting with the ACC. I dashed across and into the shop. One cashier was standing idly behind his till.

"That man who just left," I said. "The policeman. He's a colleague of mine. Don't suppose you can tell me what he bought can you?"

The youth grinned, happy to oblige. "Garth Brooks," he replied. "The Chase."

"Country and western?"

"Yeah, well. One man's poison an' all that."

"Thanks. Are you likely to have the music from Band of Brothers?"

"Try Soundtracks, in the corner."

It was there, at £13.99, which I considered a rip-off. They'd made the music for the TV series, so from now on it was all profit. I'd liked the main theme but wasn't sure about the rest of it, so I decided not to bother and went to the sandwich shop.

* * *

Back in the office everybody had materialised again and they'd set the telescope up on a desk, pointing out of the window. The troops were queuing up to take turns.

"Hey, be careful with that, it belongs to technical services," I said.

Jeff Caton was at the helm. He let out a low whistle, saying: "Just grab an eyeful of that."

"What?" the next in line demanded.

"Legal and General. You can see straight into their office. They've got flat screen monitors."

"Wow!" I exclaimed as he stood up to let a DC have a look.

"Take a dekko at her in the middle window," he advised.

After some readjusting the DC complained: "She's got her back to us."

"I know," Jeff replied, "but can't you just imagine her little skirt riding up her young thighs?"

Somebody added: "And her tiny breasts thrusting against the thin material of her blouse."

Dave said: "And her knicker 'lastic cutting into her like a cheese wire."

"Perverts!" I shouted. "You're all perverts!" and retreated into the sanctuary of my little office. The file from South Wales was on my desk. I looked through it then rang Rosie's number.

"How are you?" I asked when she answered.

"Fine, Charlie. And you?"

"I'm OK. Can I come over and see you tonight?"

"Of course you can. Have you made any progress?"

"I'd hardly call it progress but I've spoken to a couple of people. About eight-thirty?"

"Mmm. Eight-thirty. I'll bake you a cake."

"Did you know that Gareth was a country and western fan?" I asked Dave as we drove over to Grainger's supermarket headquarters.

"You're joking."

"He bought a Garth Brooks CD in HMV this morning."

"Well, well. That should be worth something, one day. We still owe him for nabbing the knicker thief."

Sharon Brown saw us in her office, after telling her secretary – a gawky girl with a ring through her nose and shoes the size of paddle steamers – to take a break. She didn't offer us coffee and sat behind her desk twiddling a pencil between her fingers. The jacket for her power suit was over the back of her chair and it was easy to see where the attraction lay for Sir Morton.

"What's company policy on shoplifters, Miss Brown?" I asked.

"We prosecute them all," she replied.

"Without fear or favour."

"That's right."

"Old ladies – and gentlemen, I suppose – sometimes become confused. Don't you make any allowances for that?"

"Those confused old ladies, Inspector, are usually wearing fur coats with big pockets, and it's always a tin of best salmon they just happen to slip into one, never the tuna."

"Are you saying that there's no such thing as Alzheimer's, or senility?"

"No, of course not, but it's up to the court to decide that."

"It's rather stressful for them, don't you think, going to court for what is most likely the first time in their lives."

"That's their problem."

I turned to Dave. "A girl called Rebecca Smith worked for Grainger's, here at this store, Miss Brown," he began. "She left under a bit of a cloud. We thought you had a policy of retraining and redeploying people who didn't immediately settle in."

"We have," she replied. "Dismissal is absolutely a last resort."

"What about bullying? Where does that come in the Grainger's management development programme?"

"If we were aware of any bullying we would take steps to deal with the causes of it."

"You didn't in this case."

"I wasn't aware of it."

"Miss Smith has been advised to sue for constructive dismissal."

Sharon Brown rotated the pencil between her fingers, glanced up at the clock and shuffled in her chair. "That will be between her and our solicitors. I'm not familiar with the case."

"But you must accept some responsibility."

"I'm not familiar with the case."

I cleared my throat and asked: "Where were you last Saturday evening?"

She switched her gaze from Dave to me. A lock of

dark hair fell across her spectacles and she brushed it away.

"Last Saturday," I reminded her.

"I…went away for the weekend."

"Where to?"

"I don't see that it's any of your business."

Back to Dave. "How long have you been shagging the boss?" he asked.

Miss Brown dropped the pencil and jerked her head to face him. "I don't know what you mean."

"Right," he said. "We'll start at the beginning. There are birds, and there are bees. And there are little birds and little bees. Shagging is what the big birds and bees do to get little birds and bees."

"What about Mr Robshaw, the manager here?" I asked. "Are you having an affair with him?"

She turned to me again, throwing her head back and laughing in an exaggerated manner, relieved to be on safer ground. "Tim Robshaw!" she scoffed. "He should be so lucky."

Dave came straight in with: "So it's just Sir Morton?"

She retrieved the pencil and carefully placed it on the blotter on her desk, exactly parallel with the edge. She stared down at it and readjusted its position, but we could see that her face had turned colour under the makeup and her lips were moving silently, as if she were chewing something unpalatable.

"We know that Sir Morton didn't go to Scotland," I said.

"So where did you spend the weekend?" Dave added.

"Paris," she whispered. "I went to Paris."

"With Sir Morton?"

She didn't reply and we didn't press her, content to see the devastation on her face, like some mediaeval merchant who'd just learned that his ship laden with bullion had sunk to the bottom of the ocean.

Chapter Nine

Rosie baked me a chocolate cake. "It's a pity you didn't come earlier," she said. "It's a lovely evening. I've been sitting outside."

"I wanted to spend an hour on my paintings," I explained. "You can only do so much at a time, then you have to wait until the paint dries."

I didn't mention the long phone call I'd received from Cambridge. "How did it go?" I demanded as soon as I realised who it was.

"I'm engaged, Uncle Charles," Sophie told me, her delight evident in her voice.

"Oh, I'm so pleased, Sophie. I'm so pleased. I told you it would be all right. You told Digby about… you know?"

"About the baby? Yes, he's delighted. He was a bit shocked at first, thought he'd let me down, but he soon came round."

"And you're engaged?"

"Unofficially, yes."

"A big ring?"

"Not yet. I'm not bothered about one."

"Congratulations, Sophie," I said. "I hope you're deliriously happy. I think you will be. Meanwhile, I'll just have to take this pair of tickets to Antarctica back to the travel agent."

"Uncle Charles…"

"Mmm."

"About Saturday. Thanks for looking after me. I'm

glad I came to you, and I'm glad... well, I'm just glad."

And so was I. My feelings had been mixed, just a little, but Sophie wasn't reduced to just another notch on my bed head, and that made me happy. We were still friends, something that lovers often can't say.

"Listen," I said. "I'm invited to lunch on Sunday but I'm scared stiff that Digby will say something to indicate we'd met before."

"I never thought of that," Sophie told me. "I suppose we could call to see you first, on Saturday on our way home."

"That would help," I agreed, "but I'll still skip lunch, if you don't mind."

"I was hoping for some moral support."

"You'll be fine."

Rosie was offering more tea. I nodded and pushed my cup and saucer across the table. "Nice cake," I said. "My favourite."

"I should have invited you for a meal," she said. "It was thoughtless of me."

"Nonsense. Chocolate cake is a treat-and-a-half."

"Have another piece."

"Well, just a small one."

Rosie told me about her day. She'd spent it stripping varnish from a pine bookcase she'd bought, and preparing visual aids for when school started again.

"Geography or geology?" I asked.

"Geog. The changing face of Eastern Europe. What with all the asylum seekers and upstart countries that nobody had heard of five years ago, suddenly everybody wants to know what's where. Good old boring geography is flavour of the month. Well, not quite, but mild interest has been aroused."

I smiled at her words. "Have you travelled much?" I asked.

"Not for a while, but I used to, when I could afford it. I had a couple of nasty experiences and it put me off. It can be difficult for an unaccompanied woman. You attract unwelcome attention."

"I can imagine. Where's your favourite place?"

"Florence," she replied, dreamily. "No doubt about it. I spent a month there one summer, and I was in heaven."

"What? No unwelcome attention?"

"It's not always unwelcome," she replied with a laugh. "Have you been to Florence?"

"Long time ago, when I was a student. Otherwise, I haven't done much travelling. It's something I regret."

I sipped my tea and replaced the cup on the saucer. "I went to see a man called Henry Ratcliffe today," I began, when happy thoughts about times spent in sunnier climes had subsided. "He was the investigating officer."

"Where was this?" Rosie asked, suddenly concerned.

"Chester. He's in a nursing home in Chester, has some wasting disease. Motor neurone or something like that. I doubt if he has much longer to live, but he's quite lucid."

"The poor man."

"Mmm. I asked him what he remembered about the case, and… about… your father."

"Was he any help?"

"Not in the way he meant, Rosie. Even allowing for the huge chip on his shoulder brought about by his condition, he didn't come across as a very nice man. Your father's politics were anathema to him, and I wouldn't be surprised if that didn't cloud his judgement."

"You mean… he may have tampered with the statement?"

"I certainly wouldn't put it past him. He belonged to that school, and no mistake." But before her hopes were raised too far I went on: "However, this morning I received a copy of the statement. I haven't brought it because I thought it might upset you. It was written by Ratcliffe and allegedly signed by your father. It looks OK to me but we could try to check the signature. It's a long name and your dad signed it in full, so it would be difficult to forge. It doesn't look good, I'm afraid, Rosie."

She bit her lip and stayed silent, holding a long-cold cup against the crook of her shoulder. The nail polish on her toenails was chipped through walking about bare-footed, and as if reading my mind she drew her feet under her, out of sight. Outside, the streetlights came on up the hillside, although it was still early. Big clouds were building up and the tops were lost in them. Rosie rose from her chair and switched on a standard lamp to give the room some illumination.

When she was seated again she said: "So we'll have to wait for the DNA tests?"

"It looks like it."

I wanted to cross over to her and swamp her in an embrace, tell her that everything was just fine, that we could see things through together, but I couldn't. It wouldn't be true. Life is for the living, I wanted to say, and we owe it to ourselves to make the most of it. God knows, it's short enough. But she was locked in the past, with a dead father who she loved. Would I have been as determined to clear my father's name under similar circumstances? I had no idea.

"Last night," I said, "I talked to Mary Dunphy on the telephone."

Rosie came back from wherever. "Mary Dunphy?" she repeated.

"You knew her as Mary Evans."

"Mary Evans? You've spoken to Mary Evans?"

"Yes. She said you were the prettiest girl in the village, and the cleverest."

"Oh, I was, I was! So where is Mary living?"

"Still in the village. Presumably she married someone called Dunphy and stayed there."

"That would be Barry Dunphy. He was a few years older than us but I remember him because he played for the school rugby team. He was expected to go on to great things in rugby, but I never heard of him again."

"That happens to lots of promising young sportsmen," I said, shaking my head wistfully. "Good at school, but never making it in the big, wide, outside world. Did I ever tell you about my goal-keeping exploits?"

"I can hardly wait," she replied, a smile briefly lightening her expression.

"I'll save them for another time. Mary spoke quite affectionately about your father. Said he was the last person she would have thought of to have... you know. Until she heard about the confession."

Talk of the rugby team had reminded me of the last piece of news I had for her. "There's just one other thing," I said. "According to Mrs Dunphy, Glynis was what she described as 'an immoral person'."

"An immoral person? In what way?"

"Apparently she wasn't averse to going up the hill-side with a gang of boys and giving them sexual favours. It happens in most villages, or so I'm led to believe."

"I didn't know that."

"There was no talk of it at the time?"

"No, but why should there have been?"

"No reason, except that if the case had gone to trial it could have made the difference between a charge of murder or one of manslaughter."

She sat silently, pondering on my words. I drained the dregs from my cup and stood up to leave. "I'll be on my way," I said. "I take it you haven't heard anything."

"No, nothing."

"Let me know if you do. Thanks for the tea and the cake."

"Thanks for coming, Charlie. I do appreciate it."

She walked to the door with me. As I stood with my hand on the handle I said:

"When this is over, Rosie, do you think we might spend some time together, get to know each other?"

She looked up at me and nodded. "Yes, I'd like that."

"Win or lose?"

"Mmm, win or lose."

"Good. And perhaps then we could catch up on all that travelling."

"That's something to look forward to."

"Secret of happiness," I said, "is having something to look forward to." I held her slim shoulders in my hands and gave her a kiss on the forehead. "And I've a lot to catch up on."

Rosie walked me to the gate and I admired her flowers. She grew roses but I failed to associate them with her name for a few seconds and made some fatuous comment. "I'm just a dumb detective," I said, giving myself a blow to the head.

"They're old varieties," she explained. "Like me."

As I opened my car door she said: "Charlie." I noticed the concern that had crept back into her voice and turned to her. "About Glynis," she continued. "What you said about her being an immoral person. It has no relevance now, has it?"

"No," I replied. "None at all."

"If it did," she went on, "if it were necessary for it to come out, I wouldn't want to continue. I'd drop the enquiry. Glynis's parents are probably still alive, and I wouldn't want to do anything to upset them more than is necessary. God knows, it will be upsetting enough for them just to resurrect it all again."

I nodded my agreement and pulled the car door shut. Rosie was prepared to go to great lengths to clear her father's name, but not if it meant destroying the living. Her words had moved me, and I decided that she was a very special lady, one I wanted in my life. And what she said was in line with the words of her father's statement: "I saw her and wanted her", not "she led me on." He was protecting the girl's reputation, as Rosie wanted to do. Like father, like daughter.

Which meant that the words in the confession were Abraham Barraclough's own words, not Detective Chief Inspector Henry Ratcliffe's.

Which meant that Abraham Barraclough was a murderer.

Thieves are opportunists, and the varying British climate throws up a variety of opportunities. In winter we dash out to the car on frosty mornings and leave the engine running while we breakfast. The local Jack-the-Lad materialises out of nowhere and makes off with it. In summer it's garden furniture and barbecues left out overnight, and burglaries through open windows. We were enjoying a hot spell and the sun-starved citizens of Heckley were desperately catching up with their Continental and Antipodean cousins. Garages and supermarkets were stockpiling charcoal like Armageddon was round the corner, and the latest price was being quoted in the financial news. A thriving black-market in it emerged, with inferior brands from the Far East undercutting the market leaders. Thieves of all persuasions were having a field day.

"Plenty to do?" I asked when I returned to the office after the morning prayer meeting, and everybody mumbled their assent.

"I've been asked about the gala again. Any thoughts on it?"

"Wrestling in a big bowl of Kellogg's Frosties," somebody suggested.

"Too late; the Girl Guides are doing that."

"Three-legged pole vaulting?"

"British Legion."

"How about self body-piercing for beginners?"

"Women's Institute, but you've obviously given it some thought so thanks for your efforts."

Dave followed me into my office. "Changed your mind about the brass band concert?" he asked.

"Er, no Dave. Sorry, but I've something on."

"I hope this Rosie isn't going to ruin a beautiful friendship."

"Oh, I doubt it, Dave."

"Any news about the exhumation?"

"No, nothing."

"So what about dinner on Sunday?"

I pulled a face. "I'm sorry, Dave, but it's a bit awkward."

He turned to leave. "OK, no problem. If my wife's Yorkshires aren't good enough for you, so be it. Not the mention my kids' disappointment."

I watched him slouch into the big office and collect his jacket. We'd been through a lot together since we first met at a house fire in Leeds. He says I saved his life. I doubted it, but he'd saved my reputation on a score of occasions since. Right then I felt as if I'd rather cut off my leg with a chainsaw before I'd hurt the big gorilla. Him and Rosie, too, but for one of them it was looking inevitable.

Sebastian answered the phone when I rang Dob Hall, but it wasn't him I wanted to talk to. It might have been useful but I wasn't in the mood and I prefer a pretty face. He put me through to Mrs Grainger.

"I'm afraid I have a hairdressing appointment in Hebden Bridge for ten o'clock, Inspector," she replied, after I'd introduced myself and asked to see her. "I could fit you in after that. What's it about?"

"Oh, just a general chat. We're not making much

headway. How about morning coffee in one of the teashops?"

"That sounds delightful."

"I'll pick you up at the hairdressers. What are they called?"

Her hair was much blonder when dry, and she wore it almost down to her shoulders and flicked up at the ends. Sandals, Bermuda shorts and a sequined T-shirt completed the ensemble. It was a familiar look: CNN newsreader or astronaut's wife. I stood to one side as we entered the teashop, held her chair for her as she sat down, showed her the menu.

"Just coffee," she said.

"Is it up to standard?" I asked, when she'd tasted it.

"It's fine."

"Are the Press still bothering you?"

"It's died down. Just the occasional phone call. They're not camped outside the gate anymore."

"Last Monday," I began, "when I spoke to you, you told me that Sebastian had taken the rest of the day off. I don't think he did."

"Have you talked to him?" she asked, but I didn't answer.

The little café was above a gift shop and the sun was streaming in through the window, casting patches of bright colour on the tablecloths. I sat opposite her with my hands on the table, feeling the sun's heat on the back of them.

After a silence she said: "He normally has Monday off. I just assumed he'd gone."

"How do you get on with Sebastian?"

"Get on with him? He's an employee of my husband's, that's all."

"Do you like him?"

"Like him?"

"I didn't mean in an affectionate way. Are you happy to have him around? He lives in, doesn't he?"

"It's a big house, Inspector. I don't normally see much of him."

"Which is how you prefer it."

"Yes." After a pause she went on: "Credit where it's due, I suppose. Sebastian has done well dealing with the Press at the gate. That took a lot of the pressure off Mort."

I was walking on unstable ground. I could hardly admit that I'd spent Monday afternoon spying on her through a 40x telescope. I said: "I detect a feeling of... disquiet when you talk about Sebastian. As if something about him makes you feel uneasy." Her hand was on the table, the tips of her fingers almost touching mine. It was an elegant hand, its length emphasised by nail extensions; an essential fashion accessory for many American women. I'd noticed that the hairdressing salon offered them as an extra service and suspected that Mrs Grainger was their main client.

She suddenly withdrew it and sat upright. "You're very perceptive," she admitted. "I don't like him. I've spoken to my husband about him but he says that Sebastian does a good job, claims he is indispensable."

"What's Sebastian's surname?" I asked.

"Brown. He's Sebastian Brown."

"Was there a scene between the two of you on Monday, after I left? Some unpleasantness?"

Two women in flowery dresses came panting up the stairs and after a discussion decided to sit at the table next to ours, near the window, making further revelations impossible. We exchanged smiles and the usual pleasantries about the weather. I went to pay our bill and followed Mrs Grainger down the stairs. I know, I know, the man is supposed to go first, but it never feels right to me.

"Let's have a look at the canal," I said when we were outside. We crossed the road and the river and walked along the towpath a short way until we found a bench to sit on near where the tourist boats tie up. Mrs Grainger appeared happy to stay with me. She wasn't showing any reluctance to be interrogated. I suspected that Hebden Bridge had little to offer compared with wherever she came from and talking to me was a welcome diversion in her otherwise boring lifestyle. She crossed her ankles and produced a pair of shades from the bag she carried. On the water a mallard and her chicks saw us and headed our way like a battleship with escort, their wakes fanning out behind them. I reminded myself that I was working.

"Where did you meet Sir Morton?" I asked, making it sound like idle conversation rather than a police interview. I twisted round to face her, my elbow on the backrest of the bench.

"In Florida." She laughed to herself at the memory.

Laughter is infectious and I smiled along with her, giving her time to explain.

"I was Miss Florida Oranges," she said. "My fifteen minutes of fame."

"Miss Florida Oranges?" I echoed.

"Don't laugh. One poor girl was Miss Ohio Potatoes and there was a Miss Oklahoma Pork Bellies."

Now I did laugh. "You're kidding!"

"I jest not."

"So who won the contest?"

"Who do you think?"

I bowed my head in contrition. "Forgive me."

"That's OK. When we were interviewed all the girls said they wanted to work with children and animals and for world peace. I said I wanted the money to pay my way through architects' school. Mort was there with a trade delegation from Britain. He sought me out and said that his company sometimes awarded scholarships to likely students. Would I be interested?"

"And you were."

"You bet. He paid all my fees, which was a great relief. Part of the deal was that he'd want an update of my progress every time he came to the States." She hesitated, before adding: "Let's just say that his visits became more and more frequent."

"And the rest is history."

"That's right." She smiled again. "Except... when I got to know him better, I learned that mine is the only scholarship Grainger's have ever awarded."

"That's a good story," I said. "And now you're a successful architect. Good for Sir Morton."

A narrow boat cruised by and the crew gave us a friendly wave. Papillon, all the way from Selby. Real geraniums were growing from old watering cans along the roof and painted ones twisted and spiralled along the length of the boat. We watched it putter away, venturing west towards Todmorden, Rochdale and the badlands of Lancashire, trailing a smell of diesel fumes, fresh paint and frying sausages behind it.

"Not that successful," Mrs Grainger admitted. "We haven't had any worthwhile contracts and it looks as if the London partnership is collapsing. We're a company in name only, I'm afraid."

"I'm sorry to hear that," I said. "I was very impressed with the office and leisure complex at Dob Hall."

"Yes," she sighed. "That was to be our flagship, but there are problems with it. One corner has subsided a little causing cracks. It was supposed to be on bedrock but the builder miscalculated, and we have a problem with condensation in winter. I didn't realise that this part of the world is semi-Arctic." She pronounced it see-my Arctic.

"I'm afraid so."

"Mort says he'll find a job for me at a checkout."

"Ha! I doubt if it will come to that."

An old lady in a woolly cardigan, her spindly legs encased in thick tights in spite of the weather, was throwing bread to the ducks, which appeared by the dozen out of nowhere. It looked as if she fed them every day. The mallards with chicks shepherded them towards the floating food, ferociously chasing away any intruders. Instincts, I thought. Protecting the family from danger and outside interference. It's all there, in the genes.

"In the café," I began, "you were telling me about Sebastian. You had some sort of confrontation with him on Monday."

"I didn't say that."

"But you did, didn't you?"

"How do you know?"

"It's my job to know."

"Have you spoken to him?"

"No."

"So you're guessing?"

"Let's call it intuition, Mrs Grainger. I read body language, think about your answers." She didn't look convinced. "And," I added, pointing at the sky, "we have a big satellite in geo-stationary orbit, twenty-thousand miles high, watching our every move. Do you want to tell me about it?"

She uncrossed her ankles, pulled her feet under the bench and sat on her hands. "He – Sebastian – made a pass at me, that's all. He does normally take Monday off, like I said, but because he knew I was in the house on my own he stayed behind and tried his luck."

"What happened?"

"It was in the afternoon, long after you'd gone. I was sunbathing, taking advantage of this beautiful weather. I thought Sebastian had gone too, that there was no one at home but me. Suddenly he joined me, on the lawn, carrying a tray with two drinks on it. Said he thought I might be in need of one. He sat down along-side of me and poured sun cream on my back, whispering what he considers to be sweet nothings. It wasn't very nice, Inspector. I'm not used to talk like that. I jumped up and went inside and that was that."

Which was exactly what I'd seen, "Will Sir Morton sack him?" I asked.

She shook her head.

"Will you tell him?"

"No. It's not the first time it's happened. He's

threatened me before, said he could bring it all down, if he wanted. If… if… if I didn't, you know."

"Grant him certain favours?" I suggested.

"Yes, that's it."

"What did he mean by bringing it all down?"

"I don't know. I can only assume that he has some sort of hold over Mort. Don't get me wrong, Mort likes him, thinks he's wonderful, but I suspect Sebastian knows something that would discredit my husband, if necessary. Has some inside information that he could use as an insurance policy against being fired. I'm not a complete fool, Inspector. I know Mort can be ruthless when necessary, and he's not afraid of cutting corners to land a deal. He's bound to have enemies."

Not to mention at least one mistress, I thought. The dark and voluptuous Sharon. A different type completely to brittle-blonde Debra Grainger.

"Can you think of any reason why Sebastian might be a suspect for contaminating the food?" I asked. "What would be in it for him?"

"I don't know."

"Do you think he'd be capable of doing it?"

"He's capable of doing anything."

We walked back to her car and I thanked her for being so frank with me. "I'm sorry to see you unhappy, Debra," I said, "but maybe when we get to the bottom of this, things will improve." She thanked me for listening, wished me luck with the investigation and we shook hands.

In the evening I pressed on with the paintings, finishing the writing on both of them and starting to fill in the circles and ellipses with a white undercoat. I think when I paint. I think when I walk, too. I do a lot of thinking, more than I ought.

I couldn't help wondering about Mrs Grainger, uprooted from sunny Florida and transplanted in to Calderdale. We'd had three days of exceptional weather but soon – tomorrow in all probability – it would be back to the usual mixture. And in winter the breeze came straight off the Urals and cut like a bread knife. It was a pleasure talking to her. She was straightforward, hadn't tried to mislead me or conveniently forget things. She'd have a lot of time to think, too, living all alone in that big house while her high-flying husband entertained his mistress. All alone, that is, except for the sinister Sebastian – the Heathcliffe of Dob Hall – skulking around, watching her every movement, dreaming his dreams and making his plans. But why would Sebastian want to contaminate the food and bring disrepute on Grainger's? It didn't make sense. And when Mrs Grainger said that she wasn't a complete fool had I detected a sudden vehemence in her voice? Was it a tacit admission that she knew of a darker side to her husband and that she was aware of his philanderings?

"Job for you," I said, when I saw Dave next morning. "See what you can dig up on Sebastian Brown."

His eyebrows shot up. "Is that what he's called – Brown?"

"According to Mrs Grainger."

"Is he related to the desirable Sharon?"

Now it was my turn to express surprise. "I don't know. I hadn't made the connection. That's something else for you to find out."

"Can I talk to them?"

"If you want."

"And Mrs Grainger?"

"Um, no. I've already spoken to her."

"I see," he said.

"No you don't," I replied. "It's just that I thought a personal, more… suave approach might be appropriate with, um, Debra."

He gave me a sideways look that spoke volumes, all of them fiction. "What about Sunday lunch?" he asked. "Changed your mind, yet?"

I shook my head. "Sorry, Dave, can't make it."

He went on his way and I made myself a coffee before having a look at the paperwork on my desk. Pete Goodfellow had made it all look neat but hadn't done much to reduce the amount. I was wondering whether to concentrate on the budget, the staff development reports, the crime figures or the guidelines for dealing with suspected illegal immigrants when the phone rang. It was the father of Robin, the boy I'd cautioned.

"You asked me for some names, Inspector," he said.

"That's right. Did you have any luck?"

"Yes. I had a heart-to-heart talk with Robin. He's a good boy, Inspector."

"I believe you. We're all allowed the odd indiscretion when we're young. The reprimand is not the end of the world, it won't impede his progress through life."

He told me two names and I wrote them down.

"We'll have a look at them," I said, "and if there's any more thieving we'll talk to them. If Robin doesn't tell anyone about the reprimand they'll never know where we got their names from."

"I think he's learned his lesson."

"I'd say so." And he has caring parents, I thought. Most of the kids that come in are accompanied by their mothers, who see the whole process as an irritation and can't get out of the station fast enough.

"There's just one other thing," he was saying, hesitantly.

"What's that?" I asked.

"Have you seen yesterday's Gazette?"

"No, I haven't had time to look at it."

"The headline story is about dog fighting. Organised dog fighting."

"Oh, good," I replied. "We'd asked them to publish something and make an appeal for help. What can you tell me?"

"It's Robin again. He says there was this boy at school, last term, called Damian. He was a bit backward, apparently, shouldn't have been at the comprehensive. Mixed ability classes and all that. Robin says he never spoke to him directly but heard this from other boys. He was always on about a dog he owned that could fight better than anybody else's. Threatening to set it on to people. Then one day he simply announced that it had been killed but he was getting another."

"Hmm, that does sound interesting," I said. "Did Robin tell you his surname?"

It's always the same. You spend weeks gathering disparate pieces of evidence, hoping that one day they will arrange themselves into some sort of order, like the stars in a galaxy, and when it happens you get this feeling that starts in your toes and gradually creeps upwards until your whole body is tingling.

"Yes," he replied, "he's called Brown, Damian Brown."

Chapter Ten

The problem with High Clough farm was that it was on the highest piece of ground for miles, so there was nowhere we could set up an observation post. The comprehensive school headmaster was hiking in the Dolomites, but we'd sweet-talked the school secretary into letting us have a look at the records. Damian Brown lived at High Clough farm, and the secretary wasn't at all surprised that he was in trouble. Anything else she could have done to put him away for a long time was ours for the asking. We drove back and forth on the lane that went near the farm and eventually decided on an unofficial lay-by used as a rubbish dump by the fairies. It's easy to blame townies for coming into the country to dispose of the odd three-piece suite, but they don't leave the weedkiller drums and fertilizer bags.

"You can see the end of the track that leads to the farm," Dave said.

"And a transit parked here won't attract attention," I added.

X-ray 99, our helicopter, was making slow passes over the moor, about a mile away, as if on a search. It worked its way towards the farm and as it passed over we heard the frantic barking of dogs over the thrum of the chopper's blades. It banked away, the sun flashing off its sides, to resume its search on the other side. After a minute or two stooging around for the sake of credibility it turned and sped off towards its base near Wakefield.

"When will the photos be ready?" Dave asked.

"They've promised them for this afternoon."

The Browns were a big, extended family, Dave had discovered, and Sebastian and Sharon were tenuous relatives. One branch still lived in the style of travellers, even if they were permanently settled on a council site; another had abandoned the old ways a couple of generations ago and lived in a more conventional manner. This side of the family was fully integrated with local society. Two were solicitors, some owned small businesses and a few had criminal records, including Sebastian. He'd done three months for credit card fraud. High Clough farm was the home of the latest member to come under our scrutiny: Damian.

"So Sharon was happy to talk to you?" I said.

"She came round after a few minutes. I think she's proud of her romantic gypsy origins."

"Except they're not gypsies, they're tinkers," I said.

"Gypsies, tinkers, Romanies, travellers, they're all the same, nowadays."

"Whatever, she managed to break away from it and get an education."

"That's true." We both knew that illiteracy was a very useful characteristic for some people when trying to negotiate their way past modern living's more oppressive obstacles, like income tax returns, court warrants and job applications.

"Did you ask if they ever had family get-togethers?"

"Yeah, weddings mainly. She said they had great parties."

"I bet. C'mon, let's go."

* * *

The pictures showed High Clough farm to be a tumbledown dump, falling apart after years of neglect. If it hadn't been for the Land Rover Defender parked outside we'd have thought the place was derelict. Hill farmers have been encouraged to diversify to stay solvent, and, like so many of them in this part of the world, High Clough had diversified into rusting farm machinery and old tyres. Mr Wood came down to the CID office and we all poured over the pictures.

"You reckon this is where they hold the dog fights, do you?" he asked.

"No. I think they're involved, but whether they stage the fights I don't know."

"It would be the ideal place," Dave said.

Jeff Caton was peering at the photos through a big magnifying glass. "There's a chicken run," he said, "on the paved area in front of the house."

"It's a farm," I told him. "They keep a few chickens."

"There's a big chicken run next to the barn. With real chickens. You can see them. I reckon this other one is where the dogs fight."

"Outside?" I wondered aloud.

"Why not, especially this weather?"

"No reason. I'd just assumed it was an indoor sport."

"The idle boasts of a retarded boy and a chicken run outside the front door are not enough for a search warrant," Gilbert said, "but we might manage twenty-four hour surveillance."

I thought about it. "No need for twenty-four hours," I said. "Not if they hold the fights in daylight. And I don't suppose they have them in the early morning. Ten till ten should cover it."

"Look at this," Jeff said, and we all turned to him. The chopper had taken pictures as it approached the farm, from a fairly low angle, and others as it passed directly overhead. We'd concentrated on the overhead ones, to study the layout of the buildings, but now Jeff was looking at one of the oblique views.

"What is it?"

"There's some cages, four of them," he said, "down the side of the barn. If you look carefully you can see that whatever are in the middle two are looking at the chopper." He passed me the magnifying glass.

I could see two pale smudges against the gloom of the cage interiors, like two faces painted by an impressionist with a deft dab of the brush. "Rabbits?" I suggested after studying them.

"No, they're not rabbits. Look at the ears."

Dave took over. After a few seconds he said: "They're cats. That's what they are: cats."

I was in my office, clearing up and determined to go home on time, when Rosie rang.

"You sound despondent," she said after I'd introduced myself.

"Hello Rosie," I replied. "It'll soon pass now I'm talking to you."

"Are you working hard?"

"Not really, just musing on the behaviour of some of my fellow men."

"The producer telephoned me a few minutes ago," she said without further ceremony. "The coroner has signed a warrant giving permission for my father's body to be exhumed and the chancellor of the diocese has given his approval."

"Oh," I said. "And are you pleased?"

"Of course I am. Now we can do the tests."

"Have they given you a date?"

"No, but he wants to do it as soon as possible."

I bet he did. "So it's all up to the DNA."

"Yes, that's right. It's all up to the DNA."

I let that thought hang in the air, then said: "If you're not doing anything tonight, Rosie, do you fancy that Chinese?"

"Oh, yes, I'd like that. Thank you."

"Do you mind if we make it early? I'm starving."

"That's fine by me."

"I'll pick you up."

We didn't bother with the banquet, that's for special occasions, settling for a pair of dishes from the a la carte menu. Rosie was her old self: witty and mischievous, happy that things were moving along. She told me a few of the things that the schoolchildren had said, like the boy who thought the Atlas Mountains were stockpiles of school books, and I related a few of my own about our clients.

"One youth who was given a community service order thought he'd been given a community singing order," I said. "He asked which church choir he'd be in."

"One of my pupils, a girl this time, wrote in her exam paper that the European Market was held in Brussels every Wednesday afternoon."

"It's the quality of the teaching that does it."

"Oh, definitely."

I paid the bill and took her home. On the way we saw the police helicopter in the distance, its searchlight on as it quartered the ground.

"They're having a busy day," I said. "We had them out this morning."

"Aren't you going to dash over to see if you can be of any assistance?"

I glanced at her, then back at the road and at her again. "No way," I stated.

As I parked outside her gate Rosie asked me if I was coming in for a cuppa.

"Is there any chocolate cake left?"

"There might be."

"In that case, yes please."

The weather was changing and the temperature had dropped. Rosie shivered and switched on the gas fire, and went somewhere to turn up the thermostat. I stood behind her in the kitchen as the kettle came to the boil, wanting to put my arms around her. She cut the remains of the cake into two uneven halves and gave me the larger one.

"How long have you lived here?" I asked when we were seated in the lounge, her on the settee, me in an easy chair. She gave me a potted history of her movements, first of all living in a succession of rented accommodations before splashing out, rather late in life for a first-time-buyer, on the bungalow.

"You did the right thing," I said. "The only advice my dad ever gave me was to get on the housing ladder, as soon as possible. It was good advice."

But a stupid thing to say, I thought, even as the

words came out. It killed the conversation for a few moments.

"I bought at a bad time," she said, eventually. "Prices were high."

"There's never a good time," I told her. Profound words straight from the financial pages. "Just think of all those grotty flats and bedsits, where your rent goes straight to pay for the landlord's villa in the Bahamas."

"Yes, I had a few of those." She refilled our cups, then said: "When... when I left Gary – he was called Gary – I moved to Derby, landed a teaching job there. Supply teaching, not permanent. I had a horrible bedsit. Peeling paper, damp walls, the lot. Why I stayed so long I can't imagine."

"What was Gary's problem?" I ventured.

"Gambling. He was a gambler. You don't back horses, do you?"

I shook my head. "It was a courageous thing to do," I told her. "Making the break like that, moving on. It's a pity more women don't do it."

"They're trapped, Charlie, that's why. And it didn't feel courageous at the time." She put her cup down and sat in silence for a while. I was about to mention that we might have had a breakthrough with the dog fighting saga when she said: "I had a breakdown, Charlie. I lost the plot, completely."

"What sort of a breakdown?"

She heaved a big sigh that said she'd let the genie out of the bottle and there was no getting it back in. "I don't know. What sorts are there? I moved to Derby, into this awful bedsit, with nothing but the clothes I wore and what I could stuff into a Ford Fiesta. I worked one term as a supply teacher and then it was the summer holiday. I didn't know if I'd have a job when it was over. I was so lonely I just… gave up. I sat in that ghastly, smelly room and cried my eyes out for three weeks. I didn't wash, didn't eat, didn't take any interest in the outside world. I just let everything close in on me. I wanted to die, Charlie, but wasn't brave enough to do anything about it."

"What happened?"

"Nothing. One day, I thought, what am I doing? Nobody was going to come and sort me out, I had to do it myself. There was nothing organically wrong with me, I was fairly young, had a brain, could find work almost anywhere. I took a shower and found some clean clothes, went out and did some shopping. I telephoned the headmaster and he said he couldn't offer me a permanent position just yet but there was plenty of work for me. I took him at his word and had an expensive hair-do, complete with silver streaks. Oh, and I put the deposit on a new car. Watch me go became my creed."

"And eventually you moved to Yorkshire."

"I landed a permanent post, and it was further away from him. I told you I came with baggage, Charlie. Now you know what I meant."

"That's not baggage, Rosie," I assured her. "It's what gave you those tiny little creases in the corners of your eyes when you smile, that's all. It's what goes towards making you a caring human being. It's… it's all part of the recipe that made Rosie Barraclough, and why I find her so damned attractive."

She looked at me, her chin trembling. "Do you, Charlie?"

I moved over to her, engulfed her in my arms, held her tight. "Yes," I said. "Yes I do. All that's behind you. You're with me, now."

We sat like that for a long while as it grew dark around us. I tipped her face towards mine and kissed her on the lips. I wanted to stay the night, but didn't ask. There was a ghost watching us, the ghost of her father. Soon we'd dig him up, do the tests and discover the truth. Win or lose, we'd come through it together. I drove home praying that he'd not done the deed, just so I could see the happiness it would bring Rosie. If he really were the murderer then it would be up to me to make her happy. I could do it, I was confident of that. It would just take a little longer, that was all.

I always go into the office on a Saturday morning, to clear up any paperwork and prioritise any jobs that came in overnight. Friday night brings out the worst in some people. I hadn't left home when the phone rang. It was Dave.

"Have you heard?" he asked.

"Heard what?"

"About us, last night?"

"Us? Who's us?"

"Me, Pete, Jeff and Don."

"You went to the brass band concert."

"That's right, but we had a spot of bother on the way home."

"Oh no," I sighed. A spot of bother could only mean one thing: drinking and driving.

"It's not that," he assured me, reading my mind. "It's something else."

"Go on."

"Well, we didn't stay until the end. We'd heard the set piece three times and that was enough. We decided to come a bit nearer home and have a drink. Heading along the Heckley Road, towards the Babes In The Wood, Pete just happened to notice that we were following a convoy of four-wheel-drives. Three of them. Suddenly they all slowed and turned off into this little lane that didn't look as if it led anywhere. We called in the Babes and had a couple of pints. When we came out Pete said 'I wonder what they went up that lane for? Let's go see what's up there.' He was driving and Don encouraged him so off we went. After about a mile we found the three off-roaders, parked and empty."

"Aliens," I said. "They'd been abducted by aliens."

"You're nearer than you think," Dave replied. "We assumed they were poachers, but then we saw these lights in a corn field, wandering up and down. We waited for ages but they just kept on wandering up and down, so we telephoned Dewsbury and told them all about it. We thought that maybe they were looking for badgers."

"What did Dewsbury do?"

"They sent in the heavy mob, and the helicopter, and they were all arrested. Seven of them. They thought it was great fun, laughing and joking and taking the piss."

"So what were they up to?"

"Crop circles. They were making crop circles in the

corn. Said it would create interest in the area, generate publicity, help the tourist trade and all that."

"Ha ha! And what did your colleagues from the Dewsbury force have to say to you?"

"They suggested, very politely, that in future we restrict our activities to Heckley and district."

"They can do them for criminal damage. It's a face-saver. Not much of one but a result just the same."

"No they can't."

"Why not?"

"Because it was their own chuffing field, that's why."

We get a fair number of UFO sightings around Heckley. Apparently there's a vortex somewhere up in the hills. That's a fault in the structure of the Earth that allows magnetic energy to leak out, providing a source of power for alien spacecraft. They hover overhead and recharge their power packs. Foggy nights are particularly propitious, as this allows the energy to flow more freely. It also conveniently blurs the evidence. Anybody with more than half a brain puts the sightings down to the police helicopter with its Night-Sun searchlight on, or airliners groping their way towards Manchester airport, or to too many Carlsberg Specials, but they could be wrong. The Great Crop Circle Massacre was destined to be written into the annals of Her Majesty's East Pennine Police Force, and those involved would be spoken of in hushed tones for the rest of their careers. I had a couple of hours in the office and went home to work on the paintings.

* * *

Sophie and Digby came to visit, on their way to her parents', and Digby said it was nice to see me again and it had been really generous of me to run Sophie home last week, which made me glad that we weren't holding the conversation in front of her mum and dad. Tea and coffee were refused but they insisted on seeing the paintings. Digby thought they were great, and appreciated the irony of the beautiful poetry and the careless lover's doodles. He offered to ask his father to make a telephone bid for them, but I said they weren't that good and discouraged him.

The troopers on observation at High Clough rang to tell me that all was quiet. They were in regular contact with the control room but I'd told them to give me the occasional call. The Land Rover had left at nine and returned two hours later. The postman had driven straight past.

Rosie had never visited my house but I'd have to invite her round soon, so I did a big clean-up, right through to the oven and the tops of the doors. I had a cleaning lady, once, but when she told her husband I was a cop he stopped her coming. He must have been scared she'd reveal more than she ought when we shared the obligatory pot of tea. Sunday I did all the usual Sunday things: cleaned the car; went to the supermarket; drove past the church and cursed the traffic jam near the garden centre. I rang Rosie and left a message, said I was just wondering how she was, but she didn't come back to me. Not much moved up at High Clough.

Mad Maggie Madison, one of my two female DCs, was back at work on Monday morning after a fortnight in Tenerife. She looked fit and tanned and had lost a couple of pounds.

"You look well, Maggie," I said when I saw her. "Good holiday?"

"Brilliant, thanks. Have you missed me?"

"You'd never believe how much. It's been unbridled sexism for the last two weeks. We desperately need the woman's touch."

"Saveeta still on her course?" she asked.

"My little bit of Eastern promise? Yeah, she's another week to do."

"Uh!" Maggie snorted. "You're as bad as the rest of them."

I met Gareth Adey on the stairs as we went up to Mr Wood's office for the morning briefing and he said something about my boys being busy on Friday night. I resisted the urge to tip him over the banister. They were already in there when we knocked and entered: Dave, Jeff, Pete and Don; the Crop Circle Four. Dave winked at me and Gilbert wore the expression of a father who has just learned that his teenage son has rodgered the vicar's wife: a struggle between anger and amusement.

"Have you heard about this lot?" Gilbert asked, looking at me.

"I've heard the expurgated version."

Gareth, in his usual smug manner, said: "I'd rather not intrude into private grief."

"What do you reckon we should do with them?" Gilbert asked.

"Latrine duties," I said. "Put them on latrine duties for three months. Maggie's back so we won't miss them."

"We could do it, Boss," Pete replied. "We'd have the cleanest bogs in the division, guaranteed. We could put those little blue things in the cisterns, and maybe even have a few flowers."

"I could supply the flowers," Jeff said. "Grape hyacinths would go well with the blue water. We'd need some vases, though."

"Coffee jars would do," Pete suggested. "Not plain ones. Those fancy Kenco ones. We could start collecting them."

"OK, OK," Gilbert interrupted, holding up his hands. "We'll spare you the latrine duties. But could we please have a little less gallivanting round the countryside like a bunch of cowboys? Dewsbury are threatening to sting us for the cost of the operations support unit and the chopper. Now, haven't you any work to do?"

They trooped out through the door, Dave at the rear. He paused, one hand on the handle, turned and said: "That might be an idea, Mr Wood."

Oh no, I thought. Don't say it, Dave, whatever it is, please don't say it.

"What's that, David?" Gilbert asked.

"What you said about cowboys. It might be an idea for the gala. They could dress up like sheriffs and their deputies. Lawmen and all that. It might go down well with the kids."

Gilbert looked doubtful, started to voice his misgivings, but Gareth interrupted him. "Um, well, in the absence of any other suggestions, Mr Wood, it might be worth considering," he said, as I glared after Dave as he pulled the door shut behind him.

I was thinking about a mid-morning coffee when the man himself brought me one. "You're a mind reader," I said. "Pull up the chair," and placed two beer mats on the end of my desk. "Gareth took the bait," I told him.

"He's a twat."

"That's no way to talk about a senior officer. So, how did the weekend go?"

"Terrific, Chas. He's a good lad, I really liked him."

"That's what I thought. They called to see me on the way." I sighed inwardly: with a bit of luck that disclosure would eliminate the need for any more untruths.

"He plays rugby, and he's devoted to Sophie. He asked me if he could marry her. Can you believe that? He actually asked me. Bet that doesn't happen too often, these days."

"That's great. So they're engaged?"

"I suppose so. He didn't have a ring or anything."

"What does Shirley think?"

"Oh, she's over the moon one second, tearing her hair out the next. She spent all last week doing the house, now she's scared stiff about meeting his parents. They seem to be quite well off."

"That's good. What are they called?"

"I knew you'd ask that, so I wrote it down." He pulled a pay-and-display ticket from his pocket. "Here we are: Merriman hyphen Flint."

I said: "Wow! That's a mouthful."

"That's what I thought. Sophie says they own half of Somerset."

It was nearly my undoing. I thought Sophie had said Shropshire, so I responded with: "You mean Sh… Sh… Sh… she's, er, she's marrying into a wealthy family?"

"It looks like it."

"Good for her."

"That's neither here nor there, Charlie. They looked good together, and she's 'appy. That's all I care about."

He asked me about my weekend and I was blustering again when the phone rang. How the crooks we work with keep track of their various subterfuges escapes me. Perhaps they're cleverer than I think they are. It was Control.

"Things are happening up at High Clough, Charlie. Four vehicles have arrived in the last fifteen minutes."

"That's interesting. Tell the OSU to start their engine and tell the FOP to give me a ring."

Five minutes later the pair in the Transit were telling me that another three vehicles had arrived. "That'll do," I said. "Stay put and direct the heavy mob straight in when they arrive. You watch out for escapees."

The operations support unit used to be called the task force. We had one van with a sergeant and six PCs standing by, all in heavy riot gear. I told them where to rendezvous with my team, in a lay-by about a mile from the farm. I raised an armed response unit off the motorway, because there was certain to be a shotgun at the farm, plus two pandas and three unmarked vehicles with my lads in them. A video cameraman was in one of the pandas, with a bobby to act as his personal bodyguard as he recorded the scene. The chopper was up above. It's compulsory, these days. What did we do before Heinrich von Helicopter invented the craft that made him into a household name? On the drive over I told Dave to let the RSPCA know what was happening.

We were the last to arrive at the rendezvous. I jumped out and briefed the OSU sergeant, who didn't think they'd meet any resistance. We agreed that the best tactic would be to tear straight up the drive and block their vehicles in. The only other way out was to leg it over the fells.

"Let's go!" I shouted, because I get all the best bits.

The FOP Transit saw us coming and pulled across the lane. The passenger got out and directed our convoy into the dirt drive that led to High Clough farm, as nonchalantly as if he were on crossing duty. We bounced up the drive, dust billowing from the vehicles in front, gravel rattling underneath us.

"Oh, my springs," I complained.

"Oh, my giddy aunt," Dave said.

"Oh, my sausage sandwiches," Pete added as we bounced out of a particularly deep hole.

"Don't be sick in my car," I snapped, glancing at him through the rear-view mirror.

The buildings were arranged in a quadrangle. The house was single storey with a stone flagged roof encrusted in two hundred years'-worth of lichen and moss. From either side there sprang outbuildings with sagging doors and roof tiles awry. Grass grew from gutters and drainpipes hung away from walls. Apparatus with mysterious applications stood in every corner, rotting away on punctures tyres: Heath Robinson contraptions for spinning, shredding, flinging and spreading, and uses I didn't want to know about.

They heard us coming and started to dash for the shelter of the buildings. Our OSU Transit tore straight into the middle of the quadrangle and the crew baled out and started running. Jeff was right about the chicken run. A mean-looking bull mastiff-type dog with a black patch over one side of its face was leaping and snarling inside it, bouncing off the wire in its frantic desire to be part of the action and tear something apart. Another dog, equally enraged, was inside a small cage against the wall, where we'd seen the cats. I said a little prayer about the strength of wire netting and looked for someone not too physical to chase.

A few of the participants gave themselves up, turning to meet their attackers, arms raised. Others were followed inside and dragged out, protesting. I saw a figure run to a door, find it locked and run into an open outhouse. A figure I thought I recognised.

I stood gaping at him for a moment, not believing my eyes, until I saw one of the OSU officers emerge from the house leading a woman by the arm. I jogged over to the outhouse as one of the PCs from the pandas looked inside, and put my hand on his arm.

"This one's mine," I whispered.

It was a pig sty. There were two stalls inside with fat sows asleep in them. I tiptoed past, looking into the corners while my eyes accustomed themselves to the gloom. The stink of ammonia made me weep and my feet squelched in the muck on the floor. The next stall had quarter-grown piglets in it which dashed squealing to meet us, hoping we were bearers of food. The next one was used for storage, with several long planks leaned up in the corner. He was pressed against the wall, trying to make himself invisible behind them, while the ordure on the floor lapped over the tops of his highly polished brogues. The PC produced a torch and shone it on him.

"Hello, Sir Morton," I said. "It looks as if you're in the shit."

He was a knight, after all, so I handcuffed his hands to the front.

"I can explain, Inspector," he protested. "This is all a mistake."

I put my finger in front of my lips to hush him. "Not now," I said, and led him out into the sunshine.

Sharon Brown was standing near the transit, also in handcuffs, with a group of men. Some wore flat caps and dirty jackets, with collarless shirts; others were in leather jackets, smart trousers and enough gold ornamentation to pay off the national debt of a South American republic. I stood Sir Morton near my car and brought Sharon to join him. They faced each other without speaking.

"You wanted a word," I said to him.

"Er, yes, Inspector. I was saying, this is all a mistake. I've never done anything like it before. I was appalled by what I've seen, totally appalled."

"Well, you'll be able to explain all that when we take a statement from you back at the station." I led him over to a panda and removed his handcuffs, saying: "I don't think these are necessary, do you?" and placed a protective hand on his head as he ducked into the car, all for the benefit of the watching Sharon.

I was walking across to talk to the OSU sergeant and congratulate him on a job well done when I saw one of the uniformed PCs sitting on his heels, looking at something between the cages.

"What is it?" I asked, stooping beside him.

He was young but no doubt he'd seen some unpleasant sights in his short career. Sometimes it's not what you expect that gets through to you. His face was ashen as he looked up at me and moved aside.

Blood and fur, that's all I could see. A matted mass of blood and fur. Then a tail became visible, and an eye and the gory socket where its partner should have been, an ear and a leg. Underneath was the head of another creature, its jaw torn off, the teeth exposed like a saw blade. They were the cats we'd seen in the photos of the cages.

"Sorry, Claudius," I whispered. "I just wasn't quick enough."

We took Sir Morton and the desirable Sharon to Heckley and most of the others to Halifax, although Ms Brown looked anything but desirable with her mascara resembling the run-off from a coal tip, her lipstick like she'd been smacked in the mouth with a ketchup bottle and her expression one of loathing for us. Within half an hour I was removing her cuffs and telling her to sit down at the table of interview room number one. Dave was with us.

"Did the cats put up much of a fight?" I demanded.

"I don't know what you mean."

"Are you saying they weren't thrown to the dogs?"

"I'm not saying anything."

"Do they hold dog fights at High Clough farm?"

"I don't know."

"Proud of yourself, are you?"

"I've done nothing to be ashamed of."

"Watching dog fights nothing to be ashamed of?"

"I'm saying nothing."

"Do you want a solicitor?"

"No."

"You'll need one, when I've finished."

"I don't want one."

"Do you think Sir Morton won't be asking for a solicitor? Do you think he won't be telling us all about it – from his point of view, of course. You heard him, Sharon, wheedling his way out of it before we'd gathered our breath. Soon you'll all be in front of the magistrate, who he probably plays golf with. I assume he does play golf, occasionally. The prosecuting barrister is probably the grand master of his lodge, and the judge, if he ever reaches a judge, will probably hold shares in Grainger's. I assure you, Sharon, that Sir Morton certainly won't be saying nothing. He'll be singing like a ..."

I was choosing between a canary on hemp and a Welsh wedding when there was a knock at the door and a PC poked his head in.

"Have a word, Boss?" he said.

Outside he handed me a video cassette in its box. "Found these at the farm. Seven of them, all the same. It's a dog fighting video, almost certainly recorded there, with evidence to suggest they were doing mail order."

I thanked him and went back inside, carrying the video. "Put some tapes in, Dave," I said. "We'll do this properly."

It was his idea," she told us. "It… it turned him on."

"His? Who's he?"

"Mort. Sir Morton."

"That would be Sir Morton Grainger?"

"Yes."

"So one day, right out of the blue, he said: 'Let's organise a dog fight and video it?'"

"No."

"What, then? Perhaps you'd better start at the beginning."

Her instinct was to tell us nothing, leave it to us to prove what we could. Admit nowt, say nowt, remember nowt; that was the creed. But she knew that her lover boy had a different armoury of defences, and he'd be pulling every string he could to put the blame elsewhere. Perhaps this was another of the old values that had served its time.

"It was… a couple of years ago," she began, hesitantly, her confidence gone, feeling for the words. "My cousin telephoned me, asked me to do him a favour."

"Which cousin was this?"

"I'm not saying."

"OK. Go on."

"He wanted me to copy a video he had. I didn't know what was on it."

"Why did he ask you?"

"Because he'd seen a film I'd made for Grainger's. It was a training video and I'd produced it. We did it all ourselves, from the camera work to making copies. I was proud of it and took a copy home to give to my parents. I was on it for a few seconds, doing the introductions. He must have seen it there."

"Did you look at his video?"

"Yes. I thought it was going to be pornographic, but it was only a dog fight. The production was terrible, a typical home video."

"Only a dog fight?"

"They're animals, Inspector. Wolves, underneath. We don't have the sentimental views about them that you have."

"You copied the video for your cousin."

"Yes."

"So where does Grainger come in?"

"He wanted a copy of the training video to have a look at. I wasn't in my office so he went in my drawer and found the wrong one. That night it was all he could talk about. He… it… he was… you know…"

"It turned him on."

"Yes." She was blushing, but she still managed a defiant stare.

"And afterwards?" I asked. At his age there's always a lot of afterwards.

"He wanted me to take him to a fight. My cousin arranged one a fortnight later and we went. He was full of it, excited. He suggested organising a better one, more professional, and videoing it properly. We had all the equipment at Grainger's. Since then we've held one almost every month. He took over the betting, with him as the bookmaker. He loved every minute of it. The cats were his idea."

"The cats?"

"Yes. Cats against the Clock, he called it."

I dreaded to think what Cats against the Clock was, but no doubt all would be revealed when I watched the video. I turned to Dave and asked him if he had any questions.

"Yes," he replied, shuffling in his seat. "Where does Sebastian fit into all this?"

"Sebastian?" she echoed.

"Your distant cousin. Sir Morton's home help."

"He doesn't come into it."

"How did he get the job?"

"It was years ago. He worked for Grainger's and made assistant manager, but he wasn't qualified to go any higher and he wasn't happy. Mort mentioned that he wanted a Man Friday and I suggested Sebastian. It's worked out very well, I'm told."

"But Seb isn't part of the dog fighting club?"

"No, he…" She hesitated.

"He what?" Dave prompted.

"He doesn't believe in all that."

"All what?"

"The old ways. Our parents made the break and he doesn't like being reminded of his background."

"Are you saying he's ashamed of it?"

"Yes."

"But you're proud of yours?"

She stared at him with her big gypsy eyes. "Yes, I am."

According to the 1911 Protection of Animals Act the organiser of the dog fight was looking at six months inside, except that we don't put anyone away these days unless it's at least his tenth offence. There was some gobbledygook about procuring and/or receiving money that we might have been able to nail Grainger with, but it looked as if we'd have to settle for a hefty fine. He'd be shamed in open court, with his name in the papers – that was the main punishment. It would make the nationals and we'd field a few plaudits for stamping out the evil business. Kids and animals. Actors don't like working with them but to us they're all in a day's work.

Jeff and Pete came in, grinning like a pair of truants at an afternoon match, closely followed by a uniformed sergeant. I looked past them at the sergeant and swivelled round in my chair to face him.

"You'll get lost up here, Max," I said.

"I could always ask a policeman, if I could find one," he replied. "Message for you, Charlie. Thought I might catch you downstairs but I missed you. It could be important."

I reached out and took the telephone report sheet from him. It was short and sweet. From Miss Barraclough, to DI Priest, personal. "Gone to Uley. The exhumation is scheduled for midnight tonight."

"Bugger," I sighed.

Max left us and Jeff said: "Bad news?"

I turned the sheet round and offered it to him. "Not sure. Depends what the result is."

He read the words and gave it back to me. "Were you hoping to go?"

"I'd have liked to."

"You can still do it. There's plenty of time for you to drive there."

I gestured towards the pile of yellow file jackets on my desk, each bulging with the blank forms that needed completing before we could put the dogfighters in front of a magistrate. "What about this lot?"

"We can manage, can't we, Pete?"

Pete shrugged. "Yeah, no problem. Where were you hoping to go?"

"To an exhumation in Gloucestershire. It's the father of a woman I know. Jeff'll tell you all about it."

"Get yourself off, then. We'll have a word with Mr Wood and manage this lot. It's just a matter of taking statements and letting them go, isn't it?"

I thought about it for a second or two. "I'm a bit worried about Sir Morton," I said, pursing my lips and shaking my head. "He was sounding off about it not being his idea and all that. He could be at risk of violence from the others if we let him out. Some of them are really mean types. It would look bad if anything happened to him, wouldn't it?" The codes of practice said we should release them all as soon as possible after they'd been charged, but there were exceptions. We could hold someone if there was a chance that they would interfere with witnesses, or if we ran out of time, or if we considered them to be a danger to others or be in danger themselves.

"Mmm, I see what you mean," Jeff agreed with a knowing nod. "Now you've mentioned it I did hear a few threats being muttered. In that case perhaps we should hold him overnight, for his own safety."

"Just what I was thinking, Jeffrey."

"OK. We'll leave him 'till last and see how it goes."

"Cheers," I said. "I really would like to be at this exhumation but I'll make a couple of phone calls first."

Rosie didn't answer and she doesn't own a mobile. Inconvenient but another reason to like her. After that I rang a Gloucester number and spoke to the coroner's officer in charge of the exhumation. She'd cleared all the legal obstacles and orchestrated interested parties so that the whole thing would run smoothly at midnight tonight. She was an ex-police sergeant and had no objection to my attending, even though the case was well outside my jurisdiction. I didn't explain my interest and she didn't ask.

"Presumably First Call are paying," I said.

"You bet," she replied.

"Why midnight? And why so hastily arranged?"

"Their request. We would normally have organised it for first light, about 5 a.m., but they asked for the midnight slot. It's the witching hour. They'll be able to show the church clock at that time and superimpose hooting owls on the soundtrack. We're normally seen as a bunch of obstructionists but they were in a hurry and the family member had given her permission, so we were happy to accommodate them. It shows us in a good light and the publicity for the office won't do us any harm. You know the score: everything stops for the great god television."

"And the TV crew'll be able to go there straight from the pub," I said, "instead of having to drag their hungover bodies out of bed at four in the morning."

"You're a cynic, Inspector."

"A cynic? Moi? Never."

The next call was to the Home Office laboratory at Chepstow, where I eventually found myself speaking to the scientist who was handling the case. He suggested that he ring me back.

"So what's the game plan?" I asked after we'd confirmed that we were talking about the Barraclough case.

"Not much of a plan," he replied. "We dig down to the coffin and then decide on the next step. Ideally, if it's in a good condition, we'll remove the whole caboodle and take it to the path lab, but after thirty years that's unlikely. We'll have a spare coffin standing by, a big one, and we'll probably have to lift everything into that. The best place to find uncorrupted DNA will be in the bones. We'll get what we want while it's in the lab and have the coffin back down the hole by lunchtime."

"Is Chepstow handling the profiling?"

"Not completely. The TV people have asked for samples so they can use a private lab."

"And you still have the nail-scrapings from the girl?"

"Yes, we've already done a profile on them."

"Have you given First Call a sample?"

"No. We refused, but they've got the profile."

"Are they happy with that?"

"They'll have to be."

"So why do they need a Barraclough sample? Why can't they let you do the whole job? Don't they trust you?"

"Probably not, but we have different agendas. They want to televise the process and we won't allow them in here, so they're using the private lab. And they want to beat us to it, of course. It's all to do with the great unwashed's craving for excitement. We want to get to the bottom of a murder and possibly defend the police's reputation, they want a story, preferably one that shows police incompetence."

I thought about his words for a few seconds and decided to come clean with him. "The dead man's daughter is an acquaintance of mine," I said, "so I have a slight personal involvement. She'll be there and I'm worried she'll find it upsetting."

"Hmm, I imagine it will be. I'd keep her well back if I were you. He'll be a skeleton by now and there might be a certain amount of disrespectful conduct when we're down the hole, trying to find all his bits and pieces."

"Rather you than me," I said.

"It's a living."

"Thanks for your help, and we'll see you at midnight."

"See you then. Oh, and just one other piece of advice."

"Fire away."

"Your friend. I'd keep her upwind of the grave if I were you."

Chapter Eleven

I went home and put a packet of Chorley cakes and a bottle of flavoured water in the car. The route was simple enough: A hundred and eighty miles down the M6 and M5 to J13 and follow the signs. No need to write that down. I stuffed myself with a big ham sandwich and a piece of fruitcake and set off. I was heading to an area of the country we refer to as the Cotswolds. It's a fairytale place, where princes live and call in the pub for the odd half pint with the locals; where pop stars inhabit castles and handsome girls called Cressinda and Tasha, their jodhpur-clad bums rising and falling in unison, give you a friendly wave as you drive slowly past their horses. It only rains at night in the Cotswolds, and the streets are dry again by seven fifteen.

The drive down was hellish. You switch off, regard it as five hours taken out of your life and keep an eagle eye on the brake lights of the car in front. Some people, I reminded myself, have to do this every day. I arrived about eight thirty and pulled off the road for a look at the map and a swig of water. As I drove into Uley the sun was low behind me, giving the lighting a magical quality.

It's a one-street village, the one street being called, simply, The Street. It clings to the valley wall rather than following the bottom, giving long views across to the other side. Cotswold stone has a yellow colour, and the angle of the sun and some obscure property of light, to do with frequencies and reflection, conspired to make the walls of the cottages glow. They were made of limestone or sandstone, or perhaps a mixture of the two. I should have paid more attention during those first geology lessons.

Rose Cottage was now an antique shop but the King's Head had seen better days. I drove slowly with my window down, heading uphill to where I could see the church with its square tower and a small, offset spire overlooking the whole valley. There was a village store and post office and some ancient petrol pumps that someone had saved from the scrap heap. The Old Crown pub, bedecked with window boxes, was straight out of the English Heritage brochure.

Marl, I thought. That was the name of the stone. I'd check with Rosie when I saw her. During my drive through the village I didn't see a single estate agent's sign announcing 'House for Sale'. The people of Uley were content with their lot, and I couldn't blame them.

I parked outside the church, St Giles, and went for an explore. There was a graveyard next to the church and another, more modern one across the road. I wandered around this one and read the dates on the headstones. 1950, 1952, 1969, continuing right up to the present time, many of the later ones bearing flowers in granite vases. In Heckley they'd be stolen. The grass was mown short and grasshoppers whirred away from my feet. The graves covered the period in question but I couldn't see one with the right name on it, or any sign of preparatory work done by the gravediggers. I crossed the road to the graveyard proper.

The ground here was uneven, with the graves crowding against each other as if seeking comfort in their neighbour's proximity. Some had sunk and some were still heaped up, with the headstones leaning at angles. None had flowers on them and no lawnmower could deal with this terrain. Lichen, moss and acid rain had taken their toll, making it difficult to read dates but they must have stretched back at least two hundred years. The graveyard was surrounded by high trees, firs and yew, and sloped down away from the church. Behind the church was a substantial manor house, which I took to be the vicarage or rectory. Or, more likely these days, the Old Vicarage or Old Rectory. I couldn't see Rosie's car but there was one of those miniature JCB excavators parked nearby, ready for action.

The line of least resistance took me downhill and I found myself in the lowest corner of the graveyard. There were planks of wood alongside an unmarked grave, with folded tarpaulins laid next to them and bags of lime under the hedge. I'd found the last resting place of Abraham Barraclough. The sun never penetrated this secret corner but it was a warm, clear evening, the birds were singing and the grass was dry under my feet. So why was the hair on the back of my neck standing on end? I thought of Stephen King and turned back uphill, towards my car and sanctuary.

Dinner in a pub would have made sense but I settled for coffee at the motorway services and had a snooze in the car. Uley was a different place when I returned, just after midnight, the glow of stone replaced by the soft colour of an occasional lighted window, and beyond them an infinity of blackness. It was a moonless night but the stars put on a show for us. I parked my car behind the long line of vehicles near the church and glanced up at them as I zipped my jacket and closed the car door. Maybe that's my way of praying: a casual glance up at the stars; a tacit acknowledgement that there's something out there that's beyond our comprehension and always will be.

The drone of a generator disturbed the night as it fed a couple of floodlights on a column, and blue police tape held back a silent straggle of people who were watching the gravediggers and TV crew at work. I stumbled on the uneven ground and worried about falling through into one of those sunken graves. A uniformed PC saw me approach and detached himself from the onlookers. I introduced myself and asked him to indicate the coroner's officer and the boffin from Chepstow.

"They're disappointed," the scientist told me, nodding towards the cameras after I found him. "The coffin's in good condition – solid oak at a guess – so we're enlarging the hole and trying to lift it out fairly intact. Saves me and my assistant getting messed up. They were hoping for some good shots of the lid being smashed open and me climbing out of the grave holding a thigh bone or even the skull." He gave a little laugh at the thought. "Bloody ghouls. I don't know why we're helping them. All they want to do is prove that you got it wrong, all those years ago."

"Perhaps we did," I replied.

He was silent for a few moments, wondering where my interest lay, then: "Did you say that you were a friend of the deceased's daughter?"

"Yes."

"Is she here?"

"I believe so."

"I need a mouth swab from her. Could you point her out to me?"

"When I find her."

Rosie was at the edge of the group of people, standing with the vicar and the coroner's officer. They all turned as I approached and Rosie started as she recognised me, then stepped towards me and accepted a hug.

"I didn't expect to see you," she said but I couldn't think of a reason for being there and just gave her an extra squeeze.

The vicar was called Duncan and had a handshake in proportion to the six-foot-six he stood, while the coroner's officer's was soft and warm. She'd been standing with her hands in her pockets.

"We talked on the phone," I said to her. "You must have worked hard, organising all this so quickly."

"You know what they say, Inspector: Ask a busy woman…"

I turned to Rosie. "Did you drive down?" I asked.

"Yes. Duncan and his wife are putting me up at the vicarage."

"That's kind of them. I wish I'd known, I could have brought you."

"You have work to do."

"Look at that lot," the coroner's officer said. "He'll fall in if he gets any closer."

The cameraman was pointing his huge shoulder-mounted camera down into the grave while the director endeavoured to hold him back and look over his shoulder at the same time. A third member of the team, the sound man, waved what looked like a fluffy animal on the end of a pole over them. Rosie gave a sniff and a sudden swirl of a breeze stirred the tree-tops, as if some restless spirit were up there, trying to find its way back home.

"C'mon," I said, taking Rosie by the arm and turning her away from the activity. I switched my hand to hers and she allowed me to lead her towards the church. The light was behind us, so the footing was more secure, and when we were on the paving stones I put my arm across her shoulders.

"You shouldn't be here, Rosie," I told her, when we were standing inside the doorway of St Giles. "I can understand you coming, but there's nothing else you can see, nothing you can do. I think you should go to bed."

"What about you?"

"I'll go home, or book in at the Holiday Inn if I feel tired. I'll be OK, it's you I'm worried about. Listen, Rosie. It's obviously upsetting for you. It would be for anyone. Let them get on with it in their own way. They'll take the coffin to the hospital lab and open it. Apparently they'll have it back here by lunchtime. Maybe you'll be able to say your goodbyes to your dad then, without all this… all this circus."

"That's what they said," she admitted. "Duncan said we could have a little service of interment."

"That's good of him. Would you like me to be there?"

"I don't know. No, I don't think so. I'd prefer to be on my own. Lay him to rest, one way or another, once and for all."

"That would be best," I said. "From what I've heard

of him, from what I've gathered, he was a special person. That's the memory to cling to."

Rosie wiped her eyes and pressed her face against my chest. "Shall I tell them you've seen enough?" I asked, and felt her nod her acquiescence.

"Inspector!" I turned to face the voice. It was the scientist from the Chepstow lab. "Is this the lady I'm looking for?"

"Yes," I replied, releasing Rosie and making the introductions. "He needs a sample of your buccal cells," I told her, "from inside your mouth."

The scientist produced his kits and removed the screwed lid from one of the plastic tubes. He extracted the swizzle stick with its cotton wool bud and handed it to Rosie. "Just give it a good rub round the inside of your cheek, please." Rosie did as she was told, silent and compliant, and he placed the swab back inside its tube. "And another, please, just to play safe."

He sealed the samples in their envelopes and filled in the details before saying thanks and wandering off again. It was going to be a long night for him.

"What's the purpose of that?" Rosie asked as he vanished into the gloom.

"It's just a check," I replied.

"A check for what?"

"He wants to compare your DNA with that from the body, to prove it's the right grave. We inherit half our DNA from our father, half from our mother. They'll be able to verify that you're a close relative to… to the person in the grave."

"I see." Then, after a long pause: "First Call haven't asked me for a sample."

"No? Well, let's just say that we're more thorough than they are."

The vicar insisted I go back with them for a coffee and we had it seated on high stools in his big kitchen. He wanted to make me a flask and a sandwich for the trip home, but I managed to convince him that it wasn't necessary. When I was in the car again I put Gavin Bryars' The Sinking of the Titanic in the CD player and pointed north. It's a musical description of the liner's final journey to the bottom of the sea. The roads were mercifully quiet and I hardly dropped below eighty, almost halving the time of my outward trip. As that final, sad Amen sounded and the broken hulk settled on the ocean floor I'd covered over a hundred miles and the morning sun was in my eyes.

An exhumation isn't undertaken lightly. It can only be done in a few special cases and requires the issue of a warrant by either the local coroner or the Home Office. Other parties with an interest are the police, just so that they know it's official and not the work of grave robbers, the environmental health officer and the Church. As this was a criminal case, a police photographer was there to record every stage, and another officer was appointed to follow through the continuity of the process, so that there was no suggestion of bones being substituted. When you added the cost of the JCB, the funeral director and gravediggers, plus a new coffin and all the various materials, it was costing First Call a pretty penny. And they wanted their money's worth.

I went straight to the nick and had a toasted teacake and mug of tea in the canteen, joshing with the dayshift woodentops as they slunk in, bleary-eyed and reluctant.

I was towelling myself dry after a shower when Gareth Adey came into the bathroom. "Morning, Charlie," he shouted to me. "Had a busy night?"

"So-so, Gareth. So-so."

I combed my hair with my fingers, hardly able to see my reflection in the steamed-up mirror, and pulled my pants on. Gareth had a pee and washed his hands.

"If you could start all over again, Charlie," he said, "what would you do differently? What changes would you make?"

That's Gareth's way of making conversation, and as profound as he ever gets. I pulled a sock over my toes, wriggled them about and pulled it fully on.

"If I could start all over again?"

"That's what I said."

"There is one thing."

"What's that?"

"I'd eat more roughage."

"Ha ha!" he laughed. "Ha ha! Eat more roughage! I like it, Charlie, I like it." He wandered out into the real world and I reached for a shoe. Another day had begun.

I went through the motions but my mind was else-where. We'd made twelve arrests at the dog fight and they'd all been sent home on police bail, Sir Morton being the last to go, earlier this morning. He'd brought in a high-flyer of a solicitor and admitted nothing, claiming to have been taken to the farm by one of his employees who apparently was under the illusion that a little escapism would do him good, be a relief from the pressure he'd recently been under. But she was wrong. He'd been disgusted and dismayed by the whole thing. Jeff and the CPS prosecutor had the case in hand, so I left it to them. Two burglars were in the cells but I let Dave and one of the DCs do the interviewing. Jeff came into my office to ask how it had all gone and I told him.

"You look knackered," he said. "Why don't you take the afternoon off?"

"I'm thinking about it."

"We can manage." He bent down and opened my bottom drawer. "Have a watch of this," he told me, handing me a video box, "but not before you go to bed."

"What is it? The dog fight?"

"Yeah."

I did some shopping and went home. Sleeping in the afternoon is something I rarely do, but I could get used to it. I set the alarm for three hours and crashed on the bed, with the curtains open and the sun warming my legs. I fell asleep imagining that I was on a Caribbean beach, with Rosie on the next sun bed and an attentive waiter hovering nearby in case either of us felt the need for another pina colada. I never heard the alarm, the three hours was nearer five and I awoke shivering with a mouth like a hamster's nest.

I cleaned my teeth, had another shower, changed my clothes and put the ready meal I'd bought in the oven. Lamb in a rosemary sauce, with roast potatoes and dumplings, to be followed by bread and butter pudding. I had a can of lager while it cooked, and I was looking for somewhere to stand the glass when I saw the video.

Sometimes we do things without making a conscious decision. Our genes take over, do what they think is right or necessary for the future of the human race. An individual's feelings don't come into it. Natural selection in action? I don't know. I just knew that right then was an inappropriate time to be watching that particular video. It was wrong, it was unnecessary, it could have waited. But my arm reached out, my fingers opened the box and shoved the cassette into the machine, and I sat down and pressed the play button.

There was a blizzard of noise on the screen, quickly followed by a parade of dogs, close up and full frontal. They barked and snarled and slavered at the camera, held back by tattooed arms and hands hooked through their studded collars. A narrator told us their names: Tyson, The Wrecker, Tojo and Jaws.

The attention span of the target audience was measured in seconds rather than minutes, so they didn't waste any more time. We saw a dog inside the familiar chicken run, restrained by a chain threaded through its collar as it struggled and fought in a violent frenzy to be attacking something off camera. The camera panned slowly to the right and zoomed in on the object of the dog's fury. A wire cage sat in the middle of the run, with a cat inside it. The creature stood on its claws, back arched, tail erect, staring at the demented dog. As we watched, a rope on top of the cage pulled taut and lifted its protection away, leaving the cat exposed. A second later the chain through the dog's collar was slipped and the chase was on.

The cat reared, hissing and spitting, its claws extended and teeth bared. You saw it as it was: a wild animal stripped of its veneer of domesticity. It looked ferocious, straight from the jungle, but no match for the dog. As the dog attacked, the cat turned to flee, but there was nowhere to go. It swerved left as it hit the side of the enclosure and the dog blundered into the wire, recovered, and continued the chase. The cat headed into a corner, realised its mistake and climbed the wire.

The dog leapt and grasped it by the tail. The cat screamed and fell to the ground, turning to face its tormentor. The dog went for a better hold and its jaws clamped round the cat's back, severing its spine. The poor creature turned, its rear end paralysed, and raised one defiant claw as the dog finished it off with a bite to the head. As it shook the carcass a spray of blood arced away from it and the dog trotted proudly round the enclosure, stump of a tail wagging, more blood trailing on to the concrete floor from the lifeless body dangling from its jaws.

"Fifteen seconds," I heard someone announce, and there was a smatter of jeering from the audience.

The next cat was a long-haired Persian type that had eaten too many chocolate drops and had never faced anything more threatening than Jerry Springer on daytime TV. Instinct kicked in as the cage was raised and the leash slipped, but it was no contest. The cat turned as it reached the wire, losing fur off its back as it dodged the snapping jaws, but the next time it tried the manoeuvre the dog cut the corner and grabbed a leg. The cat rolled on its back and tried to fight but dogs like that don't feel pain and it ignored the flashing claws and went for the cat's belly.

"Eight seconds," the MC told the jeering audience,

and Tojo was declared the winner of Cats against the Clock.

After that it was dog versus dog.

I ate the meal but didn't enjoy it. The last big case I had involved someone strangling young women. I couldn't reconcile my feelings for the animals with those I had for the girls. Perhaps it was impossible, futile to try. Perhaps it was the perpetrators I should focus on. I didn't know. Nobody did. It was a shit world with some shit people in it, that's all you could say. I went for a walk around the estate for some fresh air. The weather was changing, as promised by the forecasters, and the threat of thunderstorms had passed. People were saying we needed the rain. They're never satisfied.

Rosie rang. She was still at the vicarage and staying another night. She'd come home Wednesday, she told me.

"Thank you for coming down, Charlie," she said. "I was really pleased to see you. The vicar, Duncan, is very nice, but he's still, you know, a caring professional."

"Did you hold a service?"

"Yes. They had the coffin back by ten a.m. The grave was filled in again before I knew anything about it. There were just the three of us, including the vicar's wife, then they left me alone for a while. I said my goodbyes, Charlie. Now all we have to do is wait for the DNA results."

"Have they said how long it will be?"

"No. As soon as possible, that's all. What about you?"

"No. They can do it in a day, if necessary, but they charge extra. They're always busy, and this isn't an active enquiry, so it will be low priority, but they'll do their best."

We chatted for a while and I remembered an advert I'd seen in the Events column of the Gazette.

"Did you ever get to play the part of Mustard Seed?" I asked.

"Mustard Seed? No, I had to drop out."

"It just happens that A Midsummer Night's Dream is on at the Leeds Playhouse this week. It's the RSC. How do you feel about going to see it on Saturday, if I can get the tickets?"

"This Saturday?"

"Mmm." I was worried about the memories it might revive. People are irrational about some things; they look for something to blame. If Shakespeare had never written that particular play Rosie would not have stayed on at school on the fateful day, therefore her father might still be alive.

She was silent for a while, before saying: "I'd love to, Charlie. It will be wonderful, a real treat, and I need a treat. But what about the gala? Isn't that this weekend?"

"Sunday," I replied. "No problem."

"Have you finished the paintings?"

"Not quite. I'll have to spend some time on them. Hey, listen to this: the uniformed branch always have a display at the gala, and this year they were hoping to do something different. We tried to convince them that they'd look good all dressed up as cowboys, but they've refused."

"I think that's a great idea. You could go as Wyatt Earp, Charlie. You'd look splendid in a frock coat."

"No way."

"Oh, go on!"

"No way."

"Spoilsport."

"Thanks for ringing, Rosie. You've brightened my day, and it's good to hear you sounding happier."

"Well, things are moving, aren't they?"

They were, but I wasn't sure in which direction. "I'll try for those tickets," I said.

I slept well. I didn't expect to, but I fell straight into a contented sleep and was deep in the arms of Morpheus when the alarm woke me, early Wednesday morning. Had I been deep in the arms of Goldie Hawn I would have hurled it through the window, but it was only sleep and it had rained through the night, the sky was clear again and Charlie Priest was ready to raise hell amongst the thieves and robbers of Heckley.

He wasn't ready for what was waiting for him.

Chapter Twelve

"There's been another," Dave announced as I strode into the office.

"So I've just been told. Any details?"

"A baby. Swallowed some glass from a tin of baby food. That's all I've heard."

"And he's in the General?"

"Oh, yeah. And that."

"Look on the bright side, Dave," I said. "It's not Ebola. They'll be giving us a parking place down there soon. C'mon, let's go."

The doctor in charge came to meet us at the front desk and took us up to the paediatrics ward. He was black, with delicate hands and a soft, almost inaudible voice.

"The child was brought in yesterday evening," he explained as we exited the lift, "bleeding from a cut inside his lower lip. His mother said she found pieces of broken glass in a tin of baby food she fed him with and that she found blood in his nappy. We've X-rayed him but small pieces of glass don't show up very well."

"How serious is it?"

"Hard to say. Small pieces in his stomach will make him feel unwell, but in themselves they need not be dangerous." He stopped, his hand on the door handle. "Have you ever seen a goat eating leaves off a thorn bush, Inspector?"

"No," I admitted, stooping to hear him, hoping I hadn't misunderstood.

His face split into a grin. "Neither have I, but they do it without hurting themselves, even though their mouth parts are extremely soft. Babies' mouths and digestive tracts are similar. Ingesting broken glass is not to be recommended but it should not cause any damage if the pieces are small enough, and it should pass through relatively harmlessly. Powdered glass is not considered a problem. Bigger pieces may cause damage, of course, and we will analyse his stools for blood. Otherwise we just wait and see."

"There's been a spate of contaminated food at supermarkets," I told him. "No doubt you've read about it in the papers. It's what started the Ebola scare. We thought it had subsided, but evidently not."

He pushed the door open. "I'm afraid this was something more complicated than contaminated food. I'll show you."

Rory Norcup was asleep in an oversize cot, wearing only a disposable nappy and an adhesive strip that underlined his bottom lip. He kicked his legs and waved his arms as if deep in a disturbing dream. Sadly for him, it wasn't a dream.

"He's thirty-one weeks old, but has the weight of a baby half that age. There is also evidence of bruising on his arms, as if he has been gripped tightly, plus some old bruising on his back. He was clean when he came in but he has a severe nappy dermatitis, as if it was rarely changed."

"Where's his mother?" I asked.

"She brought him in and sat with him most of the night, but we sent her home not long ago."

"How was she?"

"Distraught with grief and concern for her poor baby." He paused between each word, implying that they meant exactly the opposite of what they said.

"You think she had something to do with it?"

"Almost certainly. Take a look at his face."

We peered at him, his eyes screwed shut, his expression contorted as he fought with demons that he had no name for.

"He's not the bonniest baby I've ever seen," Dave said, "but he's not Down's Syndrome, is he?"

"No, he's not a Down's baby."

"Alcohol whatsit?" I suggested.

"That's right, Inspector. FAS – foetal alcohol syndrome, caused by his mother drinking whilst pregnant."

"How serious is that?" Dave asked.

"It's a setback," the doctor replied, "but it can be overcome with a caring, nourishing upbringing."

"Which he won't get."

"Not with his present mother."

"You reckon she was trying to get rid of him?"

"No, she loves him, she says, but she's inadequate, has as many problems as he has, so she uses him to alleviate her own difficulties."

Dave leaned over the cot's high side and started making noises. "Hi, Rory," he whispered. "We haven't given you the best start in life, have we?" He reached in and covered the child's legs with the cellular blanket that he'd kicked off.

"I know what you're getting at, Doc," I said, "but my brain's not working. Tell me its name."

"Munchausen syndrome by proxy. She damages the

child to win sympathy for herself. I've come across it before."

"That's a serious accusation."

"I know, and Munchausen mothers are plausible liars. They appear to be overly protective of their children, take great interest in their treatment and become familiar with medical procedures. It's not always to win admiration as a wonderful mother – sometimes they do it to strike up a relationship with medical staff and impress them with their concern. I'd say Mrs Norcup is a classical example."

"Have you seen her before?"

"Yes. Rory was in about a month ago, with an undiagnosed rash on his back."

"And you think she caused it?"

"It cleared up in two days with minimum treatment. She stayed by his bedside throughout."

"Perhaps we ought to talk to her GP."

"I'd think you'd find, Inspector, that he's completely taken in by her. He'll say she's a caring mother."

"We see the self-inflicted part often enough," I said, "but not the by proxy bit. Will he go into care?"

"Yes. We've notified social services."

"You'd better give me the mother's address."

"Why do they have kids if they don't want them?" Dave said as we drove through Heckley towards Gaitskill House, where Mrs Norcup lived. "There's no excuse for it these days. They teach them birth control before they teach them their times tables, hand out free condoms to the juniors, and still every teenage girl you see has at least one youngster following her around."

I looked sideways at him. "It just happens."

"Well it happens too often. Booze and sex, that's what does it, if you ask me."

"Well, yes, sex does play a part," I agreed.

A traffic light fifty yards ahead turned amber and Dave braked. Two cars behind us in the right hand lane accelerated through as it turned to red.

"Look at those two bastards," he cursed. "Did you get the numbers?"

"The second one," I told him, reaching into my pocket for my notebook. "Tell me the make and colour."

The light switched to green and we moved off again. "We could always adopt him," Dave suggested.

"Who?"

"Young Rory."

"What? You and me?"

"No, Dumbo. The police station. Not adopt him, just buy him treats, keep a weather eye on him, wherever he goes. Uncle Police."

"Or Uncle Nick?"

"Something like that. It needn't cost much. The surplus on the coffee money would cover it."

"Uncle Bill?"

"Are you taking the piss?"

"Not at all, Dave. It's a great idea." I shook my head and smiled. There was a temptation to say that he'd probably have another of his own clinging to his legs before much longer, but I resisted.

Gaitskill House was one block in what was known as the Project, on the opposite side of Heckley to the Sylvan Fields estate. The tenants of the Project aspire to live in the Sylvan Fields. It had sounded like a noble idea, back in the Sixties. Housing for everyone, at an affordable price because of new construction methods. Modular design, prefabricated units, pre-stressed concrete. The councillors banded the terms around as if they knew what they meant, and the ugly, pebble-dashed façade of the Project soon scarred the landscape.

The underfloor heating was expensive and unreliable, the joints between the prefabricated sections leaked and you could hear your neighbour clack his false teeth. In the eighties the half-empty flats were condemned and marked down for demolition, but sociological trends were at work, the sanctity of marriage was under threat and there was an upsurge in demand for accommodation for one-parent families. Now the council regarded them as a dumping ground for problem tenants, and the influx of asylum seekers had put a further demand on them.

A researcher had estimated that one parking place for every two flats would be generous, but the single burned-out Sierra standing in front of them showed the error of that calculation. Dave parked well away from it, where his car was highly visible from the upper balconies. Mrs Norcup lived in number 419.

I gazed up at the bleak concrete walls, streaked with rust from the reinforcing bars, and felt as if I were part of Rumania's secret police when Ceausescu was in power. "Third floor," I said, warning my nostrils to brace themselves. "We'll walk."

"Just a tick," Dave said, and strolled over to where four industrial-size dumpsters stood, next to the stairwell. He lifted a lid, looked in, closed the lid and looked in the next one. "Bugger!" he declared. "They're empty. Looks as if the bin men have just been."

Mrs Norcup answered the door at the fourth knock, probably after doing a high-speed tidy of the flat. Her face was flushed pink but etched with concern as Dave made the introductions.

"Is it about Rory?" she demanded, a hand nervously raised to her face, her hair untidy. "Is he all right? Has something happened to him? I was just about to go back to the hospital…"

"Rory's fine," I assured her with a smile. "We've just left him and he was chatting up the nurses. May we come in and have a word?"

She looked at me, bewildered.

"Rory's fine. Can we come in, please?"

The flat was about what I expected: cheap furniture; untidy and smelling of cooking. I try not to be judgemental, lest others judge me. It was reasonably clean and the carpets didn't stick to your feet as you walked across them, for which I am always grateful. The electric fire was on low and the television on high. A man with a toupee and an orange face was talking about antiques. Dave switched off the telly and settled into the only easy chair that didn't have something on it, giving me a smile that said: "Beat you to it." I found an upright one and invited Mrs Norcup to sit on her own settee.

"The doctor told us that Rory should make a full recovery, Mrs Norcup," I said, "with no after-effects."

"Oh, thank God for that. I've been so worried about the little mite. I wanted to stay with him but I had to tell his daddy what had happened. I hadn't taken his phone number to the hospital."

"Where is Rory's dad?" Dave asked.

"He lives in Sheffield."

"Are you together?"

"No, we split up just before Rory was born. It was amicable. No one else was involved."

"Did you get through to him?"

"No, I missed him. I'll go back to the hospital and try him again tonight. I don't know what I'd do if anything happened to Rory. I just don't know what I'd do." She started to cry and excused herself. Dave pulled a face at me. I walked over to the window and looked down to where the car was parked. It still had its wheels on.

Mrs Norcup came back looking slightly tidier, her face newly washed and her hair tied back, dabbing her nose with a tissue.

"You told the doctor that Rory had eaten some baby food with glass in it," Dave said.

"That's right. Can you believe it? Who'd do something like that to a little baby?"

"What happened?"

"I was feeding him. Do you have any children?"

"No," Dave lied and I shook my head.

"It's a special time, feeding them. It's when you bond. I loved to feed him, watch him watching me. I'd tease him and he'd laugh. He has a lovely laugh. It was peach and banana, Rory's favourite."

"From a tin?"

"Yes," she replied, looking at me as if to say: "What other sort is there?"

"Go on."

"That's it. Suddenly he was crying and blood was

pouring out of his mouth. I poked my fingers in, cleared his mouth out, and cut my finger on a piece of glass." She looked at her finger but decided not to offer it as evidence.

"How much had he eaten?" Dave asked.

"About half the tin."

"Have you kept the rest of it?"

"Yes, it's in the fridge."

We moved into the tiny kitchen and she produced the offending item. It was one of those with a pull-tab on the top and she'd saved the lid, too.

"Did you open the tin yourself?" I asked.

"Yes, I suppose so."

"Was there any evidence of it having been tampered with?"

"Not that I noticed. You don't look for things like that, do you? You don't expect anybody to poison your baby's food, do you? What sort of people are there who could do such a thing?"

"There are some strange people about, Mrs Norcup." I spooned some of the gooey mixture out of the tin and rubbed it between my fingers. I found a piece of glass, about four millimetres square and gave it to Dave.

"Where did you buy this?" I asked.

"At Lidl, yesterday. I still have the receipt." She found it immediately, on the windowsill, together with another one. "I bought some shampoo, too, at Wilkinson's."

I took the receipts that she offered me, looked at them and handed them to Dave. The sum of her shopping trip was one tin of baby food and one bottle of shampoo. Hardly worth the journey into town.

"It's lightbulb glass," Dave declared, passing the piece back to me. "I'll tell you what's 'appened. They make this stuff by the ton, and have conveyor belts filled with it. A lightbulb above the conveyor has broken and fallen in the food. That's what 'appened. Nobody tried to poison your baby, Mrs Norcup."

Her face lightened, the crumpled brow smoothed out and she almost smiled. "You mean… you mean, it was an accident?"

"I'd say so."

"Oh, that is a relief. I'd never have slept again if I'd thought someone had tried to kill poor Rory. An accident! Oh, that's wonderful."

"Glad to be of assistance. Now, do you think I could use your toilet, please? I've drunk rather a lot of coffee this morning."

I took Mrs Norcup back into the other room and closed the door behind us while Dave went to the loo and had a wander round. "How do you get on with your neighbours?" I asked.

"I don't," she replied. "There's a white girl lives below who's on the game, a West Indian crack dealer above, Chinese on one side who have gambling parties that last for days and two Bosnian refugees on the other side. It's not a good place to bring up a child. We'll be out of here as soon as we can find somewhere else. Rory's dad said he'd try to help."

"It's like the United Nations." I heard the sound of flushing and the creak of floorboards. "Do you see Rory's dad very often?"

"Not really. He does his best, always sends Rory a present, but he works hard. He's on oilrigs."

I didn't know if they had oilrigs in Sheffield, and Rory hadn't seen a birthday or Christmas, yet, but I let it go. Dave came in and raised an eyebrow.

"We'll need a full statement from you, Mrs Norcup," he said. "I think you ought to come to the station with us."

Alarm flashed across her face. "But what about Rory?" she said. "I ought to be with him. He'll be missing me."

"Rory'll be fine. Do you have a coat?"

She produced a big blue and yellow anorak with Michigan in four-inch letters across the back. We locked the door behind us and led her down to the car. When I'd put her safely in the back seat Dave jerked his head at me and walked a few paces away from the car.

"There's glass fragments embedded in the kitchen worktop and glass in the rug," he told me. "We need a SOCO here, soon as possible."

I made the phone call and we took Mrs Norcup to Heckley nick. There was a good chance that she'd never see Rory again.

I was making a brew when Gilbert came in to ask about developments. He accepted the offer and I spooned Nescafe into a clean mug. Pete joined us, complaining about the roadworks that had sprung up on the bypass. I pushed the coffee jar his way and gave mine a vigorous stir.

"Why do they have to cone off half a mile of road when they're only working on about five yards of it?" he asked. "They don't realise that the amount of delay is proportional to the length of time you slow the traffic for. There's a critical point when the traffic slows so much it becomes stationary."

"It's a conundrum, Peter," Gilbert told him. "Where's the sugar?"

"Write to the Gazette," I suggested. "It's in the Coffee Mate tin."

Pete handed out beer mats and we cleared spaces on desks in the big office to make room for our drinks. Maggie came in, asked if it was a private party and we told her to join us.

"So," Gilbert began. "What's the state of play with the lady you have downstairs?"

"According to the doc at the hospital she's a classic case of Munchausen syndrome by proxy," I replied. "I've invited the child protection unit to talk to her – it's a bit outside my experience."

Gilbert sipped his coffee and replaced it on the desk, adjusting the position of the beer mat until it was just right. "Dodgy jobs, these involving mothers and babies," he said. "One wrong step and we're accused of misogyny, or matricide or something. Be careful how you go with this one, Charlie."

"Matricide's killing your mother," Pete told us. "There was a bad case of MSBP reported in Norwich earlier this year. Mother of twins and they had about a hundred visits to hospital and operations and all sorts before she was found out. There's probably more of it about than we realise. Doctors are not as aware of it as they should be."

"Dave's at her flat right now," I told Gilbert, cutting off Pete before he could start telling us more about the Great Norwich Twins case. "He reckons there were fragments of glass on the worktop and on the rug in the kitchen. He has a SOCO with him. If they find any glass we should be able to match it with that from the tin of food."

"Good," Gilbert said. "Good. That's what we want – good, solid forensic evidence. So how does this fit in with the Grainger's job? Was that her handiwork, too?"

"I'm afraid not," I replied. "The two are unrelated."

"That's a shame. What's the state of play there?"

"We're struggling. There's been no new case reported for over a fortnight, so the scare may be over, but we're no nearer catching the culprit."

"Anybody in the frame?"

"Not really. Chief suspect is the wife of the warfarin victim, but it's a long shot."

Gilbert looked puzzled, then said: "Oh, I see. She poisoned her husband's pineapple and placed the other tins on the supermarket shelves to divert the blame elsewhere."

"That's right."

"There was a similar case in America a few years ago," Pete informed us. "Poisoned her husband with stuff you clean aquariums with after taking out a big insurance policy on him."

"Have another word with her, eh, Charlie," Gilbert said. "It's a high profile case with a lot of public interest. People in high places will start asking questions before too long so we need to draw a line under it as soon as possible."

"The wife works at the electronics factory," Pete added, "soldering components on printed circuit boards. One of the contaminated tins of pineapple had been soldered."

"There you go, then," Gilbert said. "You have a volunteer."

Gilbert stumped off back to his office and Pete found the file and swatted up on the warfarin victim. I indicated for Maggie to follow me and carried my coffee into my little office.

"You didn't sound convinced about the wife," Maggie stated as she manoeuvred the visitor's chair to a more favourable position.

"No," I replied as I hung my jacket behind the door, "but it gets Pete out of the way. There've been too many cases for it to be her. The crime is the poisoning of the tins, not the poisoning of Mr Johnson. It's either done for pure mischief or it's aimed at Grainger's. Enough of that, what was Tenerife really like?"

She laughed. "It was brilliant, Charlie, just brilliant. You'd love the place. OK, so it's a bit chicken-and-chipsy in some parts, but it's incredibly beautiful in others. And the weather is gorgeous. That's what you go for, isn't it?"

"It's been sunny here while you were gone. You missed the summer."

"So I've heard. Ah, well, you can't have everything. And what about you? How have you been, Charlie?"

"Pretty good. A couple of juicy cases to solve, with no personal involvement. Old-fashioned detective work, just like we joined for. I've been enjoying myself."

"And the love life?"

"Um, looking up, Maggie. Looking up."

The phonecall came about ten minutes later. "That's brilliant," I said. "Well done," and "Keep me informed."

I replaced the receiver. "She's coughed," I said. "Mrs Norcup has just confessed to poisoning her son with broken glass."

"Congratulations," Maggie said. "More brownie points for the department."

She went to tell Pete and make some more coffee while I rang Gilbert. It was a tidy conclusion to a difficult case, but we didn't rejoice or jump up and down with jubilation at a crime solved. It was a sad ending, and two lives would never be the same again. I stood looking out of the window at the traffic down below, marvelling at the way it kept going without all piling into each other. There were simple rules. That's why it kept moving, and in each vehicle was a driver with a pair of eyes and a brain and a desire to survive. So they obeyed the rules, or most of them, and everybody rubbed along.

"Do you take sugar these days?" Maggie asked.

I turned around and held the door for her as she manoeuvred in, holding two more coffees. "I don't mind," I replied.

"What'll happen to her?" Maggie asked, when she was seated again.

"I don't know. Little Rory's going into care. Dave thinks the department should adopt him."

"Hey, that's a brilliant idea."

I found a KitKat in my drawer and broke it into two. "There's this woman," I said, munching on my half of the biscuit. "She's all alone in a house and has nobody to talk to all day. No neighbours, no friends. Her relationship, if you can call it that, is on the rocks and she's reached the end of her tether, so she decides to do something about it. She damages the person she says she loves. Does it make sense, Maggie? Why would a woman do something like that?"

"Who can say? When you're in an emotional state there's no knowing what the human mind can rationalise. People do things like that to attract attention to themselves. They have bleak, loveless lives. Abject poverty with no possible way out of it, never any treats, never the centre of attention. It must grind away at you, a life like that."

"But it's not the sole prerogative of the poor, Maggie. It happens to rich people, too."

"I know, and that's more difficult to explain. But you can still be well off and have a loveless life, be downtrodden. And poverty's relative, isn't it? Most of us realise that our lives are in our own hands, we can do something about them, but some people don't see that, or they're trapped. They make a cry for help. Slash their wrists, take an overdose. You've seen it often enough, Charlie."

"That's true, but money helps, doesn't it?"

"Usually, but not always. And I draw the line at damaging the baby. That's cowardly, unforgivable, in my opinion."

"The baby?"

"Young Rory."

"Oh yes, young Rory. No, Maggie, I'm not talking about Mrs Norcup. I'm not talking about her at all."

"Sorry, Chas, but you've lost me."

"How do you feel about having your hair done, in the firm's time, on expenses?"

"Now you've really lost me."

Chapter Thirteen

I collected the frames, tried them for size on the unfinished pictures and painted them white. It was looking promising. I filled in the loops of the letters in bright colours and gave some of them ears and tails, so they looked like owls, cats, mice and Mr Smileys. Typical doodles. I was enjoying myself. If I could have started again I'd have made the writing even larger, with only five or six well-selected words covering the board, but I was happy with the first attempt.

Rosie rang to say she was home, and I told her that I'd ordered the tickets for A Midsummer Night's Dream. It's not my favourite Shakespeare, but I'd survive.

"Have you ordered your outfit for the gala?" she asked.

"What outfit?"

"Your Wyatt Earp outfit."

"That outfit. There'll be enough hoots of derision when they see my pictures," I told her, "without me dressing up like a clown."

I was tempted. Long coat, big hat, cowboy boots and moustache. It'd be good for a laugh and Gareth would be green with envy. But there are some temptations I can resist, and this was another of them.

Thursday morning I read the transcript of the interview with Mrs Norcup. Rory was the result of a brief fling with a married man she met when he was working on the bypass, who had gone AWOL when the Child Support Agency tried to serve him with a summons. The original Mr Norcup left her when they were both eighteen, after the inquest that recorded the death of their daughter as a cot death.

Dave poked his head round the door. "What're you doing for lunch, Sunshine?" he asked.

"Um, going shopping," I replied.

"Shopping? You?"

"Yeah. There's a shop on the High Street advertising trousers at three pairs for ten pounds. Sounds a bargain to me so I thought I'd have a look, see what they're like."

"Three pairs for ten pounds?"

"That's what it says in the window."

"Whereabouts on the High Street?"

"Next to Jessup's."

"That's a dry cleaner's, you dozy wazzock."

"Is it? Oh, in that case I'm free. Sandwich in the pub?"

"Sounds like a good idea to me."

Have a day off and the work piles up. Nobody thinks to come in and empty my In tray for me. I spent the rest of the day catching up, paying for my trip down to the Cotswolds. In the evening I fixed the pictures in their frames and stood them in the kitchen where I could study them while I ate my tea. I made a few minor adjustments where I'd left ragged edges and declared them finished. Final touch was my initials in the bottom corner.

"It suits you," I told Maggie, next morning.

"Cut and blow dry," she said. "I was tempted to

sting you for a full work over, complete with hair extensions and braiding, but common sense prevailed."

"Good. Did you remember the corned beef?"

"Right here." She placed the tin on my desk.

"Super."

I dusted down my briefcase, put everything in it and looked in my notebook for a number. When I was through I said: "It's Detective Inspector Priest here. I'd like to come and see you. Now."

Debra Grainger opened the door before I could reach for the bell push. I thanked her for seeing me so early and she led me inside. We went into a drawing room I hadn't been in before, with uncomfortable wing-backed chairs covered in a tapestry material that you could have struck a match on. They sat upright in those days, spine straight and not touching the back of the chair. Give me a beanbag, any day. I sat down and refused a coffee.

"What's it about?" Debra asked.

"I think you've a good idea, Mrs Grainger," I said.

"Is it about Mort?"

"Partly. What has he told you?"

"That he spent the night in a cell. Said he was asked to go to this farm. He didn't know what it was about. They held a dog fight. He said it was horrible but he couldn't get away. Then the police came and arrested everybody."

"Do you believe him?"

"I don't know what to believe."

She was wearing a blouse and skirt, with modest heels on her shoes and no tights. A thin chain with a crucifix hung round her neck but the rings had vanished from her fingers and she looked as if she hadn't had much sleep.

"Where is Sir Morton now?" I asked.

"He said he was going to London to have a word with his lawyer."

"And Sebastian? Where's he today? I thought you didn't like being left alone with him."

"I don't know where he is. He knows the score, so he's keeping a low profile. Is he behind all this?"

I shook my head. "No. Sebastian comes out of it shining white. He had nothing to do with it. Just the same, I think you should insist on your husband moving him. It may not be possible to sack him, these days, but he could transfer him back to one of the branches."

"That won't be necessary, Inspector."

"Why's that?"

"I'm going home, back to the States, soon as I can arrange the flight. Then I'll have a word with my lawyers. My marriage is over, I want out of here."

"That might not be possible," I said.

"Why not?" She looked at me, alarmed by my words, and fidgeted with the cuffs of her blouse. She should have been puffing nervously on a cigarette or gulping at a large brandy and soda, but I suspected that she'd never done either.

"There are certain legal processes to be followed," I told her. "You'll have to stay here for a while."

"Until when?" Disappointment filled her voice like she'd heard that the Easter Bunny had died.

"As long as it takes."

An original oil painting hung on the wall over the

fireplace, of girls in long skirts gathering cockles or mussels from the sea. I'd have swapped it for both my efforts. The sun came out briefly, lighting the room, then went behind a cloud again.

"You're leaving him?" I said.

"Yes."

"Divorce?"

"Yes."

"Because he went to a dog fight and spent the night in police custody?"

Her cheeks flushed and she plucked at her sleeve with those long fingernails as if something objectionable were sticking to it. "This isn't easy for me," she said.

"I know."

"He's having an affair, isn't he?"

"Who with?" I asked, turning the question back at her.

"I can guess." She jumped up, fetched a mobile phone from a drawer and pressed a pre-set button. "Could I speak to Sharon Brown, please," she said, then: "Is she? Do you know when she'll be back? Thank you, I'll contact her then."

She put the phone down. "Ms Brown is on a course and won't be back until Monday. Guess when Mort will be back. Was she at this dog fight, Inspector?"

"Mmm."

"Well, at least there'll have been one bitch there." She jumped up again and strode over to the window, looking out, hiding her tears.

"I'm sorry," I said, walking over to stand beside her.

"It's happened before, it's not your fault."

"How long have you known?"

"About Sharon? A year or so. She was one of his brighter employees. He encouraged her, put her through college. It's a familiar story, Inspector, a tried and trusted formula. There were others before her, but nothing I could prove."

A grey squirrel galloped across the lawn where I'd watched her sunbathing, sending a pair of collared doves flapping off, and in the distance I could see Stoodley Pike.

"Have you heard the expression 'trailer trash', Inspector?" she asked.

"Yes."

"Well that's what we were, as my husband likes to remind me. My parents moved to Florida from Virginia when I was a baby, looking for a better life for them and me. They swapped one trailer park for another, but the winters were milder. Things didn't go well for them but they stayed together through thick and thin because that's what they believed in. That and in Jesus Christ. They didn't want me to marry Mort, said he was too old for me, that I wasn't sophisticated enough for him, but I wanted to escape from that life so I leapt at the opportunity. Now I've got to go back to them and admit that they were right, and it's not easy."

I told her to come and sit down again, and she followed me. "You can afford a good lawyer," I said, "and he's a wealthy man. You'll come out of it OK. You'll be able to build your parents that villa with the ocean view they've always dreamed of. I know it's not the best solution but it helps."

"Look on the bright side?"

"That's right."

"When will I be able to go home?"

"It's not that simple," I said, reaching down for my briefcase which I'd left on the floor at the side of my chair. I removed a large manila envelope and extracted the photo of the woman in the long coat and gloves.

"Is this you, Mrs Grainger?" I asked.

She studied it for much longer than necessary, weighing the implications of her reply.

"It… could be," she decided upon, eventually.

"Is it or isn't it?"

"I think it is."

"Do you still have that coat?"

"Yes."

"Can I see it, please?"

"The coat?"

"Yes."

"Why?"

"To prove to myself that it's you in the picture."

"I'll fetch it." She stood up and left the room. I was wondering if I should have followed her, how it would look if she hurled herself from an upstairs window while I was sitting there twiddling my toes, when she returned with the coat over her arm. I took it from her and held it up by the shoulders.

It was a navy blue Burberry, lightweight, with an expensive feel to it, and exactly like the one in the photo. I delved into a pocket and found a leather glove. Its partner was in the other pocket. That saved me having to ask to see the gloves.

"I was worried about these," I said, flapping the

gloves at her. "I didn't think you'd be able to wear them over your nail extensions, so we made enquiries with your hairdresser. Apparently you had short nails up to last week."

"What's all this about, Inspector?"

"I think you have a good idea, but I'll show you." I reached into the briefcase again and retrieved the tin of corned beef. "This is a tin of corned beef exactly like the one that poisoned Maureen Wall, nearly three weeks ago. Somebody had pierced the tin, and the others that were found, with something small and sharp, like a drawing pin." I produced one from my briefcase. "Let's see if it works," I said.

It was awkward, holding the tin steady while trying to balance the pin under my thumb with the point against the hard metal. When it was stable I placed my other thumb over the first one and squeezed. The thumbnail turned pink with the pressure until, without a sound, the pin penetrated the steel and slid effortlessly into the meat.

"There," I said. "Nothing to it."

"I don't know what all this has to do with me," she said, but her expression told a different story.

"You're a practical person, Mrs Grainger," I told her. "I'm told you made the model of the office and leisure complex with your own hands. You know how to use tools, have access to them, no doubt know all about soldering and super glue and saturated solutions. I think it was you that contaminated all the food at Grainger's superstore."

She was staring down at her hands and I noticed that one of her nail extensions had become detached.

She tried to press it back in place. "It's absurd," she declared. "Why would I do such a thing?"

"To hurt your husband," I suggested. "You'd had as much as you could take and this was revenge for all his philandering." She stayed silent, as I expected, so I threw her the lifeline: "Or perhaps you did it to save your marriage. You saw it as a way to win Sir Morton's affection back by giving him your full support and understanding during these difficult times? If the Press were hounding him everywhere he turned perhaps he'd spend more time at home instead of gallivanting off every weekend? Or maybe you thought that by putting pressure on the company you'd create stress between him and his staff, in other words, between him and Sharon Brown. You tell me."

"You haven't any evidence. None at all."

The gloves were on the arm of my chair. "That's true," I conceded, "and you saw how fiddly it was holding the pin against the tin. Doing that whilst at the shelves might attract attention; might be picked up by the CCTV cameras. But if you put the pin inside your glove, poking out of the thump, it would look perfectly natural to pick up a tin, appear to read the label and then replace it, after piercing it with the drawing pin. That's what you did, Mrs Grainger."

She shook her head but was unable to speak.

"And if we look at your gloves," I continued, "I suspect we'll find a neat little hole in the thumb of the right hand one."

"You're very clever."

"It's what I'm paid for."

"You're right, I did it to save my marriage," she said, her voice a whisper.

"I don't think you should say any more," I told her, "until you have a solicitor present. I'll have to ask you to come to the station with me."

"Am I under arrest?"

"Not unless you refuse to come."

"Will I go to jail?"

"Two people nearly died. You put hundreds of lives at risk, scared half the population out of their wits and wasted thousands of hours of police time. If a child or someone frail had eaten that corned beef this might have been a murder enquiry. You could go to jail, but no doubt you will have a very good lawyer in your corner."

"I didn't want to hurt anybody. It's just that nothing happened."

I interrupted her – "I'd prefer you not to say anything until we're at the station," – but she ignored me.

"I pierced the corned beef and some tins of fruit, but nobody noticed. I wanted them to go bad, that's all, but nothing happened. So then I used the dye, but it was covered up by the store. Next I used the rat poison. It tastes horrible. I tried it. I didn't think anybody would actually eat the stuff."

I cautioned her. If she insisted on telling me all the details without being cautioned the whizz-kid lawyer would pick it up and make trouble. "We'll take a statement from you at the station," I said. "Can you come with me, please?"

"Do I need anything?"

"No. Just the key to lock the door."

Driving through Hebden Bridge she turned and looked out of the window at my side of the car. "I hate this place," she said. "Can you believe that? It's such a beautiful place and I hate it. Do you know what the happiest day I've had was, for months and months?"

I shook my head, not wanting to hear, not interested.

"It was last Thursday. Morning coffee with you in that quaint little café, then sitting by the river watching the birds and talking. Simple gifts. I felt happier than I've done in a long while. I… I thought I'd found a friend."

If it was meant to make me feel good it didn't work. "If it's any consolation, Debra," I said, "I think Sir Morton is every kind of fool I've ever known."

But that didn't help, either.

The Assistant Chief Constable (Crime) was delighted, and when he's happy we're all happy. The troops who were out knocking on doors, studying CCTV footage or skulking round supermarkets were pulled in and told that the job was solved, they could have the weekend off. We were sitting round in the big office, drinking more coffee, when Gilbert came down to tell us of the ACC's pleasure at clearing up two high-profile cases in one week. He then immediately destroyed the euphoria by asking what we were doing about burglaries. Two cases, no matter how big or high-profile, didn't have much impact on our figures.

"Oh, we'll sort them out Monday morning," I assured him, reaching for another chocolate digestive.

"Before elevenses," Jeff added.

Mrs Grainger had made a full confession, in the

presence of a solicitor, and was released on police bail
on condition that she brought her passport in. When
her case came to trial medical reports would be pre-
sented to the court by the best in the job, all the way
from Harley Street. They'd claim that trying to poison
half the population of Heckley was a plea for help after
years of mental cruelty. We'd try for a section 18 assault
– grievous bodily harm with intent – but settle for a
section 47 actual bodily harm after her lawyers plea
bargained. She'd probably get a community service
order and a large fine, before fleeing back to the States
and screwing Sir Morton for half his fortune.

Mrs Norcup was remanded to a safe institution
while her state of mind was investigated, and a GBH
charge would stay on her file. She'd be inside for a
long time before being pronounced cured and released
to whatever society had to offer her. Another dismal
flat in the Project if she were lucky. Whether she'd ever
see Rory again was in the hands of the gods and social
services.

"How about a celebration curry?" somebody was
suggesting.

It was a great idea, everyone agreed, and numbers
were counted.

"I'll ring the Last Viceroy," Jeff said, "and tell them
to expect us. Six o'clock?"

"You coming, Charlie?" Dave asked.

I'd intended ringing Rosie on the off-chance that
she'd baked another chocolate cake, hoping for an
invite round, but I'd been dodging Dave for the last
fortnight. The heat was off, now, and I didn't see how I
could refuse. "Yeah, fine," I said. "Six o'clock it is."

When it comes to curry I like them hot, but the following night I was seeing Rosie, taking her to the theatre, so I stayed with the mild ones. There were fifteen of us and the proprietor of the restaurant was overjoyed to have so much custom so early in the evening. Prodigious quantities of rice, naan bread, popadoms and samosas were consumed, washed down with Kingfisher beer. I stayed sober, not wanting to have to abandon my car and take a taxi home. When talk started of moving on to a club we older ones made our apologies and split.

The answerphone was bleeping as I opened the door and I pressed the play button with unseemly eagerness.

It was Rosie, just as I'd hoped: "It's Rosie, Charlie. Give me a ring, soon as you can. It doesn't matter how late." She sounded breathless.

Her number wasn't committed to my memory, yet, so I tried the 14713 shuffle and was rewarded with a ringing tone.

"Is that you, Charlie?"

"Yes. What's happened?"

"I've heard from First Call. The samples don't match. Dad is innocent. Isn't it wonderful?"

I said: "Wow! That's fantastic. Really fantastic. When did you learn this?"

"About six o'clock. I rang you at home and at the station but you weren't there."

"Did they say anything else?"

"No. I tried to ring the producer earlier in the afternoon but he'd taken the afternoon off. His secretary said she would try his home number. She came back to me and he'd told her that he'd seen the report from the lab and it said that the samples didn't match and my dad was in the clear. Oh, Charlie, I'm so excited. I wanted to tell someone but there was only you and you were out. I'm… I'm… I don't know, it's all a bit too much for me."

"I can't begin to imagine how you feel, Rosie, but I'm so pleased for you." I wanted to say something about all we had to do was prove it was the right grave, but I didn't. It seemed churlish to cast doubts on the results, and the church records had been quite specific.

"Are we still going to see A Midsummer Night's Dream tomorrow?" I asked, "or would you prefer some other celebration?"

"No," she replied, firmly. "The Dream will be perfect. It will be like picking up my life again, from where it left off. I've put a bottle of champagne that I've been saving in the fridge. We could have a little celebration here, after the show."

"That sounds a good idea," I agreed.

"Oh," she said. "I don't suppose you'd want to drink and drive, would you?"

"It's OK, there's always a taxi," I replied.

"That's an unnecessary expense, but… you could always sleep on my settee."

"Another good idea. Thanks, I'll pack my toothbrush."

The office was quiet Saturday morning, the troops having a well-earned weekend off, probably nursing hangovers. I called in as usual to tidy a few things and do any jobs that required more attention than I'm capable of giving during the hubbub of a normal day. I like being there in an empty office, surveying the blank screens and the heaps of papers, marvelling that order can come out of such chaos. It's my domain, and I feel a little tingle of pride when I survey it.

At nine o'clock exactly I rang the lab at Chepstow. He was in. "It's DI Priest," I said, "about the Glynis Williams case. Apparently First Call TV have had their samples profiled and it's good news. Can you confirm it, yet?"

"Haven't you received my report?" asked the scientist who'd extracted the DNA and done the tests.

"No. The mail hasn't arrived yet."

"Well, we've completed the profiles and I sent the results to your home address. I knew you wanted them ASAP and there was less likelihood of them being lost in the system."

"That was thoughtful of you. It'll probably be waiting for me when I go home. So what did you find?"

"Bad news, I'm afraid, Inspector, not good news."

Something churned in my stomach and I felt as if my legs had been kicked out from under me. "Bad news?" I echoed. A picture of Rosie flashed into my brain and I thought of how her happiness was about to be smashed.

"Yeah, that's what I said. You got the wrong man. The tests show that the blood from under the girl's fingernails didn't come from Abraham Barraclough."

My emotions were being blown around like a newspaper in a hurricane, plunging earthward one second only to be sent soaring a moment later. I let the words sink in and when I was certain of their meaning I yelled a silent "Yabadabadoo!" She'd done it. Rosie had done it. The scientist, I realised, had a different agenda to me. He was looking at the case from the inside, objectively and impartial. But now I was up there with the birds again, with one final obstacle before we could once and for all declare Rosie's dad innocent.

"Oh, I see," I said. "And what about the grave? Have you verified that it was the right grave?"

"Oh, yes, we got the right grave, no doubt at all about that."

Hallelujah.

Chapter Fourteen

I dashed home, not content with the verbal report. I wanted to see it written down, neatly typed in appropriate language. Only then would I believe it.

My job is to catch criminals. Juries determine who is guilty, parliament decides on the penalties, judges apply them, prison officers carry them out. I just catch them. All the rest has nothing to do with me. A jobsworth, that's what I am; just another jobsworth.

Yesterday I came within an ace of handing Debra Grainger her gloves and telling her to take more care of them. Walking away. But then I remembered Mrs Norcup, banged up in some smelly secure ward with nothing to walk away from, no one to give her a break, so I did my job and left things to the courts.

And now this. The envelope was lying on the mat when I opened the door. I ripped it open and unfolded the single sheet of paper. I read it and re-read it, standing in the doorway. Then I read the conclusions again, looking for the weasel words or double negatives or a misplaced not, but there was nothing there. What it said was what it meant, and that was exactly what the cocky young scientist had told me on the phone. I re-folded the sheet, ran my thumbnail down the folds until they were as sharp as a blade and replaced it in the envelope. I pulled the door shut and walked back to the car.

I don't know why I came all the way up here. I had to go somewhere, get in the car and drive, and this was where it started. I parked at the end of the track and ducked under the barrier. The grass was longer and browner and the trees looked heavier, more sinister. Bethesda quarry is wedge-shaped, like a piece from a cake laid on its side, and a track made by a big-wheeled vehicle runs down one edge all the way to the bottom. Two burnt out cars stand at the top of the slope, slowly returning to nature. The body shells have disintegrated but the oil-covered engines are resisting change. They might last out for five or ten years, even twenty or a hundred, but in this temple to evolution that was nothing.

Long time ago I heard a definition of eternity. Imagine a rock a thousand miles high. Once every thousand years a bird lands on the rock, wipes its beak on it and flies off. When the bird had worn the rock away, that will be the first second of the dawn of eternity.

The sky was heavy with clouds the colour of ditch-water except for one patch of blue off to the south, almost perfectly rectangular in shape and edged in silver. If you painted a sky like that people would tell you it looked wrong. Rosie had said that these rocks were laid down three hundred million years ago. The bird had hardly started its work.

I was at the bottom. I searched until I found it, standing on end in a crack in the rock face like a miniature statue in a cathedral wall. It was smaller than I remembered, less impressive. Three nondescript fossils of long-extinct creatures crushed together in a chunk of limestone, enjoying their five minutes of fame after a long, dark wait. I rubbed my thumb over them and over the marks left by Rosie's chisel. One thing was certain: nobody would be doing the same to any of us after that length of time.

It was hot down there in the secret world of the quarry, the stone walls radiating the heat they had stored in the last few days. A square of rocks and a pile of ashes marked where someone had lit a fire, their empty beer cans mixed in with the dead embers. It sounded fun. A campfire and a couple of beers; what could be nicer? What was it Debra Grainger had said? Simple gifts? I turned and hurled the clump of fossils as hard as I could into the trees at the far side. It arced through the air, spinning, until I lost it against the shadows and then found it again as it rustled the leaves in its fall to earth, its return to obscurity. No birds flew away, startled by the intrusion, or maybe they couldn't be bothered.

A spot of rain fell on me. I found a boulder and sat on it, near where the class of '02 had hung on to every word the teacher said. Well, one of them had. I reached into my inside pocket and removed two envelopes. One of them held the tickets for that evening's performance at the Playhouse. I took them out, studied them for a long minute and then tore them into thin strips that I let flutter down around my feet. If nature could return a car to its organic state it would make short shrift of a couple of theatre tickets. The Dream had turned into a nightmare, and it fell upon me to deliver it.

The next envelope held the report from the lab, sitting on my doormat as innocently as a newborn sparrow when I returned home.

"The bad news," the scientist had told me on the telephone, "is that you got the wrong man. Abraham

Barraclough didn't kill Glynis Williams." Then, when
I'd finished wittering about the right or wrong grave,
he'd added with an air of triumph: "But would you
like me to tell you the good news?"

I preferred the dispassion of the report to his gloat-
ing tones, and unfolded the single A4 sheet.

The bones from A, it said, were examined using a sex
test and ten variable regions of DNA. They were male
in origin.

The blood B from under the fingernails was examined and also found to be male in origin but it did not
match the profile obtained from A, indicating that this
blood could not have come from A.

That's all we wanted to know, but there was more:

However, the profile obtained from B did show 5 of
the 10 alleles present in the sample from A. These are
the results we would expect if B were the natural father
or son of A.

The DNA from sample C was examined and found
to be female in origin and also showed half of the alleles present in sample A such that the results fully support the allegation that C is the natural daughter of A.

My head ached with the clunking of pieces falling into
place. Rosie's father was everything she believed he
was, and a lot more. He was kind and courageous,
compassionate and wise, and he burned with a love
for his children.

But her brother, who ran away to sea, was a murderer.

Abraham Barraclough had seen his son come off the

hillside that fateful evening, and later, after the girl's body was found, he'd seen the scratches on the boy's neck. When they started testing for blood groups he knew it was only a matter of time before the truth was revealed, so he took action to protect those he loved.

He probably grilled the boy – I didn't even know his name – until he dragged out of him a few intimate details, like the colour of Glynis's underwear. Then he scratched his own neck and went to the police station to confess to a murder. A joyful DCI Henry Ratcliffe recorded his statement and later that night Barraclough hanged himself. The case was closed.

I may have had a few details wrong, but there was no doubt about the overall truth of my theory. The son would be about forty-three now. Tomorrow, or the next day, or next week, wherever he was, two detectives from Dyfed would walk up his garden path, or ask his captain if they could see him, and he'd be arrested for a murder that he thought was long forgotten. Big blobs of rain were falling on the dry grass around my feet, stirring the stalks, promising a renewal of life.

And it was my job to tell his sister. A dog barked and I heard children laughing, somewhere outside the quarry. In a few days they'd all be back at school. It was the gala tomorrow but I wouldn't be there. I didn't know where I'd be. A magpie landed about twenty feet away, saw me and flew off, complaining loudly about the intrusion. I turned my face upwards to catch the raindrops. The square of blue sky had stretched out into a rhombus and a jetliner was crawling across it, leaving a silver trail behind like a snail across a window.

I'd have given my pension to be on it.